GEORGE ELIOT

Impressions of Theophrastus Such

GEORGE ELIOT

IMPRESSIONS

OF

THEOPHRASTUS SUCH

Edited by

NANCY HENRY

University of Iowa Press, Iowa City

CONTENTS

DEDICATED TO

GRAHAM HANDLEY AND STUART TAVE

INTRODUCTION

> It is a commonplace that words, writings, measures, and per-
> formances in general, have qualities assigned them not by a
> direct judgment on the performances themselves, but by a
> presumption of what they are likely to be, considering who is
> the performer.
>
> 'The Wasp Credited with the Honeycomb'
> (XI:95–6)

When George Eliot published her first work of fiction, *Scenes of
Clerical Life* (1857), critics speculated that the author was a man.
Her last published work, *Impressions of Theophrastus Such* (1879),
looks back at the absurdity of that time when everyone was
making guesses about the author.[1] The passage quoted above
marks the transition within the chapter between the description
of Euphorion, a scholar less than scrupulous about identifying
his sources, and a story about a council of animals trying to
determine 'what sort of creature' had constructed a honeycomb.
In this fable, the animals make a series of conjectures before the
'evidence' (a wasp smeared in honey) leads them to conclude
that 'the beneficent originator in question was the Wasp.' The
animals have guessed wrongly, but their community is satisfied
with its own account of who made the honeycomb.

George Eliot's last book is a serious and playful exploration of
issues raised in this fable about authorship, origination, and
community. 'Hardly any kind of false reasoning', says George
Eliot's narrator Theophrastus, 'is more ludicrous than this on the
probabilities of origination.' When Theophrastus tells the story
of the council of animals, he does not acknowledge its source;
he is merely 'reminded' of it by Euphorion's 'communistic

principles' with regard to property in ideas. The presence of the fable in the chapter on Euphorion raises further questions about the relationship between origination and ownership, and about how the inherited intellectual property of any community binds its members and defines its character.

In 'The Wasp Credited with the Honeycomb', George Eliot confronts the issue of how much an English audience might be expected to know about its own cultural traditions. Consider some of the information needed to decipher this chapter. We must recognise that the fable is not 'original', that we could find it in a book of Aesop's fables, that Aesop is the presumed originator of the fabulist tradition, but that the difficulty of establishing a source for many fables means that his name is really just a convenient label for grouping stories which exist in multiple versions.[2] We should know that Euphorion was a third century BC Greek poet who wrote eclectic poems which borrow generously from the work of other poets, and also that the character Euphorion is the son of Faust and Helen of Troy in Goethe's *Faust*, Part II. To note the significance of Theophrastus's reference to the *Vestiges*,[3] we must know that the author of this book propounding pre-Darwinian evolutionary theories was unknown at the time George Eliot was writing. And of course, we must know some details about George Eliot's career if we are to appreciate a biographical subtext in the story her character tells.

This quotation from *Impressions* about the prejudgment of a performance based on the name of the performer recalls George Eliot's beginnings as an author, but it has become prophetic, or perhaps self-fulfilling. *Impressions* has been judged as inferior to George Eliot's other work; consequently, it is no longer read. Only Theophrastus's pastoral reminiscences about his Midlands childhood in 'Looking Backward' (II) are accepted as consistent with what is best in George Eliot. Some of the displays of learning in George Eliot's novels – the epigraphs from *Felix Holt* (1866), the historical detail of *Romola* (1863), the scientific precision in *Middlemarch* (1872), the Judaism of *Daniel Deronda* (1876) – initially distanced some readers, but these intellectual aspects of George Eliot have been examined and valued by late twentieth-century critics. The quotations and allusions in George Eliot's novels, stories and poetry, even when set as epigraphs at the head of chapters, are integral to the whole of these works. The integration of literary, scientific, or historical allusion in the structure of *Impressions* is more difficult to explain and evaluate, which accounts in part for the confusion over the work. Since there is no plot, or development of the characters from chapter to chapter, where is the coherence and how do these seemingly random and puzzling elements fit into the whole of the work?

The complexity of the title *Impressions of Theophrastus Such* and of the character Theophrastus need to be established, and each of the eighteen parts requires evaluation if *Impressions* is to be understood both as a reflection of George Eliot's previous works and an experimental departure from them. *Impressions* comes at the end of her development as a late Victorian writer of organic form, and at the beginning of what looks like early Modernist experimentation through fragmentation in form. Theophrastus is invisible and pervasive; the essays are separate and unified; English culture is multicultural and distinctly English. In *Impressions* George Eliot goes beyond even her last novel, *Daniel Deronda*, in positing the role of collective memory in the future of national cultures, and the power of literary texts in creating and preserving both.

By 1878, George Eliot was a novelist and public figure of unrivalled influence, at the centre of London literary and intellectual life, but *Impressions* is full of allusions to the period in her life before she was established. In 1851, Mary Ann Evans came to London from Coventry. She began to make her way in the literary world, working as editor, reviewer and translator. As a woman, a university education was not available to her, but she was conscious that her self-education was often superior to the university educations of men with whom she worked. In 1854, she began living with George Henry Lewes, journalist, actor, literary and drama critic, scientist. He was estranged but not divorced from his wife Agnes Lewes. As a female intellectual openly living with a married man, Marian Evans Lewes (as she now called herself) suffered. She became an exile from her family (her brother Isaac severed relations with her) and from London social life (she was shunned by polite society, even when Lewes was not). She began writing fiction at Lewes's prompting, and chose the name George Eliot to suggest her connection with him. As her success continued with the major works after *Scenes of Clerical Life*, *Adam Bede* (1859), *The Mill on the Floss* (1860), *Silas Marner* (1861), *Romola* (1863), *Felix Holt* (1866), *Middlemarch* (1872), and *Daniel Deronda* (1876), she was gradually accepted, as a celebrated author, if not a respectable 'wife'.

George Eliot composed most of the eighteen chapters of *Impressions* in the summer of 1878, which she spent in the relative isolation of 'The Heights', Witley, the country house in Surrey she and Lewes had recently purchased. While they were happy to be away from London, spending time alone and with close friends, their summer was shadowed by personal and professional concerns. They were coming to accept that Lewes's ambitious, multi-volume *Problems of Life and Mind* (1874–79) would not be appreciated by the scientific establishment, at least not in his lifetime. They had hoped it would become the most important work of his career, gaining for him the respect of institutionally accepted scientists which he never entirely commanded, because he had no university education and was considered a populariser and dilettante. Furthermore, they were confronted by the serious decline in Lewes's health, which by August 1878 made it impossible for him to work.[4]

Back in London on 21 November 1878, Lewes, who also acted as George Eliot's literary manager, sent the manuscript of *Impressions* to the publisher John Blackwood. On 30 November Lewes died, ending their twenty-four years of life together. *Impressions* remained unpublished while George Eliot mourned his death and devoted herself to completing the last two unfinished volumes of *Problems of Life and Mind*, an indication of how thoroughly involved she had been with his work. In January and February of 1879, she corrected page proofs of *Impressions*, finally agreeing to its publication in May of that year.[5]

The book marks the end of George Eliot's career and the end of her life with Lewes, making its neglect by critics and biographers particularly odd. The difficulty of the cultural allusions in *Impressions* is complicated by the presence of jokes made in a seemingly private language, and which may be a testimony to the specific time in which it was written. Towards the end of 'Looking Inward' (I), an unnamed friend turns up in Theophrastus's description of the sadistic and critical reader against whom he can only 'ask my friend to use his judgment in insuring me against posthumous mistake'. We know that Lewes protected George Eliot from harsh reviews, and that he read and commented on all of her writing. When Marian Evans Lewes was ready to submit her first story, 'The Sad Fortunes of the Reverend Amos Barton', for publication, Lewes wrote to John Blackwood on behalf of his 'friend', who did not wish to be identified.[6] The presence of Theophrastus's friend in *Impressions* is assumed thoughout, though he is never mentioned again. Through textual references – to 'poor Pol' and 'the humble mollusc',[7] George Eliot wrote her own unacknowledged collaborator into her text, part of its multi-layered questioning of how literary origination and intellectual property are assigned. Allusions to Lewes's published work as well as to George Eliot's own mix with the allusions to classical philosophy, Romantic poetry, contemporary science, and other texts, hindering the definitive identification of an origin for any idea or phrase in *Impressions*. Such elusiveness may well be the primary explanation for critical hostility or indifference to this book. To understand what purpose its self-referential game-playing serves, we have to appreciate how the jokes are 'in jokes' which are 'in character' for Theophrastus, and how his character is the book's unifying force.

George Eliot's Theophrastus is a middle-aged London bachelor of uncertain profession. From 'Looking Inward' (I) we know he has one published book and a closet full of unpublished manuscripts. As he guides the reader (whom he assumes to be hostile) through a series of brief narratives about different characters, he is a narrator not unlike those of George Eliot's novels, and he is also reminiscent of the two narrators in 'Poetry and Prose from the Notebook of an Eccentric' (1846–7), the narrator in *Scenes of Clerical Life*, and of Latimer in 'The Lifted Veil' (1859). He might also share some characteristics with Lewes's character, London theatre critic and bachelor, Vivian.[8] Theophrastus's name, like the names of all the characters he describes, tells us something immediately about his history. He is a fictional character, and *Impressions* reminds us that the genealogy of this figure is to be traced not only through the parents who raised him in the Midlands countryside, but in his name, which signifies an entire literary tradition familiar to educated members of a particular culture. In the same way that the events of his childhood will explain why he feels like an exile in London, or why he loves the English landscape, so this textual history will explain why he writes about characters.

His literary derivation is explicit. Theophrastus (c.370–288 BC), native of the city of Eresus on the island of Lesbos, was a student of Aristotle's and his successor as head of the Peripatetic School. He wrote prolifically on subjects in metaphysics and natural science, mostly in response to Aristotle. Aristotle treats 'character' in the *Rhetoric*,[9] but Theophrastus's *Characters*, thirty sketches of 'types' observed in the city of Athens, initiated its own form and tradition. The *Characters* influenced a dramatic tradition beginning with the New Comedy of Menander. Translated into Latin in 1592 by Isaac Casaubon, they became a model for a kind of formulaic character writing popular in Europe as late as the early nineteenth century.[10]

George Eliot's Theophrastus shows the accumulated traces of Theophrastan 'imitators' through the centuries – most notably Jean de la Bruyère, who translated Theophrastus's *Characters* and added to them his own observations of seventeenth-century French society in *Caractères de Théophraste, traduit du grec, avec les Caractères ou les Mouers de ce siècle* (1688). George Eliot's version of the 'Characters' is not just a series of sketches of nineteenth-century types.[11] It is a book about what defines moral character, about how fictional characters are created, and about how the author survives as his or her written text is inherited by successive generations. *Impressions* is different from previous 'imitations' of Theophrastus because in writing about characters he meets, George Eliot's Theophrastus performs the acts of literary history that have made the adaptation of the form possible – the borrowings, imitations, responses and exclusions of texts in their translation from one generation and national culture to another.

The verbal tricks that characterise *Impressions* – contorted sentences, ambiguous quotations, incessant puns – destabilise the identification of sources, the fixed meanings of words, and the readers' expectations. With each joke or allusion, readers of *Impressions* are divided into those who understand (insiders) and those who do not (outsiders). This is not a strict division, but shifts depending on what we know. Alternately, we may experience the pleasure of catching the allusions and understanding the jokes or of uncomfortably feeling we have missed something. The conditions of intelligibility of the work as a whole are dictated by Theophrastus; the density of allusions, the mysteriousness of names, the sense that arcane jokes are being made, can situate readers in an uneasy, outsider relationship to 'high' culture. A modern reader, in good company with past readers, might encounter Theophrastus's arcane jokes and coy puzzles with what the narrator of *Romola* describes as that 'half-smiling, half-humiliated expression of people who are not within hearing of the joke which is producing infectious laughter'.[12]

It was this sense of exclusivity and elitism that offended the first critics of *Impressions*. Four months after its publication, George Eliot wrote to her friend Elma Stuart that Theophrastus 'has most unexpectedly won great favour with the public whom he certainly does not flatter, and they have been magnanimous enough to buy 6000 of his "Impressions"'.[13] Critics, however, were generally unimpressed with either the intellect or the humour displayed by the great national novelist in her first book of essays. Finding little in *Impressions* to meet expectations, they took offence on behalf of the 'ordinary reader', to whom, it seemed, George Eliot had an obligation. Joseph Jacobs, in the *Athenaeum*, proclaimed that: 'No poem is great if only a small coterie admire it.' To this, George Eliot punned again: 'I think I have known other books succeed in impressing the public without the sanction of that "literary organ".'[14] The *Saturday Review* chided the author for making so many demands on a reader's 'learning and exact knowledge', and even the *Times*, which called the book 'emphatically a work of genius', doubted it could ever be popular 'in the ordinary acceptation of the word', because readers could not be expected to submit to any 'serious strain on the faculties'. The *Spectator*, in its critique of the work's overly intellectual demands, puzzled over the usually unasked and never satisfactorily answered question: 'why "Such"...?'[15]

George Eliot scoffed at the critics' complaints, and watched the book sell steadily, probably on the strength of her name. However, it was she who knew best how 'the public' (with the critics) was not flattered by Theophrastus. Most readers would be excluded by the daunting erudition which she, referring to the untranslated, unidentified Latin motto from Phaedrus' *Fabulae*, called 'the deepest dyed pedantry'.[16] Contemporary critics objected to the inappropriate presence of 'scientific theory' and to the mental 'strain' caused by obscure references to unfamiliar texts. However, it is the more recent reputation of the book as ponderous and moralising rather than as too difficult which has persisted through the mid-twentieth-century George Eliot revival, even through later feminist attention to her novels. The book was never popular on the scale of her novels, and none of the various critical perspectives on George Eliot has been able to accommodate the cryptic performance of Theophrastus. Recent critics who bother to mention *Impressions* complain that Theophrastus is a failure as a character, or refuse to acknowledge him. This critical attitude comes from not taking the work seriously enough to read it carefully. A simple example of how critics have not paid attention to *Impressions* is the misnaming of the work in criticism, a practice which ranges from the careless to the comic.

On 1 May 1879, George Eliot wrote to William Blackwood[17] in 'alarm' over a misprinted advertisment for *Impressions* which read '"*The* Impressions of etc." instead of simply 'Impressions of etc"'.[18] This was an error in *Blackwood's Magazine*, but all printed editions of the book itself bear the correct title. The ambiguity of the word 'impressions' without the limiting 'the' is crucial to the title, which refers both to impressions Theophrastus receives from the world and impressions he makes on the readers. The pun on 'impressions' as printed book is also apparent. In the light of this subtle but important distinction between 'impressions' and 'the impressions', it is telling that so many critical works misprint the title. The only critical article on *Impressions* unfortunately refers to 'The Impressions' throughout.[19] The most recent biography of Lewes informs us that Lewes's last act as George Eliot's literary agent 'was to write, on 21 November, a note to Blackwood accompanying the manuscript of her compilation of aphorisms *The Impressions of Theophrastus Such*'.[20]

The names critics have called George Eliot's last book often betray lack of familiarity rather than actual hostility toward it. One mid-twentieth-century critic was particularly imaginative, referring in his index to 'Theophrastus and Such',[21] while more recently, *An Annotated Critical Bibliography of George Eliot* does not index *Impressions* at all, but refers at one point to *The Confessions of Theophrastus Such*.[22] These difficulties with getting the title right and understanding how important the concept of 'impressions' is to George Eliot's book are really only the first indication of how successful George Eliot seems to have been in showing critics, whose misreadings and judgments had been so painful to her as an author, that she could, if she chose, write a book that seems like a simple collection of short essays on unrelated contemporary topics, but in fact is a demonstration of how much the self-proclaimed authorities on English culture don't know about their own culture and about literary form. Theophrastus defines an audience for himself in 'Looking Inward': 'The act of writing, in spite of past experience, brings with it the vague, delightful illusion of an audience nearer to my idiom than the Cherokees...' (I:12). His only other published book was translated into Cherokee. With his 'impressions', he seems to target an English-speaking audience in general, but this statement might be his way of signalling that his 'idiom' is a very restricted one.

Critics who have written about *Impressions* usually assume (perhaps uneasily) that the name of its 'shadowy' narrator is Theophrastus Such, referring to him as 'Mr. Such', or simply 'Such'.[23] Nowhere in George Eliot's book does her narrator refer to himself as 'Theophrastus'. Instead, he slips in remarks about acquaintances who are 'as forgetful of my biography and tenets as they would be if I were a dead philosopher' (I:3), or who view him as a person 'who had probably begun life with an old look, and even as an infant had given his countenance to that significant doctrine, the transmigration of ancient souls into modern bodies' (XII:102). As Theophrastus recognises in 'The Wasp Credited with the Honeycomb': 'check ourselves as we will, the first impression from any sort of work must depend on a previous attitude of mind, and this will constantly be determined by the influences of a name' (XI:96). 'Such' is placed so as to imply a patronym. This seems to modernize George Eliot's Theophrastus as compared to the Greek philosopher who is known by the single name given him by his teacher Aristotle, and which marks an intellectual rather than a blood inheritance. The 'attitude of mind' George Eliot could count on from English readers is likely to assume that 'Such' is a surname like Bede, or Marner, or Holt or Deronda.

Once we know that 'Theophrastus' refers to both the Greek 'Spoken by God' and the unnamed English author/character who fails to make an impression on others, we can consider whether this author, rather than imitating, is 'doing an impression' – an impersonation – of Theophrastus. Is the unambitious London bachelor not only borrowing the generic form but producing and parodying the character of the classical philosopher who kept his own name out of the cast of characters he produced?

Theophrastus incorporates the tradition he has inherited by embodying the 'originator' of the genre (or species) as a character in his text. But Theophrastus is interested in aspects of writing about characters which played no role in the writings of the Greek philosopher; the form has evolved from its pre-novelistic origins. There are aspects of the novelist in George Eliot's Theophrastus, hints that he embodies not only his ancient predecessor, but also the novelist who made the Greek Theophrastus into a nineteenth-century fictional character. In 'Looking Inward', Theophrastus describes authors whose writings expose aspects of their character legible to others, but not to themselves. He tells his readers:

> while I carry in myself the key to other men's experience, it is only by observing others that I can so far correct my self-ignorance as to arrive at the certainty that I am liable to commit myself unawares and to manifest some incompetency which I know no more of than the blind man knows of his image in the glass (I:5).

Classical Theophrastus does not reveal this kind of self-reflection. In explaining his purpose in writing, modern Theophrastus begins to sound like the familiar novelist George Eliot.

The title, *Impressions of Theophrastus Such* (and the reading which follows from an understanding of it), signifies the blurring of a line between the author (outside) and the character (inside). The ethical responsibilities of the author, *Impressions* suggests, may be as important for the culture to examine as the ethical dilemmas faced by characters in fiction, and it may be in this sense that George Eliot (through Theophrastus) found herself speaking, at least at one level, to an audience closer to her idiom as an author; in short, to other authors.[24] Theophrastus describes characters who hide behind their written work, unwilling to take any moral responsibility for those parts of themselves they make public by publishing. Modern Theophrastus has taken a significant step in publishing, rather than closeting, his 'impressions'. But when author becomes character, when ancient Theophrastus gets impersonated by the character of a modern author, inseparably 'typed' on the page along with his judgments of others, he, as representative author, must assume responsibility for what this character does and writes. The moral responsibility of authorship is posited in *Impressions* at the same time as the ideas of origination and authorship are called into question.

In the title, Theophrastus is no longer 'Spoken by God'. He becomes, in his modern embodiment, 'the God within, holding the mirror and the scourge for our own pettiness as well as our neighbours', (I:13). For the author/character Theophrastus, in contrast to the ancient Theophrastus, who criticised others, criticism comes from within and without in the form of a double-sided mirror held up to those around him, but ruthlessly reflecting his own image back to him, scourging him to fashion himself according to the standards he would apply to others and bringing – writing him – into a community. This morally exacting impulse in Theophrastus is typical of George Eliot's other work. What is not familiar or typical is the way we are meant to see (or not see) the relationship between ancient Theophrastus, modern Theophrastus, and George Eliot.

In the Greek, each of Theophrastus's character sketches begins with a formula: *toiontos tis, hoios*, translating literally to 'such a type who...'. *Impressions of Theophrastus Such* is a pun based on the formula used by the Greek Theophrastus as a way of introducing each of his characters. So we have 'The Garrulous Man', 'The Boorish Man', 'The Mean Man', all shaped into types by this introductory formula at the head of each chapter in the Greek.

In contrast, the title of George Eliot's book is something like a calling card, a formulaic introduction to a narrator who, at the outset, is nothing more than a name set in type: 'Impressions of Theophrastus, Such a Type Who...'. The ancient Theophrastus follows his formula with descriptions of separate character types; modern Theophrastus appropriates the 'Such a type who...' formula to himself, following it with eighteen chapters slowly revelatory of his own character as he describes the habits of other persons. The question, 'what is the type of Theophras-tus?' ('can I give any true account of my own [character]?') gets answered by a performance of his dispositions, habits, flaws, triumphs – an account of his character that can only be supplied retrospectively, from the vantage point of the last word in the book's final chapter.

The title connects the modern character writer to the 'father' of the tradition. It challenges the reader to tease out its puns. 'Impressions', 'type', and 'character' work to emphasize the materiality of the printed word, the literal engraving – 'impressing' of Theophrastus's impressions and his character on the page for preservation and transmission. Moral virtue, according to Theophrastus's teacher Aristotle, is shaped by the repetition of actions which over a period of time slowly engrave a person with the marks of habit.[25] It is the habit of Theophrastus to write, and to show, even as he says, that it is absurd and dangerous to believe that there could be a 'radical, irreconcilable opposition between intellect and morality' (XVI:134).

By reading what Theophrastus writes, we get to know him. But we might begin reading his character differently, depending on what we already know about the other Theophrastus. George Eliot's Theophrastus has no literal patronym in his title, merely the appearance of one to minds culturally predisposed to see it. What he has is a linguistic connection in 'Such' to the literary tradition of character writing. Rather than a 'family' name, he has an ellipsis: 'Such a type who...'. The formula introduces – types – Theophrastus, but can only be completed on the completion of the book, and then only in terms of what he does, not in terms of any 'first impression' of a name. Theophrastus, 'Such a type who writes this book', in writing the book, has made its writing characteristic of him.

Theophrastus's name is only the first of the challenges his readers face in *Impressions*. The second is keeping track of his voice, and in trying to do this we confront the authority of a century-old prejudice, marking *Impressions* as a set of unconnected essays strung together in no particular sequence. The parts of *Impressions* gradually develop the character of Theophrastus, and they also cohere around the idea Theophrastus develops about English culture through his descriptions of characters. The characters Theophrastus describes have allegorical names, which in most cases connect them to some kind of

textual tradition: mythical (Ganymede, Proteus), fabulist (Corvus, Reynard), historical (Lentulus, Pepin), scientific (Grampus,
Vorticella), poetic (Laura, Melissa). But these traditions and
categories are not autonomous; they intersect and overlap with
one another. The chapters mix names, titles, quotations, allusions from different centuries and different national cultures.
Understanding the associations of the names in *Impressions* requires knowing something about the diverse traditions from
which they come, and a recognition of the intertext Theophrastus calls 'the backward tapestry of the world's history'.

The subject matter of the chapters is diverse because English
culture itself is diverse, yet the pieces cohere through the
consciousness of Theophrastus, just as, with all of its various
influences, English culture, according to *Impressions*, exists as the
confluence of all its myriad traditions. To see how George Eliot
has presented this 'backward tapestry', it will be useful to give a
brief summary of the chapters.

In the first two chapters, Theophrastus sketches the circumstances of his personal life, the habitual social rejections leading
him to formulate a modest principle of observation and judgment. 'Looking Inward' (I) introduces Theophrastus: 'It is my
habit to give an account to myself of the characters I meet with:
can I give any true account of my own?' Telling the story of how
he came to write this book, he meditates on the genres of
autobiography and the first-person narrative essay. But he also
meets characters like Minutius Felix (author of the Latin dialogue *Octavius*) and Glycera (a character in a play by the Greek
playwright Menander), and he alludes repeatedly to Shakespeare's *Hamlet*, especially the play within the play. In this way,
through explicit discussion, dialogue between characters, and
allusion to specific texts, Theophrastus establishes the terms of
the essays to follow. He tells the reader there will be elements
of confession, but also of performance, and it is the reader's job
to judge the performance as well as identify the names and
allusions in order to fully understand the 'true' account of his
own character.

Theophrastus's early life provides the narrative of 'Looking

Backward' (II), but the title has a broader historical sweep, as he imagines himself living in the time of Aristotle and 'his disciple Theophrastus'. The recollections of his childhood in the Midlands combine aspects of George Eliot's early life, of her early writing (especially *Scenes of Clerical Life*), and of Romantic poetry, the literature characterising the pre-Reform Bill England she is describing and also an early influence on her. The chapter, then, is not only a look back at Theophrastus's family history, but a tracing of the dual genealogy of his writing within a tradition of classical philosophy, and of George Eliot's writing, the pastoral prose of her first fiction and the sources of its inspiration.

Theophrastus turns from himself to characters he has met in 'How We Encourage Research' (III). Proteus Merman has a first name which connects him to the Greek sea god, Proteus (who is able to assume any form), and a second mythical name, Merman, which is an emblem of his divided identity – neither fully man nor cetacean. His downfall comes when he, a humble lawyer and journalistic dabbler, attempts to join the community of 'a half-a-dozen persons, described as the learned world of two hemispheres'. He is 'pilloried' and 'as good as mutilated' by scholars figured as whales. In keeping with the associations of his own pagan name, he is made a sacrificial victim for the hubris of aspiring to join a community from which he is (metaphorically speaking) anatomically excluded. Proteus Merman, like Matthew Arnold's 'The Forsaken Merman', can only look from the outside into the world he would like to join. Although Theophrastus is critical of his flaws, Merman suffers ultimately because he is an outsider who has futilely tried to change his form and assimilate.

The next six chapters all reveal aspects of Theophrastus through his descriptions of individual characters. They also take on different literary genres. 'A Man Surprised at his Originality' (IV) tells the story of Lentulus in the form of a eulogy, which is really an attack couched in the rhetoric of praise. Lentulus was a self-proclaimed literary critic who was always promising but never managing to produce his own superior verse: '"The world has no notion what poetry will be"' (IV:44).

Hinze is the 'Too Deferential Man' (V). In German, his name suggests 'Everyman'. Hinze provides the counter example to the 'bildungsroman' because his character does not direct itself toward a goal: 'But one cannot be an Englishman and gentleman in general: it is in the nature of things that one must have an individuality, though it may be of an oft-repeated type.'

'Only Temper' (VI) is a character sketch on the Theophrastan model, describing the actions of the bad-tempered man, Touchwood. Literally, his name refers to the dry wood used to start fires, and in his case it suggests an inflammatory nature. The chapter works with the following chapters to expose inconsistencies in Theophrastus (who does not overvalue consistency). Describing Touchwood, Theophrastus objects to 'the assumption that his having a fundamentally good disposition is either an apology or a compensation for his bad behaviour' (VI:61). In 'The Watchdog of Knowledge' (VIII), he defends the bad temper of Mordax, explaining that 'my apology for Mordax was not founded on his persuasion of superiority in his own motives, but on the compatibility of unfair, equivocal, and even cruel actions with a nature which, apart from special temptations, is kindly and generous' (VIII:71). It turns out that this apology is motivated by his own temptation to act cruelly. Theophrastus does not have sufficient self-knowledge to recognise contradictions between what he says and what he does, and this negative side of Theophrastus's character is present for the reader to see in his treatment of his 'valet and factotum', named Pummel, one suspects, because of the way he is verbally pummelled by Theophrastus, who has the advantage of him in every way.

In 'A Political Molecule' (VII), Spike, a cotton manufacturer, becomes a political element by aligning himself with other businessmen for his own benefit, and in this way indirectly works for the benefit of a group. 'A Political Molecule' is one of many biological metaphors. Grampus is likened to a whale (III), Touchwood to a bear (VI), and Mordax to a dog who runs down sheep, or 'Lanigers' (VIII). Spike is a molecule, but at the same time, ape-like: 'when he was uncovered in the drawing-room, it was impossible not to observe that his head shelved off too rapidly from the eyebrows towards the crown, and that his length of limb seemed to have used up his mind so as to cause an air of abstraction from conversational topics' (VII:64). In class terms, Spike too is neither/nor, significant in light of the political reforms, which have determined the configuration of the molecules: 'If he had been born a little later he could have been accepted as an eligible member of Parliament, and if he had belonged to a high family he might have done for a member of Government' (VII:65).

'A Half-Breed' (IX) recalls Evangelical preaching in a provincial town. Mixtus had been of a reforming and religious mind, but in moving to London, marrying Scintilla and seeking wealth, he loses touch with his earlier (worthier) enthusiasms and no longer knows who he is. The chapter brings together Marian Evans's experience with Evangelicalism in Nuneaton, as well as George Eliot's representations of provincial clergymen in *Scenes of Clerical Life*. Furthermore, the chapter portrays yet another outsider: 'Indeed, hardly any of his acquaintances know what Mixtus really is, considered as a whole – nor does Mixtus himself know it' (IX:80).

'Debasing the Moral Currency' (X) is a transitional chapter marking Theophrastus's increasing anxiety about the dissolution of 'civilisation'. Ostensibly, the chapter concerns the mindless burlesque of classic texts. The tone of the chapter itself is comic, mocking those who prefer 'that enhancement of ideas when presented in a foreign tongue, that glamour of unfamiliarity conferring a dignity on the foreign names of very common things . . .' (X:81). The anxiety about national languages and literatures is expressed through a series of references to outbreaks of violence in the July Revolution of 1830, in the Revolution of 1848, and in the Paris Commune of 1872. 'We have been severely enough taught (if we were willing to learn)', says Theophrastus, 'that our civilisation, considered as a splendid material fabric, is helplessly in peril without the spiritual police of sentiments or ideal feelings' (X:86).

'The Wasp Credited With the Honeycomb' (XI) mocks the idea of a 'communist' state in which 'Mine and Thine disappear and are resolved into Everybody's and Nobody's, and one man's particular obligations to another melt untraceably into the obligations of the earth to the solar system', and also discredits the fixation on naming a definitive origin for ideas, thus marking them as property. George Eliot's Euphorion himself represents a meeting of Ancient and Romantic traditions, a synthesis of ancient and modern, like that of ancient and modern Theophrastus, or the modern retelling of the ancient fable.

'So Young' (XII) tells the strange story of Ganymede, who grew up being told how exceedingly young and 'girlishly pretty' he was, and in adulthood had not outgrown this self-image. The chapter provides an illustration of the analysis given in 'How We Come to Give Ourselves False Testimonials, and Believe in Them' (XIII). The term 'False Testimonials' has psychological and aesthetic implications: dishonesty with oneself due to a failure to see what one has become, and dishonesty to others on the part of the artist who fails to observe and represent the details of daily life. The chapter opens with an extended metaphor that brings together the needs for examining both the external and the internal as Theophrastus describes 'the natural history of my inward self'. The aesthetic imperative to represent accurately observed detail recalls George Eliot's earlier writings on the importance of realistic representation, particularly 'The Natural History of German Life' (1856).

'The Too Ready Writer' (XIV) measures the effects of irresponsible, ill-considered writing of the journalistic sort. An author who has no unpublished ideas does harm to both himself and to the public discourse he dominates. Theophrastus, as he has tried to demonstrate in his chapters, values a multiplicity of perspectives: 'Besides, we get tired of a "manner" in conversation as in painting'. This is bad enough, but when the mistaken impulse to enlighten the world with one's own originality hardens into 'style' in writing, 'the dreamy buoyancy of the stripling has taken on a fatal sort of reality in written pretensions which carry consequences' (XIV:115). Pepin's folly is also that he wants to write a 'species of romance' that would try to capture the spirit of an age ('truly Roman and world historical') without representing the common element. Pepin provides a model of the worst kind of historical fiction, an elevated, unrealistic form of representation George Eliot consciously rejected when she wrote her own historical novel, *Romola*.

In 'Diseases of Small Authorship' (XV), Vorticella is the author of 'The Channel Islands, with Notes and Appendix'. She is described by Theophrastus as flourishing in his youth. Vorticellae are parasitic, unicellular organisms described by Lewes in his *Sea-side Studies*, researched and written in Ilfracombe, Tenby, the Scilly Isles and Jersey during trips he and George Eliot took together. (Lewes also spent some time in his youth on Jersey.) Theophrastus sets up the microcosm of Pumpiter as if it were the view from a microscope in which the observer could see organisms flourishing and interacting with one another: Volvox and Vibrio (small town critics) swarm around Vorticella, while she may 'pair off with Monas', a male writer of equally magnified ego. The microscope provides yet another model for viewing the world, and these microbes are described in terms of high Shakespearian drama, personified as Lewes had personified his specimens in *Sea-side Studies*.

'Moral Swindlers' (XVI) starts with a literal example of financial swindling by mine-owner Gavial Mantrap, described by Melissa as a 'moral man', but soon turns into an indictment of verbal swindling through the misuse of the terms moral and morality in the writing of political history and literature. The issue is one of power. Men who are kind to their families but abusive of their political and financial power should not be called moral, and it is even more crucial that those who wield power in language – the poets – take the responsibility of considering the moral value of the art they produce, not turning the experiences of debauchery into polished verse. In its parody of a Frenchman (literally of Charles Baudelaire), the chapter warns against a Nietzschean 'rule of reversing all the judgments on good and evil which have come to be the calendar and clockwork of society' (XVI:135).

'Shadows of the Coming Race' (XVII), beginning with its title, evokes the genre of science-fiction writing.[26] Theophrastus's

friend Trost, a technology enthusiast, accuses Theophrastus of
'incurable dilettanteism in science as in all other things – '
because Theophrastus insists that the implication of machines
advancing to a state of doing the work of humans (applying the
Darwinian model) is that they will supersede and replace human
beings, abolishing their noisy, 'screaming consciousnesses'. His
point is that culture, as we know it, includes fallibility, inconsistency, and the tendency to blunder of every individual person.
Impressions describes a series of flawed characters, and it reveals
the flaws in Theophrastus's character. As he argues, Theophrastus metaphorically devolves: '"Take me then as a sort of reflective and experienced carp..."' (VII:140).[27]

'The Modern Hep! Hep! Hep!' (XVIII) pulls together the
themes, images, anxieties and concerns of all the preceding
chapters. By focusing on Jewish history, Theophrastus compares
his own experiences as a native-born Englishman to those of
English Jews. He does this by extending the model of exile he
applies to himself in 'Looking Backward' and also by extending
his analyses of individual 'mixed' and marginalised characters to
a group of people which is both inside and outside of English
culture.

Community is defined in *Impressions* as something one can
experience from within or without. One question 'The Modern
Hep' raises is how do members of a community exiled from that
community's place of origin maintain their sense of belonging
and connection to each other. The memories of place stored in
literature provide one answer for both Theophrastus and the
Jews with whom he has an affinity. The 'half-visionary' rural
dream he describes in 'Looking Backward' sustains him as an
exile in the 'Nation of London', and connects him to other
English people in an invisible bond of shared memories, whether
those memories be actually lived or transmitted through literature. This imagined nationality is reinforced by common habits
dictated by life in the city. Theophrastus's own everyday life in
London is marked by the view from his room: 'my bachelor's
hearth is imbedded where by much craning of head and neck I
can catch sight of a sycamore in the Square garden' (II:26). His

obstructed view reveals a symbol of his earlier experience. The sycamore tree, signifying a particular remembered landscape, has been inserted into the artificial design of the Square garden. This crafting of nature parallels the representations of English landscape in the Romantic poetry of his father's age, a central topic of 'Looking Backward'. Landscaped urban gardens, like the language of poetry, order the memories to which later generations will turn to construct and maintain their own sense of corporate, national identity.

Persecution and physical pain are other experiences which unify an exiled community. The individual outsider, as well as communities of outsiders, according to the historical perspective of *Impressions*, have always suffered at the hands of dominant groups laboring under collective delusions ('traditions') of their own superiority. Inevitably, the English inherit Christianity's history of attempting to convert the Jews, as well as a tradition of sustained attempts to re-impress colonised cultures and bodies. Representations of everyday life under the scourge of imperial discipline are handed down in texts from Virgil to Tasso to Scott, storing images both of the author's age and the historical period about which he or she writes. Nineteenth-century Theophrastus is offering a model of reading, entreating his contemporaries to see in their own writings the same combination of external detail and authorial confession they see in older texts, and consistently implying that textual performances are not only portraits held up for the present to view the past, but mirrors held up for the present to see itself.

It is in 'The Modern Hep' that the character of Theophrastus becomes most fully English. He points out that the religion claimed by the English and in the name of which Jews are persecuted is itself a legacy from them. And, because the Jews are an exiled 'nation', they live amongst the English, anglicised and assimilated, but bearing the historical scars of a persecution often perpetuated in the name of converting them to something their history and customs would not allow. Theophrastus deplores a mentality that attempts justification:

for putting it to them whether they would be baptized or
burned, and not failing to burn and massacre them when they
were obstinate; but also for suspecting them of disliking the
baptism when they had got it, and then burning them in
punishment of their insincerity... (XVIII.152).

His sympathy for persecuted peoples does not change
Theophrastus's role as one of the dominant English culture. He
keeps the 'scourge in his own discriminating hand', he 'respects
the horsewhip when applied to the back of cruelty', and he
recognises that 'we are a colonizing people, and it is we who
have punished others' (XVIII:146). He is aware that he might
not see the worst manifestations of Englishness – the self-
superiority that scourges others – in his own character, illus-
trated, for example, in his treatment of his servant Pummel.

These moral concerns about English culture emerge within a
context which might seem to undercut them. There is no doubt
that in *Impressions*, George Eliot demonstrates that author, text,
origin, and culture are complex and interrelated concepts, and
the self-conscious anxieties of modern Theophrastus are what
most distinguish him from his ancient namesake. But to insist
that by questioning the value of cultural origins and authorial
origination, George Eliot abandons the idea of authorship – that
she kills and buries the author – would make her unaccountably
postmodern, and would risk the suppression of just those ethical
concerns she consistently argues are central to the process of
writing. The problem with disowning authorship, for George
Eliot, is that without an author, no one is responsible. Not
taking responsibility for what one writes, Theophrastus implies,
is like using the text – which faces the world – as a moral shield
behind which the author can hide his or her character. It is a
'lunacy' that he likens to 'another form of the disloyal attempt
to be independent of the common lot, and to live without a
sharing of pain' (I:12), and it compares to hiding the colonising,
'punishing' aspects of English culture behind the 'glorious flag of
hospitality which has made our freedom the world-wide blessing of the oppressed[?]' (XVIII:159).

As the chapters of *Impressions* progress from the presentation of the author, to descriptions of characters, to analyses of English culture at large, the concerns about the dissolution of the individual author parallel the concerns with the dissolution of national cultures through what Theophrastus terms 'the fusion of races'. This, he sees, is an inevitability, but it is frightening in its implications for the cultural identification which has enabled noble acts and produced the texts in which the 'national memories' of such acts are stored. An argument emerges in *Impressions*, which goes something like this: authors produce written texts; written texts are foundational to traditions which make up culture; the authors within any culture must take responsibility for the character of the culture to which they contribute texts. *Impressions* suggests that it is impossible to fix a stable origin for the ideas expressed by any one author. Likewise it is futile to insist on a single origin for what we know as English culture. Nonetheless, George Eliot remains Victorian in her assertion that despite the threat of dissolution, an author is responsible for acknowledging her debts in the recording and transmitting of inherited ideas. She is also responsible for making her own, distinct contribution, made possible by the way her historical circumstances have shaped her. It is as necessary to acknowledge 'our parents', says Theophrastus, as to monitor the value of what we pass on to the next generation. The present generation need not assert definitive origins, thereby effacing the signs of its own enriching diversity, but it must rather act ethically in acknowledging its debts and making its own contributions to the future.

One more example from the text will help illustrate what George Eliot considered to be an erudite joke, and also a test to her readers measuring their knowledge of 'high' culture. It will also show just how far George Eliot had gone in her proto-Modernist impulse to write the author into the text, seeming to complicate the distinction between author and character.

In 'Debasing the Moral Currency' (X), Theophrastus takes on the problem of the present's disregard for past models of artistic accomplishment. To do this he pits mindless mockery against

wit refined to such a point that his own example of a good joke
depends upon an allusion so obscure, it seems even to have
eluded scholars approaching the text today.[28] He begins with a
quotation from La Bruyère. He likes, he says, to quote French
testimony, and in this case, English Theophrastus is using La
Bruyère (as La Bruyère had used Greek Theophrastus) to begin
his description of the 'manners of his century'. Theophrastus,
however, refuses to translate La Bruyère, as La Bruyère had
translated him. In 'Looking Backward', he refers to 'the undeniable testimony' of Theophrastus. In 'How We Give Ourselves
False Testimonials', the 'worn and soiled testimonial' in the
pocket of the tippler is a symbol of how debased the status of
some forms of written confession can become. So even as he
mocks the lady who feebly tries to quote La Bruyère as at the
beginning of 'Debasing', he quotes French testimony, which is
indirectly, a way of quoting himself.

He ends this chapter with a story from Athenaeus, a classical
writer whose *Deipnosophistae* ('The Learned Banquet', c. AD 192),
like *Impressions*, is a pastiche of literary quotations and cultural
references. The story is a warning about the dangers of mockery
and burlesque, and the implicit contrast is to wit, 'an exquisite
product of high powers', while the chapter as a whole asks what
those high powers might be:

> The Tirynthians, according to an ancient story reported by
> Athenæus, becoming conscious that their trick of laughter at
> everything and nothing was making them unfit for the conduct
> of serious affairs, appealed to the Delphic oracle for some means
> of cure. The god prescribed a peculiar form of sacrifice, which
> would be effective if they could carry it through without
> laughing. They did their best; but the flimsy joke of a boy upset
> their unaccustomed gravity, and in this way the oracle taught
> them that even the gods could not prescribe a quick cure for a
> long vitiation, or give power and dignity to a people who in a
> crisis of the public wellbeing were at the mercy of a poor jest
> (X:86–7).

In addition to the work this story and its moral do within the essay, emphasising the dangers of habituation to barbarous laughter, the full force of 'exquisite wit' comes only through the realisation that there is an unsignalled joke at play, another layer to the chapter's experimentation with and commentary on the relationship between testimony and authority.

Athenaeus does in fact report this story in his *Deipnosophistae*. But what one could only know by reading Athenaeus, is that buried in Book VII of the 'Learned Banquet' is a discourse on comedy which begins:

> And Theophrastus, in his treatise on comedy, tells us that the Tirynthians, being people addicted to amusement, and utterly useless for all serious business, betook themselves once to the oracle at Delphi in hopes to be relieved from some calamity or other. And that the god answered them, 'That if they sacrificed a bull to Neptune and threw it into the sea without once laughing, the evil would cease'. And the oracle forbade any of the boys to be present at the sacrifice; however, one boy, hearing of what was going to be done, mingled with the crowd, and then they hooted him and drove him away, 'Why', said he, 'are you afraid lest I should spoil your sacrifice?' and when they laughed at this question of his, they perceived that the god meant to show them by a fact that an inveterate custom cannot be remedied.[29]

Modern Theophrastus's joke is that in citing a classical source to fix an origin for his story – to authorise it – he is in fact citing 'himself' as the authority for the joke which is the last word of the chapter. This citing of 'Theophrastus' as the origin and source of this anecdote 'on comedy', and on the relationship of laughter to social stability means the 'author' himself is the only authority. Within his own cultural context (rather than in the 'original' Greek, or in seventeenth-century French), he is laughing to himself at an allusion only a handful of readers could be expected to understand. Author, text, origin, culture are the ambiguous and interrelated concepts with which Theophrastus is playing. This may be 'fine wit' and also an 'inside' joke. It is difficult to know what community, outside of herself, George Lewes, and a few classicist friends, George Eliot is testing.

In 'How We Encourage Research' (III), Theophrastus describes the behaviour of the cetaceans who exclude poor Merman: 'but the more learned cited his blunders aside to each other and laughed the laugh of the initiated' (III:33). Here, Theophrastus is both sympathetic and complicitous – an outsider and an insider, both and neither. To know whether any person or any group of people is inside or outside a particular culture, we have to know what that culture is. What is English culture? This is the ultimate question George Eliot asks in response to change in English culture, such as language and racial composition.

The nature of the fable from 'The Wasp Credited with the Honeycomb' (XI), which began this Introduction, invites the question: what are the cultural texts and traditions the English can claim as their own? And is it possible that 'we' have as little 'evidence' and as little knowledge on which to base our claims about the origins of our artistic and intellectual traditions as the animals had in drawing their conclusions about the origination of the honeycomb? In *Impressions* George Eliot is testing a new form not only to express, but to stage her anxieties about the perpetuation of a culture which seems to her to be devaluing the written word, and therefore the author. The work suggests that by the end of her career she had concluded the author was an outsider as measured against the 'ordinary reader' and was likely to be misunderstood and likely to be pilloried as a result. The defence of the author Theophrastus is to look for a community of insiders by writing in an 'idiom' that is, on one level, accessible and applicable to most people likely to read it, and on another level, a self-conscious attempt to constitute an inside-community of readers who are also writers, and who will recognise a subtext, in the form of humour as well as erudition.

The jokes and allusions, unattributed, esoteric, coy, which contribute to the past critical assessment of *Impressions* as fragmented, can be seen as an attempt to reconstitute a minority community of people who understand them. It is not easy to locate an author or a source for what is said in *Impressions*. Attempts to trace names often turn up multiple possibilities.

Quotations are introduced by 'it is said' or 'he virtually says'. Stories and phrases are freely borrowed. The concepts of originality and authorship are being questioned. That Theophrastus is able to draw on such a vast amount of material tells us something about how he has spent his life and what texts have been available to him. The pieces of past and foreign cultures that have been assimilated into English culture over the centuries are integrated by and in him, and his preoccupation with the 'debasing' of English culture and with its 'fusion' with other cultures is motivated by an anxiety about his own survival. Without national memory, there will be no national future, and Theophrastus, the childless bachelor writing unpublished manuscripts, imagines himself splintering into the pieces which he has until now managed to hold together through memory and consciousness.

The passionate argument against a too rapid fusion of cultures which comes in 'The Modern Hep' is superseded by the hysterical fear that 'consciousnesses' themselves will disappear and with them the 'race' of humans: 'Thus the feebler race, whose corporeal adjustments happened to be accompanied with a maniacal consciousness which imagined itself moving its mover, will have vanished, as all less adapted existences do before the fittest – ' (XVII:141). 'Shadows of the Coming Race' was originally placed by George Eliot after 'The Modern Hep',[30] and it is worth considering the logic of that organisation. If we imagine reading 'Shadows' after 'The Modern Hep', it might be easier to see how this chapter about the future of the 'human race' and its relationship to inhuman machines follows from the 'The Modern Hep', which ultimately argues that the individual person can only be fully human within a community. The tone of 'Shadows' is frantic not because George Eliot believed that human beings would evolve out of existence, only to be replaced by machines, but because the double consciousness of Theophrastus is simultaneously textual and human. In 'Shadows', Trost develops a 'theory of human' wellbeing, assuring Theophrastus, who gets depressed about 'the sight of the extremely unpleasant and disfiguring work by which many of our fellow-creatures have to get their bread'. '"All this"', says Trost, '"will soon be done by machinery"'.

'Shadows' was, in George Eliot's initial conception, to serve as an example of the 'blinding superstition' with which 'The Modern Hep' ends, 'the superstition that a theory of human wellbeing can be constructed in disregard of the influences which have made us human' (XVIII:165). In the dialogue of 'Shadows', Theophrastus is beside himself: he 'gets a little out of it' in discussing this theory with Trost because he is closer to the human average and 'imagines certain results' better than Trost can. Theophrastus seems to fear on behalf of his humanness, but he also fears on behalf of his fictiveness. In 'Shadows of the Coming Race', Theophrastus fears the obliteration of memory, which would end the 'effective bond of human action' coming from attachment to a national community, inevitably shaped by the texts it inherits and responsible for those it produces. The obliteration of memory through neglect of tradition (failure to see what makes us human, that we have flaws, that we are stronger within a community than outside of it) would be the end of the national, cultural identity which has made the production of a self-conscious, responsible author/character like Theophrastus possible. Memory, text, culture converge in Theophrastus, who fears in a terrible, comic moment of insight in 'Shadows of the Coming Race' that he – author, character, human – may be evolving out of existence.

The ultimate published order of the chapters changes the emphasis of the book. In 'Shadows', Theophrastus fears he will lose his control over the world around him and consequently of himself, and this fear leads to a temporary fragmentation. 'The Modern Hep' reconstitutes Theophrastus fully within a community. He regains himself and demonstrates the moral authority an author can have in addressing the urgent social and political issues of the present.

In beginning *Impressions*, we start with the title. By the end we know the book has kept its implied promise to describe 'Such a type who...'. Reading Theophrastus, we witness the unfolding of character, a 'typically' English character whose perspective in

'The Modern Hep' is Eliot's version of a characteristic English perspective: fair, tolerant, self-critical, flawed. Theophrastus has been called a 'mask' disguising the author George Eliot. More accurately, the name 'George Eliot' has disguised Theophrastus, such a type of character who would write this book, and who has always been there, if we had been willing to see him.

NOTES

[1] When Marian Evans Lewes anonymously published *Scenes of Clerical Life* (1857), there was a great deal of speculation about what sort of 'man' had written it. After she published *Adam Bede* (1859) under the pseudonym George Eliot, a popular theory developed that Joseph Liggins was the author. Liggins did not deny this, and thus became a source of annoyance (and amusement) for the Leweses. See Gordon S. Haight, *George Eliot: A Biography* (Oxford: Oxford University Press, 1968), pp. 211–94.

[2] The question of who made the honeycomb can be read as an allegory for who wrote the fable, recalling the late seventeenth-century 'battle' between the Ancients and the Moderns. Jonathan Swift parodied the debate between William Temple and Richard Bentley over the antiquity of *The Fables of Aesop* in his *The Battle of the Books* and *A Tale of a Tub*, both published in 1704.

[3] In 1844 the Scottish publisher Robert Chambers (1802–71) anonymously published *Vestiges of the Natural History of Creation* (1844), which popularised current evolutionary theories. In 1878, the authorship of that work was still unknown.

[4] See Rosemary Ashton, *G. H. Lewes: A Life* (Oxford: Clarendon Press, 1991).

[5] George Eliot insisted that a publisher's note be inserted: 'The Manuscript of this Work was put into our hands towards the close of last year, but the publication has been delayed owing to the domestic affliction of the Author'.

[6] *The George Eliot Letters*, 9 vols (Oxford: Oxford University Press, 1954–78), 2:269–70 (6 November 1856), hereafter *GEL*.

[7] Polly was George Lewes's nickname for Marian Lewes. Molluscs and other organisms are attributed with human characteristics in the book Lewes wrote during their first years together, *Sea-side Studies* (London and Edinburgh: William Blackwood and Sons, 1858).

[8] Lewes wrote theatre reviews in the *Leader* under the name 'Vivian' (1851–2). See *Versatile Victorian*, ed. Rosemary Ashton (London: Bristol Classical Press, 1992), pp. 29–41.

[9] Aristotle, *Rhetoric*, Bk. II.12,1388b,32–37.

[10] See *The Characters of Theophrastus* (London and Cambridge: Macmillan, 1870), translated and edited by R. C. Jebb, friend of the Leweses. See also J.W. Sneed, *The Theophrastan 'Character'* (Oxford: Clarendon Press, 1985).

[11] She considered calling the book, 'Characters and Characteristics or Impressions of Theophrastus Such, Edited by George Eliot'. See *GEL*, 7:111 (5 March 1879).

[12] George Eliot, *Romola*, ed. Andrew Brown (Oxford: Clarendon Press, 1993), p. 218.

[13] *GEL*, VII:200 (11 September 1879).

[14] *GEL*, VII:165 (12 June 1879).

[15] See the *Times* (5 June 1879), p. 4; the *Athenaeum* (by Joseph Jacobs, 7 June 1879) pp. 719–20; *Saturday Review* (28 June 1879) pp. 805–6; *Spectator* (June 1879); *Contemporary Review* (July 1879), pp. 765–6; *Fraser's* (July 1879), pp. 103–24; *Edinburgh Review* (October 1879), pp. 557–86. The last was by W. H. Mallock, whose satirical novel *The New Republic* (1877) was a likely target in 'Debasing the Moral Currency' (X). See *GEL*, 7:179, n. 9. In a letter, George Eliot called it 'a bastard kind of satire that I am not disposed to think the better of because Aristophanes used it in relation to Socrates'; see *GEL*, 6:406–7 (17 October 1877).

[16] *GEL*, 7:130 (9 April 1879).

[17] When George Eliot's publisher John Blackwood died on 29 October 1879, his nephew William Blackwood took over the correspondence about *Impressions*.

[18] *GEL*, 7:144 (1 May 1879).

[19] G. Robert Stange, 'The Voices of the Essayist', *Nineteenth-Century Fiction* 35 (December 1980), pp. 312–30. This essay makes a number of important observations about the place of *Impressions* in the moral essay tradition.

[20] Ashton, p. 276.

[21] Robert Speaight, *George Eliot* (London: Arthur Barker Ltd, 1954).

[22] George Levine, *An Annotated Critical Bibliography of George Eliot* (Brighton: Harvester Press, 1988), p. 6.

[23] See Joseph Jacobs's review in the *Athenaeum*, and Stange's article, both referred to above.

[24] See George Eliot's essay 'Authorship' in *Essays and Leaves from a Notebook* (London and Edinburgh: Blackwood and Sons, 1884). This essay appears in the same notebook in which George Eliot drafted early versions of some chapters in *Impressions*.

[25] *Nichomachean Ethics*, Bk. II.I, 1103b, 12–11036,26.

[26] The title is clearly taken from the science fiction novel by George Eliot's friend Edward Bulwer Lytton, *The Coming Race* (1871).

[27] Perhaps another allusion to *Sea-side Studies*, in which Lewes numbers the carp among the 'fish that ruminate' under the larger heading of 'Fish Paradoxes' (p. 238). In *Middlemarch* (Ch.29), Carp, Pike, and Tench are mentioned as rivals of Mr. Casaubon.

[28] 'Debasing the Moral Currency' is one of the few chapters to have been published in collections of Eliot's writings. See F.B. Pinion, *A George Eliot Miscellany* (London: Macmillan, 1982), pp. 158–67. George Eliot, *Selected Essays, Poems, and other Writings*, ed. A. S. Byatt and Nicholas Warren (London: Penguin Books, 1990), pp. 437–46.

[29] It is perhaps significant that Isaac Casaubon translated both Theophrastus's *Characters* and Athenaeus's *Deipnosophistae* from Greek into Latin. George

Eliot's choice of these classical texts might suggest another indirect allusion to her own Mr Casaubon, a joke which enhances the play between author, character, and translator in *Impressions*.

[30] In the manuscript of *Impressions*, the order of 'Shadows of the Coming Race' (marked by George Eliot Chapter XVIII) and 'The Modern Hep' (marked by her XVII) is the reverse of that in all published versions. The change in order presumably took place at the proof stage.

CHRONOLOGY

1819   (22 November) Mary Anne Evans born at South Farm, Arbury, near Nuneaton, Warwickshire

1836   (3 February) Mother, Christiana Pearson Evans, dies

1841   Moves with her father, Robert Evans, to Foleshill, Coventry

1846   Translation of David Strauss's *Life of Jesus*

1849   (30 May) Robert Evans dies

1850   Moves to London; now calls herself Marian Evans

1851   Begins editing the *Westminster Review* for John Chapman

1854   Translation of Feuerbach's *The Essence of Christianity*; (July 20) goes to Germany with George Henry Lewes

1855   Begins living with Lewes in London and calling herself Marian Lewes; Lewes's *Life of Goethe* published

1856   'Natural History of German Life' and 'Silly Novels by Lady Novelists' in the *Westminster Review*

1857   *Scenes of Clerical Life* begins with 'The Sad Fortunes of the Reverend Amos Barton' in *Blackwood's Magazine*

1858   *Scenes of Clerical Life*, 2 vols.; Lewes's *Sea-side Studies*

1859   *Adam Bede*

1860   *The Mill on the Floss*

1861   *Silas Marner*

1862   *Romola* begins in the *Cornhill Magazine*

1863   *Romola*, 3 vols.

1866   *Felix Holt*

1868   *The Spanish Gypsy*

1871–2   *Middlemarch*

1876   *Daniel Deronda*

1878   Writes *Impressions of Theophrastus Such*; (November 30) Lewes dies

SELECT BIBLIOGRAPHY

Annotated paperback editions of George Eliot's novels are available in the Penguin English Library Series and the Oxford World's Classics Series.

Ashton, Rosemary, *G.H. Lewes: A Life* (Oxford: Clarendon Press, 1991)

—— (ed.), *Versatile Victorian: Selected Writings of G.H. Lewes* (London: Bristol Classical Press, 1992).

Baker, William, *George Eliot and Judaism*, Salzburg Studies in English Literature (Institut für Englische Sprache und Literatur, University of Salzburg, 1975).

—— (ed.), *Some George Eliot Notebooks: An Edition of the Carl H. Pforzheimer Library's George Eliot Holograph Notebooks, MSS 707, 708, 709, 710, 711*, 4 vols (Institut für Englische Sprache und Literatur, University of Salzburg, 1976–85).

—— (ed.), *The Letters of G.H. Lewes* (Ohio University Press, forthcoming).

Collins, K.K., 'George Henry Lewes Revised: George Eliot and the Moral Sense', *Victorian Studies* 21 (Summer 1978): 463–492.

—— 'Reading George Eliot Reading Lewes's Obituaries', *Modern Philology* (November 1987): 153–169.

Cross, John Walter, *George Eliot's Life as Related in Her Letters and Journals*, 3 vols (William Blackwood and Sons, 1885).

Eliot, George, *Essays and Leaves from a Notebook* (William Blackwood and Sons, 1884).

—— *Selected Essays, Poems, and Other Writings*, ed. A.S. Byatt and Christopher Warren (Harmondsworth: Penguin Books, 1991).

Haight, Gordon S., *George Eliot: A Biography* (Oxford: Oxford University Press, 1968).

—— (ed.), *The George Eliot Letters*, 9 vols (Yale University Press, 1954–78).

McCormack, Kathleen, 'The Saccharissa Essays: George Eliot's Only Woman Persona,' *Nineteenth Century Studies* 4 (1990): 41–59.

Pinney, Thomas (ed.), *The Essays of George Eliot* (London: Routledge and Kegan Paul, 1963).

—— 'More Leaves from George Eliot's Notebook,' *Huntington Library Quarterly* 29 (1966): 353–376.

Stange, G. Robert, 'The Voices of the Essayist', *Nineteenth-Century Fiction* 35 (December 1980): 312–330.

Vogeler, Martha, 'George Eliot as Literary Widow', *Huntington Library Quarterly* (Spring 1988): 73–87.

NOTE ON THE TEXT

This text is based on the First British Edition of George Eliot's *Impressions of Theophrastus Such* (Edinburgh and London: William Blackwood and Sons, 1879). George Eliot's holograph MS is at the British Library [Add. MS 34043]. Corrected page proofs for both the first edition and the Cabinet Edition (Edinburgh and London: William Blackwood and Sons, 1880) are at the Harry Ransom Humanities Research Center at the University of Texas at Austin. George Eliot's working notebook, containing drafts of Chs. VI, VII, and XIII of *Impressions* is at the Huntington Library in San Marino, California [HM 12993]. Two deleted passages, one from the Huntington notebook [Appendix I] and one from the corrected proofs [Appendix II] have been published here for the first time. Significant variants in the MS, First Edition, and Cabinet Editions are noted, and a few spelling errors have been silently corrected.

ACKNOWLEDGMENTS

I would like to thank Jonathan Ouvry, The Huntington Library (especially Sara S. Hodson), and the Harry Ransom Humanities Research Center at the University of Texas at Austin for permission to print previously unpublished George Eliot material. I thank the Division of Humanities at the University of Chicago for subsidising my travel to the Huntington. I thank the entire staff at Pickering and Chatto for sharing their expertise and their office.

For help in annotating and interpreting *Impressions*, I thank William Baker, Lauren Berlant, David Bevington, Tony van den Broek, and Rachana Kamtekar. I wish to thank my friends in London, Nick Shah, Ritula Shah, and Barbara Handley. For help in preparing the text, I would like to thank Janelle Taylor and John O'Brien, and for his matchless persistence with George Eliot's prose (and patience with my own) I thank Joel Snyder. Stuart Tave read the parts of this edition in between chapters of my dissertation and Graham Handley (I think) read as many sets of proofs as I did. I dedicate this edition to them both, with personal thanks and in recognition of their influence as teachers and scholars.

'Suspicione si quis errabit sua,
Et rapiet ad se, quod erit commune omnium,
Stulte nudabit animi conscientiam.
Huic excusatum me velim nihilominus:
Neque enim notare singulos mens est mihi,
Verum ipsam vitam et mores hominum ostendere.'

– Phædrus.[1]

IMPRESSIONS

OF

THEOPHRASTUS SUCH

BY

GEORGE ELIOT

WILLIAM BLACKWOOD AND SONS
EDINBURGH AND LONDON
MDCCCLXXIX

Title page to the First Edition

LOOKING INWARD

IT is my habit to give an account to myself of the characters I meet with: can I give any true account of my own? I am a bachelor, without domestic distractions of any sort, and have all my life been an attentive companion to myself, flattering my nature agreeably on plausible occasions, reviling it rather bitterly when it mortified me, and in general remembering its doings and sufferings with a tenacity which is too apt to raise surprise if not disgust at the careless inaccuracy of my acquaintances, who impute to me opinions I never held, express their desire to convert me to my favourite ideas, forget whether I have ever been to the East, and are capable of being three several times astonished at my never having told them before of my accident in the Alps, causing me the nervous shock which has ever since notably diminished my digestive powers. Surely I ought to know myself better than these indifferent outsiders can know me; nay, better even than my intimate friends, to whom I have never breathed those items of my inward experience which have chiefly shaped my life.

Yet I have often been forced into the reflection that even the acquaintances who are as forgetful of my biography and tenets as they would be if I were a dead philosopher, are probably aware of certain points in me which may not be included in my most active suspicion. We sing an exquisite passage out of tune and innocently repeat it for the greater pleasure of our hearers. Who can be aware of what his foreign accent is in the ears of a native? And how can a man be conscious of that dull perception which causes him to mistake altogether what will make him agreeable to a particular woman, and to persevere eagerly in a behaviour which she is privately recording against him? I have had some confidences from my female friends as to their opinion of other men whom I have observed trying to make themselves amiable, and it has occurred to me that though I can hardly be so blundering as Lippus[1] and the rest of those mistaken candidates for favour whom I have seen ruining their chance by a too elaborate personal canvass, I must still come under the common fatality of mankind and share the liability to be absurd without knowing that I am absurd. It is in the nature of foolish reasoning to seem good to the foolish reasoner. Hence with all possible study of myself, with all possible effort to escape from the pitiable illusion which makes men laugh, shriek, or curl the lip at Folly's likeness, in total unconsciousness that it resembles themselves, I am obliged to recognise that while there are secrets in me unguessed by others, these others have certain items of knowledge about the extent of my powers and the figure I make with them, which in turn are secrets unguessed by me. When I was a lad I danced a hornpipe with arduous scrupulosity, and while suffering pangs of pallid shyness was yet proud of my superiority as a dancing pupil, imagining for myself a high place in the estimation of beholders; but I can now picture the amusement they had in the incongruity of my solemn face and ridiculous legs. What sort of hornpipe am I dancing now?

Thus if I laugh at you, O fellow-men! if I trace with curious interest your labyrinthine self-delusions, note the inconsistencies in your zealous adhesions, and smile at your helpless endeavours in a rashly chosen part, it is not that I feel myself aloof from you: the more intimately I seem to discern your weaknesses, the stronger to me is the proof that I share them. How otherwise could I get the discernment? – for even what we are averse to, what we vow not to entertain, must have shaped or shadowed itself within us as a possibility before we can think of exorcising it. No man can know his brother simply as a spectator. Dear blunderers, I am one of you. I wince at the fact, but I am not ignorant of it, that I too am laughable on unsuspected occasions; nay, in the very tempest and whirlwind of my anger,[2] I include myself under my own indignation. If the human race has a bad reputation, I perceive that I cannot escape being compromised. And thus while I carry in myself the key to other men's experience, it is only by observing others that I can so far correct my self-ignorance as to arrive at the certainty that I am liable to commit myself unawares and to manifest some incompetency which I know no more of than the blind man knows of his image in the glass.

Is it then possible to describe oneself at once faithfully and fully? In all autobiography there is, nay, ought to be, an incompleteness which may have the effect of falsity. We are each of us bound to reticence by the piety we owe to those who have been nearest to us and have had a mingled influence over our lives; by the fellow-feeling which should restrain us from turning our volunteered and picked confessions into an act of accusation against others, who have no chance of vindicating themselves; and most of all by that reverence for the higher efforts of our common nature, which commands us to bury its lowest fatalities, its invincible remnants of the brute, its most agonising struggles with temptation, in unbroken silence. But the incompleteness which comes of self-ignorance may be compensated by self-betrayal. A man who is affected to tears in dwelling on the generosity of his own sentiments makes me aware of several things not included under those terms. Who has sinned more against those three duteous reticences than Jean Jacques?[3] Yet half our impressions of his character come not from what he means to convey, but from what he unconsciously enables us to discern.

This *naïve* veracity of self-presentation is attainable by the slenderest talent on the most trivial occasions. The least lucid and impressive of orators may be perfectly successful in showing us the weak points of his grammar. Hence I too may be so far like Jean Jacques as to communicate more than I am aware of. I am not indeed writing an autobiography, or pretending to give an unreserved description of myself, but only offering some slight confessions in an apologetic light, to indicate that if in my absence you dealt as freely with my unconscious weaknesses as I have dealt with the unconscious weaknesses of others, I should not feel myself warranted by common-sense in regarding your freedom of observation as an exceptional case of evil-speaking; or as malignant interpretation of a character which really offers no handle to just objection; or even as an unfair use for your amusement of disadvantages which, since they are mine, should be regarded with more than ordinary tenderness. Let me at least try to feel myself in the ranks with my fellow-men. It is true, that I would rather not hear either your well-founded ridicule or your judicious strictures. Though not averse to finding fault with myself, and conscious of deserving lashes, I like to keep the scourge in my own discriminating hand. I never felt myself sufficiently meritorious to like being hated as a proof of my superiority, or so thirsty for improvement as to desire that all my acquaintances should give me their candid opinion of me. I really do not want to learn from my enemies: I prefer having none to learn from. Instead of being glad when men use me despitefully, I wish they would behave better and find a more amiable occupation for their intervals of business. In brief, after a close intimacy with myself for a longer period than I choose to mention, I find within me a permanent longing for approbation, sympathy, and love.

Yet I am a bachelor, and the person I love best has never loved me, or known that I loved her. Though continually in society, and caring about the joys and sorrows of my neighbours, I feel myself, so far as my personal lot is concerned, uncared for and alone. 'Your own fault, my dear fellow!' said Minutius Felix,[4] one day that I had incautiously mentioned this uninteresting fact. And he was right – in senses other than he intended. Why should I expect to be admired, and have my company doated on? I have done no services to my country beyond those of every peaceable orderly citizen; and as to intellectual contribution, my only published work was a failure, so that I am spoken of to inquiring beholders as 'the author of a book you have probably not seen.' (The work was a humorous romance, unique in its kind, and I am told is much tasted in a

Cherokee translation, where the jokes are rendered with all the serious eloquence characteristic of the Red races.)[5] This sort of distinction, as a writer nobody is likely to have read, can hardly counteract an indistinctness in my articulation, which the best-intentioned loudness will not remedy. Then, in some quarters my awkward feet are against me, the length of my upper lip, and an inveterate way I have of walking with my head foremost and my chin projecting. One can become only too well aware of such things by looking in the glass, or in that other mirror held up to nature[6] in the frank opinions of street-boys, or of our Free People[7] travelling by excursion train; and no doubt they account for the half-suppressed smile which I have observed on some fair faces when I have first been presented before them. This direct perceptive judgment is not to be argued against. But I am tempted to remonstrate when the physical points I have mentioned are apparently taken to warrant unfavourable inferences concerning my mental quickness. With all the increasing uncertainty which modern progress has thrown over the relations of mind and body, it seems tolerably clear that wit cannot be seated in the upper lip, and that the balance of the haunches in walking has nothing to do with the subtle discrimination of ideas. Yet strangers evidently do not expect me to make a clever observation, and my good things are as unnoticed as if they were anonymous pictures. I have indeed had the mixed satisfaction of finding that when they were appropriated by some one else they were found remarkable and even brilliant. It is to be borne in mind that I am not rich, have neither stud nor cellar, and no very high connections such as give to a look of imbecility a certain prestige of inheritance through a titled line; just as 'the Austrian lip'[8] confers a grandeur of historical associations on a kind of feature which might make us reject an advertising footman. I have now and then done harm to a good cause by speaking for it in public, and have discovered too late that my attitude on the occasion would more suitably have been that of negative beneficence. Is it really to the advantage of an opinion that I should be known to hold it? And as to the force of my arguments, that is a secondary consideration with audiences who have given a new scope to the *ex pede Herculem*[9] principle, and from awkward feet infer awkward fallacies. Once, when zeal lifted me on my legs, I distinctly heard an enlightened artisan remark, 'Here's a rum cut!' – and doubtless he reasoned in the same way as the elegant Glycera[10] when she politely puts on an air of listening to me, but elevates her eyebrows and chills her glance in sign of predetermined neutrality: both have their reasons for judging the quality of my speech beforehand.

This sort of reception to a man of affectionate disposition, who has also the innocent vanity of desiring to be agreeable, has naturally a depressing if not embittering tendency; and in early life I began to seek for some consoling point of view, some warrantable method of softening the hard peas I had to walk on, some comfortable fanaticism which might supply the needed self-satisfaction. At one time I dwelt much on the idea of compensation; trying to believe that I was all the wiser for my bruised vanity, that I had the higher place in the true spiritual scale, and even that a day might come when some visible triumph would place me in the French heaven of having the laughers on my side. But I presently perceived that this was a very odious sort of self-cajolery. Was it in the least true that I was wiser than several of my friends who made an excellent figure, and were perhaps praised a little beyond their merit? Is the ugly unready man in the corner, outside the current of conversation, really likely to have a fairer view of things than the agreeable talker, whose success strikes the unsuccessful as a repulsive example of forwardness and conceit? And as to compensation in future years, would the fact that I myself got it reconcile me to an order of things in which I could see a multitude with as bad a share as mine, who, instead of getting their corresponding compensation, were getting beyond the reach of it in old age? What could be more contemptible than the mood of mind which makes a man measure the justice of divine or human law by the agreeableness of his own shadow and the ample satisfaction of his own desires?

I dropped a form of consolation which seemed to be encouraging me in the persuasion that my discontent was the chief evil in the world, and my benefit the soul of good in that evil. May there not be at least a partial release from the imprisoning verdict that a man's philosophy is the formula of his personality? In certain branches of science we can ascertain our personal equation, the measure of difference between our own judgments and an average standard: may there not be some corresponding correction of our personal partialities in moral theorising? If a squint or other ocular defect disturbs my vision, I can get instructed in the fact, be made aware that my condition is abnormal, and either through spectacles or diligent imagination I can learn the average appearance of things: is there no remedy or corrective for that inward squint which consists in a dis- satisfied egoism or other want of mental balance? In my con- science I saw that the bias of personal discontent was just as misleading and odious as the bias of self-satisfaction. Whether we look through the rose-coloured glass or the indigo, we are equally far from the hues which the healthy human eye beholds in heaven above and earth below. I began to dread ways of consoling which were really a flattering of native illusions, a feeding-up into monstrosity of an inward growth already dis- proportionate; to get an especial scorn for that scorn of man- kind which is a transmuted disappointment of preposterous claims; to watch with peculiar alarm lest what I called my philosophic estimate of the human lot in general, should be a mere prose lyric expressing my own pain and consequent bad temper. The standing-ground worth striving after seemed to be some Delectable Mountain,[11] whence I could see things in proportions as little as possible determined by that self-partiality which certainly plays a necessary part in our bodily sustenance, but has a starving effect on the mind.

Thus I finally gave up any attempt to make out that I preferred cutting a bad figure, and that I liked to be despised, because in this way I was getting more virtuous than my successful rivals; and I have long looked with suspicion on all views which are recommended as peculiarly consolatory to wounded vanity or other personal disappointment. The consola- tions of egoism are simply a change of attitude or a resort to a new kind of diet which soothes and fattens it. Fed in this way it is apt to become a monstrous spiritual pride, or a chuckling satisfaction that the final balance will not be against us but against those who now eclipse us. Examining the world in order to find consolation is very much like looking carefully over the pages of a great book in order to find our own name, if not in the text, at least in a laudatory note: whether we find what we want or not, our preoccupation has hindered us from a true knowledge of the contents. But an attention fixed on the main theme or various matter of the book would deliver us from that slavish subjection to our own self-importance. And I had the mighty volume of the world before me. Nay, I had the struggling action of a myriad lives around me, each single life as dear to itself as mine to me. Was there no escape here from this stupidity of a murmuring self-occupation? Clearly enough, if anything hindered my thought from rising to the force of passionately interested contemplation, or my poor pent-up pond of sensitiveness from widening into a beneficent river of sympathy, it was my own dulness; and though I could not make myself the reverse of shallow all once, I had at least learned where I had better turn my attention.

Something came of this alteration in my point of view, though I admit that the result is of no striking kind. It is unnecessary for me to utter modest denials, since none have assured me that I have a vast intellectual scope, or – what is more surprising, considering I have done so little – that I might, if I chose, surpass any distinguished man whom they wish to depreciate. I have not attained any lofty peak of magnanimity, nor would I trust beforehand in my capability of meeting a severe demand for moral heroism. But that I have at least succeeded in establishing a habit of mind which keeps watch against my self-partiality and promotes a fair consideration of what touches the feelings or the fortunes of my neighbours, seems to be proved by the ready confidence with which men and women appeal to my interest in their experience. It is gratifying to one who would above all things avoid the insanity of fancying himself a more momentous or touching object than he really is, to find that nobody expects from him the least sign of such mental aberration, and that he is evidently held capable of listening to all kinds of personal outpouring without the least disposition to become communicative in the same way. This confirmation of the hope that my bearing is not that of the self-flattering lunatic is given me in ample measure. My acquaintances tell me unreservedly of their triumphs and their piques; explain their purposes at length, and reassure me with cheerfulness as to their chances of success; insist on their theories and accept me as a dummy with whom they rehearse their side of future discussions; unwind their coiled-up griefs in relation to their husbands, or recite to me examples of feminine incomprehensibleness as typified in their wives; mention frequently the fair applause which their merits have wrung from some persons, and the attacks to which certain oblique motives have stimulated others. At the time when I was less free from superstition about my own power of charming, I occasionally, in the glow of sympathy which embraced me and my confiding friend on the subject of his satisfaction or resentment, was urged to hint at a corresponding experience in my own case; but the signs of a rapidly lowering pulse and spreading nervous depression in my previously vivacious interlocutor, warned me that I was acting on that dangerous misreading, 'Do as you are done by.' Recalling the true version of the golden rule,[12] I could not wish that others should lower my spirits as I was lowering my friend's. After several times obtaining the same result from a like experiment in which all the circumstances were varied except my own personality, I took it as an established inference that these fitful signs of a lingering belief in my own importance were generally felt to be abnormal, and were something short of that sanity which I aimed to secure. Clearness on this point is not without its gratifications, as I have said. While my desire to explain myself in private ears has been quelled, the habit of getting interested in the experience of others has been continually gathering strength, and I am really at the point of finding that this world would be worth living in without any lot of one's own. Is it not possible for me to enjoy the scenery of the earth

without saying to myself, I have a cabbage-garden in it? But this
sounds like the lunacy of fancying oneself everybody else and
being unable to play one's own part decently – another form of
the disloyal attempt to be independent of the common lot, and
to live without a sharing of pain.

Perhaps I have made self-betrayals enough already to show
that I have not arrived at that non-human independence. My
conversational reticences about myself turn into garrulousness
on paper – as the sea-lion plunges and swims the more energeti-
cally because his limbs are of a sort to make him shambling on
land. The act of writing, in spite of past experience, brings with
it the vague, delightful illusion of an audience nearer to my
idiom than the Cherokees, and more numerous than the visionary One for whom many authors have declared themselves
willing to go through the pleasing punishment of publication.
My illusion is of a more liberal kind, and I imagine a far-off,
hazy, multitudinous assemblage, as in a picture of Paradise,
making an approving chorus to the sentences and paragraphs of
which I myself particularly enjoy the writing. The haze is a
necessary condition. If any physiognomy becomes distinct in the
foreground, it is fatal. The countenance is sure to be one bent on
discountenancing my innocent intentions: it is pale-eyed, incap-
able of being amused when I am amused or indignant at what
makes me indignant; it stares at my presumption, pities my
ignorance, or is manifestly preparing to expose the various
instances in which I unconsciously disgrace myself. I shudder at
this too corporeal auditor, and turn towards another point of
the compass where the haze is unbroken. Why should I not
indulge this remaining illusion, since I do not take my approving
choral paradise as a warrant for setting the press to work again
and making some thousand sheets of superior paper unsaleable?
I leave my manuscripts to a judgment outside my imagination,
but I will not ask to hear it, or request my friend to pronounce,
before I have been buried decently, what he really thinks of my
parts, and to state candidly whether my papers would be most
usefully applied in lighting the cheerful domestic fire. It is too
probable that he will be exasperated at the trouble I have given

him of reading them; but the consequent clearness and vivacity with which he could demonstrate to me that the fault of my manuscripts, as of my one published work, is simply flatness, and not that surpassing subtilty which is the preferable ground of popular neglect – this verdict, however instructively express- ed, is a portion of earthly discipline of which I will not beseech my friend to be the instrument. Other persons, I am aware, have not the same cowardly shrinking from a candid opinion of their performances, and are even importunately eager for it; but I have convinced myself in numerous cases that such exposers of their own back to the smiter were of too hopeful a disposition to believe in the scourge, and really trusted in a pleasant anointing, an outpouring of balm without any previous wounds. I am of a less trusting disposition, and will only ask my friend to use his judgment in insuring me against posthumous mistake.

Thus I make myself a charter to write, and keep the pleasing, inspiring illusion of being listened to, though I may sometimes write about myself. What I have already said on this too familiar theme has been meant only as a preface, to show that in noting the weaknesses of my acquaintances I am conscious of my fellowship with them. That a gratified sense of superiority is at the root of barbarous laughter may be at least half the truth. But there is a loving laughter in which the only recognised superior- ity is that of the ideal self, the God within, holding the mirror and the scourge for our own pettiness as well as our neigh- bours'.

LOOKING BACKWARD

MOST of us who have had decent parents would shrink from wishing that our father and mother had been somebody else whom we never knew; yet it is held no impiety, rather, a graceful mark of instruction, for a man to wail that he was not the son of another age and another nation, of which also he knows nothing except through the easy process of an imperfect imagination and a flattering fancy.

But the period thus looked back on with a purely admiring regret, as perfect enough to suit a superior mind, is always a long way off; the desirable contemporaries are hardly nearer than Leonardo da Vinci, most likely they are the fellow-citizens of Pericles, or, best of all, of the Æolic lyrists whose sparse remains suggest a comfortable contrast with our redundance.[1] No impassioned personage wishes he had been born in the age of Pitt,[2] that his ardent youth might have eaten the dearest bread, dressed itself with the longest coat-tails and the shortest waist, or heard the loudest grumbling at the heaviest war-taxes; and it would be really something original in polished verse if one of our young writers declared he would gladly be turned eighty-five that he might have known the joy and pride of being an Englishman when there were fewer reforms and plenty of highwaymen, fewer discoveries and more faces pitted with the small-pox, when laws were made to keep up the price of corn, and the troublesome Irish were more miserable. Three-quarters of a century ago is not a distance that lends much enchantment to the view. We are familiar with the average men of that period, and are still consciously encumbered with its bad contrivances and mistaken acts. The lords and gentlemen painted by young Lawrence[3] talked and wrote their nonsense in a tongue we thoroughly understand; hence their times are not much flattered, not much glorified by the yearnings of that modern sect of Flagellants[4] who make a ritual of lashing – not themselves but – all their neighbours. To me, however, that paternal time, the time of my father's youth, never seemed prosaic, for it came to my imagination first through his memories, which made a wondrous perspective to my little daily world of discovery. And for my part I can call no age absolutely unpoetic: how should it be so, since there are always children to whom the acorns and the swallow's eggs are a wonder, always those human passions and fatalities through which Garrick[5] as Hamlet in bob-wig and knee-breeches moved his audience more than some have since done in velvet tunic and plume? But every age since the golden may be made more or less prosaic by minds that attend only to its vulgar and sordid elements, of which there was always an abundance even in Greece and Italy, the favourite realms of the retrospective optimists. To be quite fair towards the ages, a little ugliness as well as beauty must be allowed to each of them, a little implicit poetry even to those which echoed loudest with servile, pompous, and trivial prose.

Such impartiality is not in vogue at present. If we acknowledge our obligation to the ancients, it is hardly to be done without some flouting of our contemporaries, who with all their faults must be allowed the merit of keeping the world habitable for the refined eulogists of the blameless past. One wonders whether the remarkable originators who first had the notion of digging wells, or of churning for butter, and who were certainly very useful to their own time as well as ours, were left quite free from invidious comparison with predecessors who let the water and the milk alone, or whether some rhetorical nomad, as he stretched himself on the grass with a good appetite for contemporary butter, became loud on the virtue of ancestors who were uncorrupted by the produce of the cow; nay, whether in a high flight of imaginative self-sacrifice (after swallowing the butter) he even wished himself earlier

born and already eaten for the sustenance of a generation more
naïve than his own.

I have often had the fool's hectic[6] of wishing about the
unalterable, but with me that useless exercise has turned chiefly
on the conception of a different self, and not, as it usually does
in literature, on the advantage of having been born in a different
age, and more especially in one where life is imagined to have
been altogether majestic and graceful. With my present abilities,
external proportions, and generally small provision for ecstatic
enjoyment, where is the ground for confidence that I should
have had a preferable career in such an epoch of society? An age
in which every department has its awkward-squad[7] seems in my
mind's eye to suit me better. I might have wandered by the
Strymon under Philip and Alexander[8] without throwing any
new light on method or organising the sum of human knowledge; on the other hand, I might have objected to Aristotle as
too much of a systematiser, and have preferred the freedom of
a little self-contradiction as offering more chances of truth. I
gather, too, from the undeniable testimony of his disciple
Theophrastus that there were bores, ill-bred persons, and de-
tractors even in Athens, of species remarkably corresponding to
the English, and not yet made endurable by being classic; and
altogether, with my present fastidious nostril, I feel that I am
the better off for possessing Athenian life solely as an inodorous
fragment of antiquity.[9] As to Sappho's Mitylene, while I am
convinced that the Lesbian capital held some plain men of
middle stature and slow conversational powers, the addition of
myself to their number, though clad in the majestic folds of the
himation[10] and without cravat, would hardly have made a
sensation among the accomplished fair ones who were so precise in adjusting their own drapery about their delicate ankles.
Whereas by being another sort of person in the present age I
might have given it some needful theoretic clue; or I might have
poured forth poetic strains which would have anticipated theory
and seemed a voice from 'the prophetic soul of the wide world
dreaming of things to come;'[11] or I might have been one of
those benignant lovely souls who, without astonishing the public

and posterity, make a happy difference in the lives close around them, and in this way lift the average of earthly joy: in some form or other I might have been so filled from the store of universal existence that I should have been freed from that empty wishing which is like a child's cry to be inside a golden cloud, its imagination being too ignorant to figure the lining of dimness and damp.

On the whole, though there is some rash boasting about enlightenment, and an occasional insistance on an originality which is that of the present year's corn-crop, we seem too much disposed to indulge, and to call by complimentary names, a greater charity for other portions of the human race than for our contemporaries. All reverence and gratitude for the worthy Dead on whose labours we have entered, all care for the future generations whose lot we are preparing; but some affection and fairness for those who are doing the actual work of the world, some attempt to regard them with the same freedom from ill-temper, whether on private or public grounds, as we may hope will be felt by those who will call us ancient! Otherwise, the looking before and after,[12] which is our grand human privilege, is in danger of turning to a sort of other-worldliness, breeding a more illogical indifference or bitterness than was ever bred by the ascetic's contemplation of heaven. Except on the ground of a primitive golden age and continuous degeneracy, I see no rational footing for scorning the whole present population of the globe, unless I scorn every previous generation from whom they have inherited their diseases of mind and body, and by conse-quence scorn my own scorn, which is equally an inheritance of mixed ideas and feelings concocted for me in the boiling caldron of this universally contemptible life, and so on – scorning to infinity. This may represent some actual states of mind, for it is a narrow prejudice of mathematicians to suppose that ways of thinking are to be driven out of the field by being reduced to an absurdity. The Absurd is taken as an excellent juicy thistle by many constitutions.

Reflections of this sort have gradually determined me not to grumble at the age in which I happen to have been born – a natural tendency certainly older than Hesiod.[13] Many ancient beautiful things are lost, many ugly modern things have arisen; but invert the proposition and it is equally true. I at least am a modern with some interest in advocating tolerance, and notwithstanding an inborn beguilement which carries my affection and regret continually into an imagined past, I am aware that I must lose all sense of moral proportion unless I keep alive a stronger attachment to what is near, and a power of admiring what I best know and understand. Hence this question of wishing to be rid of one's contemporaries associates itself with my filial feeling, and calls up the thought that I might as justifiably wish that I had had other parents than those whose loving tones are my earliest memory, and whose last parting first taught me the meaning of death. I feel bound to quell such a wish as blasphemy.

Besides, there are other reasons why I am contented that my father was a country parson, born much about the same time as Scott and Wordsworth;[14] notwithstanding certain qualms I have felt at the fact that the property on which I am living was saved out of tithe before the period of commutation, and without the provisional transfiguration into a modus.[15] It has sometimes occurred to me when I have been taking a slice of excellent ham that, from a too tenable point of view, I was breakfasting on a small squealing black pig which, more than half a century ago, was the unwilling representative of spiritual advantages not otherwise acknowledged by the grudging farmer or dairyman who parted with him. One enters on a fearful labyrinth in tracing compound interest backward, and such complications of thought have reduced the flavour of the ham; but since I have nevertheless eaten it, the chief effect has been to moderate the severity of my radicalism (which was not part of my paternal inheritance) and to raise the assuaging reflection, that if the pig and the parishioner had been intelligent enough to anticipate my historical point of view, they would have seen themselves and the rector in a light that would have made tithe voluntary. Notwithstanding such drawbacks I am rather fond of the mental furniture I got by having a father who was well acquainted with all ranks of his neighbours, and am thankful that he was not one of those aristocratic clergymen who could not have sat down to a meal with any family in the parish except my lord's – still more that he was not an earl or a marquis. A chief misfortune of high birth is that it usually shuts a man out from the large sympathetic knowledge of human experience which comes from contact with various classes on their own level, and in my father's time that entail of social ignorance had not been disturbed as we see it now. To look always from overhead at the crowd of one's fellow-men must be in many ways incapacitating, even with the best will and intelligence. The serious blunders it must lead to in the effort to manage them for their good, one may see clearly by the mistaken ways people take of flattering and enticing those whose associations are unlike their own. Hence I have always thought that the most fortunate Britons are those whose experience has given them a practical share in many aspects of the national lot, who have lived long among the mixed commonalty, roughing it with them under difficulties, knowing how their food tastes to them, and getting acquainted with their notions and motives not by inference from traditional types in literature or from philosophical theories, but from daily fellowship and observation. Of course such experience is apt to get antiquated, and my father might find himself much at a loss amongst a mixed rural population of the present day; but he knew very well what could be wisely expected from the miners, the weavers, the field-labourers, and farmers of his own time – yes, and from the aristocracy, for he had been brought up in close contact with them and had been companion to a young nobleman who was deaf and dumb. 'A clergyman, lad,' he used to say to me, 'should feel in himself a bit of every class;' and this theory had a felicitous agreement with his inclination and practice, which certainly answered in making him beloved by his parishioners. They grumbled at their obligations towards him; but what then? It was natural to grumble at any demand for payment, tithe included, but also natural for a rector to desire his tithe and look well after the levying. A Christian pastor who did not mind about his money

was not an ideal prevalent among the rural minds of fat central
England, and might have seemed to introduce a dangerous laxity
of supposition about Christian laymen who happened to be
creditors. My father was none the less beloved because he was
understood to be of a saving disposition, and how could he save
without getting his tithe? The sight of him was not unwelcome
at any door, and he was remarkable among the clergy of his
district for having no lasting feud with rich or poor in his parish.
I profited by his popularity, and for months after my mother's
death, when I was a little fellow of nine, I was taken care of first
at one homestead and then at another; a variety which I enjoyed
much more than my stay at the Hall, where there was a tutor.
Afterwards for several years I was my father's constant companion in his outdoor business, riding by his side on my little pony
and listening to the lengthy dialogues he held with Darby or
Joan,[16] the one on the road or in the fields, the other outside or
inside her door. In my earliest remembrance of him his hair was
already grey, for I was his youngest as well as his only surviving
child; and it seemed to me that advanced age was appropriate to
a father, as indeed in all respects I considered him a parent so
much to my honour, that the mention of my relationship to him
was likely to secure me regard among those to whom I was
otherwise a stranger – my father's stories from his life including
so many names of distant persons that my imagination placed no
limit to his acquaintanceship. He was a pithy talker, and his
sermons bore marks of his own composition. It is true, they
must have been already old when I began to listen to them, and
they were no more than a year's supply, so that they recurred as
regularly as the Collects.[17] But though this system has been
much ridiculed, I am prepared to defend it as equally sound
with that of a liturgy; and even if my researches had shown me
that some of my father's yearly sermons had been copied out
from the works of elder divines, this would only have been
another proof of his good judgment. One may prefer fresh eggs
though laid by a fowl of the meanest understanding, but why
fresh sermons?

Nor can I be sorry, though myself given to meditative if not active innovation, that my father was a Tory who had not exactly a dislike to innovators and dissenters, but a slight opinion of them as persons of ill-founded self-confidence; whence my young ears gathered many details concerning those who might perhaps have called themselves the more advanced thinkers in our nearest market-town, tending to convince me that their characters were quite as mixed as those of the thinkers behind them. This circumstance of my rearing has at least delivered me from certain mistakes of classification which I observe in many of my superiors, who have apparently no affectionate memories of a goodness mingled with what they now regard as outworn prejudices. Indeed, my philosophical notions, such as they are, continually carry me back to the time when the fitful gleams of a spring day used to show me my own shadow as that of a small boy on a small pony, riding by the side of a larger cob-mounted shadow over the breezy uplands which we used to dignify with the name of hills, or along by-roads with broad grassy borders and hedgerows reckless of utility, on our way to outlying hamlets, whose groups of inhabitants were as distinctive to my imagination as if they had belonged to different regions of the globe. From these we sometimes rode onward to the adjoining parish, where also my father officiated, for he was a pluralist, but – I hasten to add – on the smallest scale; for his one extra living was a poor vicarage, with hardly fifty parishioners, and its church would have made a very shabby barn, the grey worm-eaten wood of its pews and pulpit, with their doors only half hanging on the hinges, being exactly the colour of a lean mouse which I once observed as an interesting member of the scant congregation, and conjectured to be the identical church mouse I had heard referred to as an example of extreme poverty, for I was a precocious boy, and often reasoned after the fashion of my elders, arguing that 'Jack and Jill' were real personages in our parish, and that if I could identify 'Jack' I should find on him the marks of a broken crown.

Sometimes when I am in a crowded London drawing-room (for I am a town-bird now, acquainted with smoky eaves, and tasting Nature in the parks) quick flights of memory take me

back among my father's parishioners while I am still conscious
of elbowing men who wear the same evening uniform as myself;
and I presently begin to wonder what varieties of history lie
hidden under this monotony of aspect. Some of them, perhaps,
belong to families with many quarterings; but how many 'quarterings' of diverse contact with their fellow-countrymen enter
into their qualifications to be parliamentary leaders, professors
of social science, or journalistic guides of the popular mind?[18]
Not that I feel myself a person made competent by experience;
on the contrary, I argue that since an observation of different
ranks has still left me practically a poor creature, what must be
the condition of those who object even to read about the life of
other British classes than their own? But of my elbowing neighbours with their crush hats, I usually imagine that the most
distinguished among them have probably had a far more instructive journey into manhood than mine. Here, perhaps, is a
thought-worn physiognomy, seeming at the present moment to
be classed as a mere species of white cravat and swallow-tail,
which may once, like Faraday's,[19] have shown itself in curiously
dubious embryonic form leaning against a cottage lintel in small
corduroys, and hungrily eating a bit of brown bread and bacon;
there is a pair of eyes, now too much wearied by the gas-light of
public assemblies, that once perhaps learned to read their native
England through the same alphabet as mine – not within the
boundaries of an ancestral park, never even being driven
through the county town five miles off, but – among the
midland villages and markets, along by the tree-studded hedgerows, and where the heavy barges seem in the distance to float
mysteriously among the rushes and the feathered grass. Our
vision, both real and ideal, has since then been filled with far
other scenes: among eternal snows and stupendous sun-
scorched monuments of departed empires; within the scent of
the long orange-groves; and where the temple of Neptune looks
out over the siren-haunted sea. But my eyes at least have kept
their early affectionate joy in our native landscape, which is one
deep root of our national life and language.

And I often smile at my consciousness that certain conservative

prepossessions have mingled themselves for me with the influences of our midland scenery, from the tops of the elms down
to the buttercups and the little wayside vetches. Naturally
enough. That part of my father's prime to which he oftenest
referred had fallen on the days when the great wave of political
enthusiasm and belief in a speedy regeneration of all things had
ebbed, and the supposed millennial initiative of France was
turning into a Napoleonic empire, the sway of an Attila with a
mouth speaking proud things in a jargon half revolutionary, half
Roman.[20] Men were beginning to shrink timidly from the
memory of their own words and from the recognition of the
fellowships they had formed ten years before; and even reforming Englishmen for the most part were willing to wait for the
perfection of society, if only they could keep their throats
perfect and help to drive away the chief enemy of mankind from
our coasts. To my father's mind the noisy teachers of revolutionary doctrine were, to speak mildly, a variable mixture of the
fool and the scoundrel; the welfare of the nation lay in a strong
Government which could maintain order; and I was accustomed
to hear him utter the word 'Government' in a tone that charged
it with awe, and made it part of my effective religion, in contrast
with the word 'rebel,' which seemed to carry the stamp of evil
in its syllables, and, lit by the fact that Satan was the first rebel,
made an argument dispensing with more detailed inquiry. I
gathered that our national troubles in the first two decades of
this century were not at all due to the mistakes of our adminis-
trators; and that England, with its fine Church and Constitution,
would have been exceedingly well off if every British subject had
been thankful for what was provided, and had minded his own
business – if, for example, numerous Catholics of that period
had been aware how very modest they ought to be considering
they were Irish. The times, I heard, had often been bad; but I
was constantly hearing of 'bad times' as a name for actual
evenings and mornings when the godfathers who gave them that
name appeared to me remarkably comfortable. Altogether, my
father's England seemed to me lovable, laudable, full of good
men, and having good rulers, from Mr Pitt on to the Duke of

Wellington,[21] until he was for emancipating the Catholics; and it was so far from prosaic to me that I looked into it for a more exciting romance than such as I could find in my own adventures, which consisted mainly in fancied crises calling for the resolute wielding of domestic swords and firearms against unapparent robbers, rioters, and invaders who, it seemed, in my father's prime had more chance of being real. The morris-dancers[22] had not then dwindled to a ragged and almost vanished rout (owing the traditional name probably to the historic fancy of our superannuated groom); also, the good old king was alive and well, which made all the more difference because I had no notion what he was and did – only understanding in general that if he had been still on the throne he would have hindered everything that wise persons thought undesirable.

Certainly that elder England with its frankly saleable boroughs, so cheap compared with the seats obtained under the reformed method, and its boroughs kindly presented by noblemen desirous to encourage gratitude; its prisons with a miscellaneous company of felons and maniacs and without any supply of water; its bloated, idle charities; its non-resident, jovial clergy; its militia-balloting; and above all, its blank ignorance of what we, its posterity, should be thinking of it, – has great differences from the England of to-day. Yet we discern a strong family likeness. Is there any country which shows at once as much stability and as much susceptibility to change as ours? Our national life is like that scenery which I early learned to love, not subject to great convulsions, but easily showing more or less delicate (sometimes melancholy) effects from minor changes. Hence our midland plains have never lost their familiar expression and conservative spirit for me; yet at every other mile, since I first looked on them, some sign of world-wide change, some new direction of human labour has wrought itself into what one may call the speech of the landscape – in contrast with those grander and vaster regions of the earth which keep an indifferent aspect in the presence of men's toil and devices. What does it signify that a lilliputian train passes over a viaduct amidst the abysses of the Apennines,[23] or that a caravan laden with a nation's offerings creeps across the unresting sameness of the desert, or that a petty cloud of steam sweeps for an instant over the face of an Egyptian colossus immovably submitting to its slow burial beneath the sand?[24] But our woodlands and pastures, our hedge-parted corn-fields and meadows, our bits of high common where we used to plant the windmills, our quiet little rivers here and there fit to turn a mill-wheel, our villages along the old coach-roads, are all easily alterable lineaments that seem to make the face of our Motherland sympathetic with the laborious lives of her children. She does not take their ploughs and waggons contemptuously, but rather makes every hovel and every sheepfold, every railed bridge or fallen tree-trunk an agreeably noticeable incident; not a mere speck in the midst of unmeasured vastness, but a piece of our social history in pictorial writing.

Our rural tracts – where no Babel-chimney scales the heavens – are without mighty objects to fill the soul with the sense of an outer world unconquerably aloof from our efforts. The wastes are playgrounds (and let us try to keep them such for the children's children who will inherit no other sort of demesne);[25] the grasses and reeds nod to each other over the river, but we have cut a canal close by; the very heights laugh with corn in August or lift the plough-team against the sky in September. Then comes a crowd of burly navvies with pickaxes and barrows, and while hardly a wrinkle is made in the fading mother's face or a new curve of health in the blooming girl's, the hills are cut through or the breaches between them spanned, we choose our level and the white steam-pennon flies along it.[26]

But because our land shows this readiness to be changed, all signs of permanence upon it raise a tender attachment instead of awe: some of us, at least, love the scanty relics of our forests, and are thankful if a bush is left of the old hedgerow. A crumbling bit of wall where the delicate ivy-leaved toad-flax hangs its light branches, or a bit of grey thatch with patches of dark moss on its shoulder and a troop of grass-stems on its ridge, is a thing to visit. And then the tiled roof of cottage and homestead, of the long cow-shed where generations of the

milky mothers have stood patiently, of the broad-shouldered
barns where the old-fashioned flail once made resonant music,
while the watch-dog barked at the timidly venturesome fowls
making pecking raids on the outflying grain – the roofs that have
looked out from among the elms and walnut-trees, or beside the
yearly group of hay and corn stacks, or below the square stone
steeple, gathering their grey or ochre-tinted lichens and their
olive-green mosses under all ministries, – let us praise the sober
harmonies they give to our landscape, helping to unite us
pleasantly with the elder generations who tilled the soil for us
before we were born, and paid heavier and heavier taxes, with
much grumbling, but without that deepest root of corruption –
the self-indulgent despair which cuts down and consumes and
never plants.

But I check myself. Perhaps this England of my affections is
half visionary – a dream in which things are connected according to my well-fed, lazy mood, and not at all by the multitudinous links of graver, sadder fact, such as belong everywhere to
the story of human labour. Well, well, the illusions that began
for us when we were less acquainted with evil have not lost
their value when we discern them to be illusions. They feed the
ideal Better, and in loving them still, we strengthen the precious
habit of loving something not visibly, tangibly existent, but a
spiritual product of our visible tangible selves.

I cherish my childish loves – the memory of that warm little
nest where my affections were fledged. Since then I have
learned to care for foreign countries, for literatures foreign and
ancient, for the life of Continental towns dozing round old
cathedrals, for the life of London, half sleepless with eager
thought and strife, with indigestion or with hunger; and now
my consciousness is chiefly of the busy, anxious metropolitan
sort. My system responds sensitively to the London weather-
signs, political, social, literary; and my bachelor's hearth is
imbedded where by much craning of head and neck I can catch
sight of a sycamore in the Square garden: I belong to the 'Nation
of London.'[27] Why? There have been many voluntary exiles in
the world, and probably in the very first exodus of the patriarchal

Aryans – for I am determined not to fetch my examples from races whose talk is of uncles and no fathers[28] – some of those who sallied forth went for the sake of a loved companionship, when they would willingly have kept sight of the familiar plains, and of the hills to which they had first lifted up their eyes.[29]

HOW WE ENCOURAGE RESEARCH

THE serene and beneficent goddess Truth, like other deities whose disposition has been too hastily inferred from that of the men who have invoked them, can hardly be well pleased with much of the worship paid to her even in this milder age, when the stake and the rack have ceased to form part of her ritual. Some cruelties still pass for service done in her honour: no thumb-screw is used, no iron boot, no scorching of flesh; but plenty of controversial bruising, laceration, and even lifelong maiming. Less than formerly; but so long as this sort of truth-worship has the sanction of a public that can often understand nothing in a controversy except personal sarcasm or slanderous ridicule, it is likely to continue. The sufferings of its victims are often as little regarded as those of the sacrificial pig offered in old time, with what we now regard as a sad miscalculation of effects.

One such victim is my old acquaintance Merman.[1]

Twenty years ago Merman was a young man of promise, a conveyancer[2] with a practice which had certainly budded, but, like Aaron's rod, seemed not destined to proceed further in that marvellous activity.[3] Meanwhile he occupied himself in miscellaneous periodical writing and in a multifarious study of moral and physical science. What chiefly attracted him in all subjects were the vexed questions which have the advantage of not admitting the decisive proof or disproof that renders many ingenious arguments superannuated. Not that Merman had a wrangling disposition: he put all his doubts, queries, and paradoxes deferentially, contended without unpleasant heat and only with a sonorous eagerness against the personality of Homer, expressed himself civilly though firmly on the origin of language, and had tact enough to drop at the right moment such subjects as the ultimate reduction of all the so-called elementary substances, his own total scepticism concerning Manetho's chronology, or even the relation between the magnetic condition of the earth and the outbreak of revolutionary tendencies.[4] Such flexibility was naturally much helped by his amiable feeling towards woman, whose nervous system, he was convinced, would not bear the continuous strain of difficult topics; and also by his willingness to contribute a song whenever the same desultory charmer proposed music. Indeed his tastes were domestic enough to beguile him into marriage when his resources were still very moderate and partly uncertain. His friends wished that so ingenious and agreeable a fellow might have more prosperity than they ventured to hope for him, their chief regret on his account being that he did not concentrate his talent and leave off forming opinions on at least half-a-dozen of the subjects over which he scattered his attention, especially now that he had married a 'nice little woman' (the generic name for acquaintances' wives when they are not markedly disagreeable). He could not, they observed, want all his various knowledge and Laputan ideas[5] for his periodical writing which brought him most of his bread, and he would do well to use his talents in getting a speciality that would fit him for a post. Perhaps these well-disposed persons were a little rash in presuming that fitness for a post would be the surest ground for getting it; and on the whole, in now looking back on their wishes for Merman, their chief satisfaction must be that those wishes did not contribute to the actual result.

For in an evil hour Merman did concentrate himself. He had for many years taken into his interest the comparative history of the ancient civilisations, but it had not preoccupied him so as to narrow his generous attention to everything else. One sleepless night, however (his wife has more than once narrated to me the details of an event memorable to her as the beginning of sorrows), after spending some hours over the epoch-making

work of Grampus,[6] a new idea seized him with regard to the
possible connection of certain symbolic monuments common to
widely scattered races. Merman started up in bed. The night
was cold, and the sudden withdrawal of warmth made his wife
first dream of a snowball, and then cry –

'What is the matter, Proteus?'[7]

'A great matter, Julia.[8] That fellow Grampus, whose book is
cried up as a revelation, is all wrong about the Magicodumbras
and the Zuzumotzis,[9] and I have got hold of the right clue.'

'Good gracious! does it matter so much? Don't drag the
clothes, dear.'

'It signifies this, Julia, that if I am right I shall set the world
right; I shall regenerate history; I shall win the mind of Europe
to a new view of social origins; I shall bruise the head of many
superstitions.'

'Oh no, dear, don't go too far into things. Lie down again.
You have been dreaming. What are the Madicojumbras and
Zuzitotzums? I never heard you talk of them before. What use
can it be troubling yourself about such things?'

'That is the way, Julia – that is the way wives alienate their
husbands, and make any hearth pleasanter to him than his own!'

'What *do* you mean, Proteus?'

'Why, if a woman will not try to understand her husband's
ideas, or at least to believe that they are of more value than she
can understand – if she is to join anybody who happens to be
against him, and suppose he is a fool because others contradict
him – there is an end of our happiness. That is all I have to say.'

'Oh no, Proteus, dear. I do believe what you say is right. That
is my only guide. I am sure I never have any opinions in any
other way: I mean about subjects. Of course there are many
little things that would tease you, that you like me to judge of
for myself. I know I said once that I did not want you to sing
"Oh ruddier than the cherry,"[10] because it was not in your
voice. But I cannot remember ever differing from you about
subjects. I never in my life thought any one cleverer than you.'

Julia Merman was really a 'nice little woman,' not one of the
stately Dians sometimes spoken of in those terms. Her black

silhouette had a very infantine aspect, but she had discernment
and wisdom enough to act on the strong hint of that memorable
conversation, never again giving her husband the slightest
ground for suspecting that she thought treasonably of his ideas
in relation to the Magicodumbras and Zuzumotzis, or in the
least relaxed her faith in his infallibility because Europe was not
also convinced of it. It was well for her that she did not increase
her troubles in this way; but to do her justice, what she was
chiefly anxious about was to avoid increasing her husband's
troubles.

Not that these were great in the beginning. In the first
development and writing out of his scheme, Merman had a
more intense kind of intellectual pleasure than he had ever
known before. His face became more radiant, his general view
of human prospects more cheerful. Foreseeing that truth as
presented by himself would win the recognition of his contemporaries, he excused with much liberality their rather rough
treatment of other theorists whose basis was less perfect. His
own periodical criticisms had never before been so amiable: he
was sorry for that unlucky majority whom the spirit of the age,
or some other prompting more definite and local, compelled to
write without any particular ideas. The possession of an original
theory which has not yet been assailed must certainly sweeten
the temper of a man who is not beforehand ill-natured. And
Merman was the reverse of ill-natured.

But the hour of publication came; and to half-a-dozen persons, described as the learned world of two hemispheres, it
became known that Grampus was attacked. This might have
been a small matter; for who or what on earth that is good for
anything is not assailed by ignorance, stupidity, or malice – and
sometimes even by just objection? But on examination it
appeared that the attack might possibly be held damaging,
unless the ignorance of the author were well exposed and his
pretended facts shown to be chimeras of that remarkably
hideous kind begotten by imperfect learning on the more feminine element of original incapacity. Grampus himself did not
immediately cut open the volume which Merman had been

careful to send him, not without a very lively and shifting conception of the possible effects which the explosive gift might produce on the too eminent scholar – effects that must certainly have set in on the third day from the despatch of the parcel. But in point of fact Grampus knew nothing of the book until his friend Lord Narwhal sent him an American newspaper containing a spirited article by the well-known Professor Sperm N. Whale which was rather equivocal in its bearing, the passages quoted from Merman being of rather a telling sort, and the paragraphs which seemed to blow defiance being unaccountably feeble, coming from so distinguished a Cetacean. Then, by another post, arrived letters from Butzkopf and Dugong, both men whose signatures were familiar to the Teutonic world in the *Selten-erscheinende Monat-schrift*[11] or Hayrick for the insertion of Split Hairs, asking their Master whether he meant to take up the combat, because, in the contrary case, both were ready.

Thus America and Germany were roused, though England was still drowsy, and it seemed time now for Grampus to find Merman's book under the heap and cut it open. For his own part he was perfectly at ease about his system; but this is a world in which the truth requires defence, and specious falsehood must be met with exposure. Grampus having once looked through the book, no longer wanted any urging to write the most crushing of replies. This, and nothing less than this, was due from him to the cause of sound inquiry; and the punishment would cost him little pains. In three weeks from that time the palpitating Merman saw his book announced in the programme of the leading Review. No need for Grampus to put his signature. Who else had his vast yet microscopic knowledge, who else his power of epithet? This article in which Merman was pilloried and as good as mutilated – for he was shown to have neither ear nor nose for the subtleties of philological and archæological study – was much read and more talked of, not because of any interest in the system of Grampus, or any precise conception of the danger attending lax views of the Magico-dumbras and Zuzumotzis, but because the sharp epigrams with which the victim was lacerated, and the soaring fountains of acrid mud which were shot upward and poured over the fresh wounds, were found amusing in recital. A favourite passage was one in which a certain kind of sciolist[12] was described as a creature of the Walrus kind, having a phantasmal resemblance to higher animals when seen by ignorant minds in the twilight, dabbling or hobbling in first one element and then the other, without parts or organs suited to either, in fact one of Nature's impostors who could not be said to have any artful pretences, since a congenital incompetence to all precision of aim and movement made their every action a pretence – just as a being born in doeskin gloves would necessarily pass a judgment on surfaces, but we all know what his judgment would be worth. In drawing-room circles, and for the immediate hour, this ingenious comparison was as damaging as the showing up of Merman's mistakes and the mere smattering of linguistic and historical knowledge which he had presumed to be a sufficient basis for theorising; but the more learned cited his blunders aside to each other and laughed the laugh of the initiated. In fact, Merman's was a remarkable case of sudden notoriety. In London drums and clubs[13] he was spoken of abundantly as one who had written ridiculously about the Magicodumbras and Zuzumotzis: the leaders of conversation, whether Christians, Jews, infidels, or of any other confession except the confession of ignorance, pronouncing him shallow and indiscreet if not presumptuous and absurd. He was heard of at Warsaw, and even Paris took knowledge of him. M. Cachalot had not read either Grampus or Merman, but he heard of their dispute in time to insert a paragraph upon it in his brilliant work, *L'orient au point de vue actuel*, in which he was dispassionate enough to speak of Grampus as possessing a *coup d'œil presque français* in matters of historical interpretation, and of Merman as nevertheless an objector *qui mérite d'être connu*.[14] M. Porpesse, also, availing himself of M. Cachalot's knowledge, reproduced it in an article with certain additions, which it is only fair to distinguish as his own, implying that the vigorous English of Grampus was not always as correct as a Frenchman could desire, while Merman's objections were more sophistical than solid. Presently, indeed, there appeared an able *extrait* of Grampus's article in the valuable *Rapporteur scientifique et historique*, and Merman's mistakes were thus brought under the notice of certain Frenchmen who are among the masters of those who know[15] on oriental subjects. In a word, Merman, though not extensively read, was extensively read about.

Meanwhile, how did he like it? Perhaps nobody, except his wife, for a moment reflected on that. An amused society considered that he was severely punished, but did not take the trouble to imagine his sensations; indeed this would have been a difficulty for persons less sensitive and excitable than Merman himself. Perhaps that popular comparison of the Walrus had truth enough to bite and blister on thorough application, even if exultant ignorance had not applauded it. But it is well known that the walrus, though not in the least a malignant animal, if allowed to display its remarkably plain person and blundering performances at ease in any element it chooses, becomes desperately savage and musters alarming auxiliaries when attacked or hurt. In this characteristic, at least, Merman resembled the walrus. And now he concentrated himself with a vengeance. That his counter-theory was fundamentally the right one he had a genuine conviction, whatever collateral mistakes he might have committed; and his bread would not cease to be bitter to him until he had convinced his contemporaries that Grampus had used his minute learning as a dust-cloud to hide sophistical evasions – that, in fact, minute learning was an obstacle to clear-sighted judgment, more especially with regard to the Magico-dumbras and Zuzumotzis, and that the best preparation in this matter was a wide survey of history and a diversified observation of men. Still, Merman was resolved to muster all the learning within his reach, and he wandered day and night through many wildernesses of German print, he tried compendious methods of learning oriental tongues, and, so to speak, getting at the marrow of languages independently of the bones, for the chance of finding details to corroborate his own views, or possibly even to detect Grampus in some oversight or textual tampering. All other work was neglected: rare clients were sent away and amazed editors found this maniac indifferent to his chance of getting book-parcels from them. It was many months before Merman had satisfied himself that he was strong enough to face round upon his adversary. But at last he had prepared sixty condensed pages of eager argument which seemed to him worthy to rank with the best models of controversial writing. He had acknowledged his mistakes, but had restated his theory so as to show that it was left intact in spite of them; and he had even found cases in which Ziphius, Microps, Scrag Whale the explorer, and other Cetaceans of unanswerable authority, were decidedly at issue with Grampus. Especially a passage cited by this last from that greatest of fossils Megalosaurus was demonstrated by Merman to be capable of three different interpretations, all preferable to that chosen by Grampus, who took the words in their most literal sense; for, 1°, the incomparable Saurian, alike unequalled in close observation and far-glancing comprehensiveness, might have meant those words ironically; 2°, *motzis* was probably a false reading for *potzis*, in which case its bearing was reversed; and 3°, it is known that in the age of the Saurians there were conceptions about the *motzis* which entirely remove it from the category of things comprehensible in an age when Saurians run ridiculously small: all which views were godfathered by names quite fit to be ranked with that of Grampus. In fine, Merman wound up his rejoinder by sincerely thanking the eminent adversary without whose fierce assault he might not have undertaken a revision in the course of which he had met with unexpected and striking confirmations of his own fundamental views. Evidently Merman's anger was at white heat.

The rejoinder being complete, all that remained was to find a suitable medium for its publication. This was not so easy. Distinguished mediums would not lend themselves to contradictions of Grampus, or if they would, Merman's article was too long and too abstruse, while he would not consent to leave anything out of an article which had no superfluities; for all this happened years ago when the world was at a different stage. At last, however, he got his rejoinder printed, and not on hard terms, since the medium, in every sense modest, did not ask him to pay for its insertion.

But if Merman expected to call out Grampus again, he was mistaken. Everybody felt it too absurd that Merman should undertake to correct Grampus in matters of erudition, and an eminent man has something else to do than to refute a petty objector twice over. What was essential had been done: the public had been enabled to form a true judgment of Merman's incapacity, the Magicodumbras and Zuzumotzis were but subsidiary elements in Grampus's system, and Merman might now be dealt with by younger members of the master's school. But he had at least the satisfaction of finding that he had raised a discussion which would not be let die. The followers of Grampus took it up with an ardour and industry of research worthy of their exemplar. Butzkopf made it the subject of an elaborate *Einleitung* to his important work, *Die Bedeutung des Ægyptischen Labyrinthes*;[16] and Dugong, in a remarkable address which he delivered to a learned society in Central Europe, introduced Merman's theory with so much power of sarcasm that it became a theme of more or less derisive allusion to men of many tongues. Merman with his Magicodumbras and Zuzumotzis was on the way to become a proverb, being used illustratively by many able journalists who took those names of questionable things to be Merman's own invention, 'than which,' said one of the graver guides, 'we can recall few more melancholy examples of speculative aberration.' Naturally the subject passed into popular literature, and figured very commonly in advertised programmes. The fluent Loligo, the formidable Shark, and a younger member of his remarkable family known as S. Catulus,[17] made a special reputation by their numerous articles, eloquent, lively, or abusive, all on the same theme, under titles ingeniously varied, alliterative, sonorous, or boldly fanciful; such as, 'Moments with Mr Merman,' 'Mr Merman and the Magicodumbras,' 'Greenland Grampus and Proteus Merman,' 'Grampian Heights and their Climbers, or the New Excelsior.' They tossed him on short sentences; they swathed him in paragraphs of winding imagery; they found him at once a mere plagiarist and a theoriser of unexampled perversity, ridiculously wrong about *potzis* and ignorant of Pali;[18] they hinted, indeed, at certain things which to their knowledge he had silently brooded over in his boyhood, and seemed tolerably well assured that this preposterous attempt to gainsay an incomparable Cetacean of world-wide fame had its origin in a peculiar mixture of bitterness and eccentricity which, rightly estimated and seen in its definite proportions, would furnish the best key to his argumentation. All alike were sorry for Merman's lack of sound learning, but how could their readers be sorry? Sound learning would not have been amusing; and as it was, Merman was made to furnish these readers with amusement at no expense of trouble on their part. Even burlesque writers looked into his book to see where it could be made use of, and those who did not know him were desirous of meeting him at dinner as one likely to feed their comic vein.

On the other hand, he made a serious figure in sermons under the name of 'Some' or 'Others' who had attempted presumptuously to scale eminences too high and arduous for human ability, and had given an example of ignominious failure edifying to the humble Christian.[19]

All this might be very advantageous for able persons whose superfluous fund of expression needed a paying investment, but the effect on Merman himself was unhappily not so transient as the busy writing and speaking of which he had become the occasion. His certainty that he was right naturally got stronger in proportion as the spirit of resistance was stimulated. The scorn and unfairness with which he felt himself to have been treated by those really competent to appreciate his ideas had galled him and made a chronic sore; and the exultant chorus of the incompetent seemed a pouring of vinegar on his wound. His brain became a registry of the foolish and ignorant objections made against him, and of continually amplified answers to these objections. Unable to get his answers printed, he had recourse to that more primitive mode of publication, oral transmission or button-holding, now generally regarded as a troublesome survival, and the once pleasant, flexible Merman was on the way to be shunned as a bore. His interest in new acquaintances turned chiefly on the possibility that they would care about the Magico-dumbras and Zuzumotzis; that they would listen to his complaints and exposures of unfairness, and not only accept copies of what he had written on the subject, but send him appreciative letters in acknowledgment. Repeated disappointment of such hopes tended to embitter him, and not the less because after a while the fashion of mentioning him died out, allusions to his theory were less understood, and people could only pretend to remember it. And all the while Merman was perfectly sure that his very opponents who had knowledge enough to be capable judges were aware that his book, whatever errors of statement they might detect in it, had served as a sort of divining rod, pointing out hidden sources of historical interpretation; nay, his jealous examination discerned in a new work by Grampus himself a certain shifting of ground which − so poor Merman declared − was the sign of an intention gradually to appropriate the views of the man he had attempted to brand as an ignorant impostor.

And Julia? And the housekeeping? − the rent, food, and clothing, which controversy can hardly supply unless it be of the kind that serves as a recommendation to certain posts. Controversial pamphlets have been known to earn large plums; but nothing of the sort could be expected from unpractical heresies about the Magicodumbras and Zuzumotzis. Painfully the contrary. Merman's reputation as a sober thinker, a safe writer, a sound lawyer, was irretrievably injured: the distractions of controversy had caused him to neglect useful editorial connections, and indeed his dwindling care for miscellaneous subjects made his contributions too dull to be desirable. Even if he could now have given a new turn to his concentration, and applied his talents so as to be ready to show himself an exceptionally qualified lawyer, he would only have been like an architect in competition, too late with his superior plans; he would not have had an opportunity of showing his qualification. He was thrown out of the course. The small capital which had filled up deficiencies of income was almost exhausted, and Julia, in the effort to make supplies equal to wants, had to use much ingenuity in diminishing the wants. The brave and affectionate woman whose small outline, so unimpressive against an illuminated background, held within it a good share of feminine heroism, did her best to keep up the charm of home and soothe her husband's excitement; parting with the best jewel among her wedding presents in order to pay rent, without ever hinting to her husband that this sad result had come of his undertaking to convince people who only laughed at him. She was a resigned little creature, and reflected that some husbands took to drinking and others to forgery: hers had only taken to the Magico-dumbras and Zuzumotzis, and was not unkind – only a little more indifferent to her and the two children than she had ever expected he would be, his mind being eaten up with 'subjects,' and constantly a little angry, not with her, but with everybody else, especially those who were celebrated.

This was the sad truth. Merman felt himself ill-used by the world, and thought very much worse of the world in consequence. The gall of his adversaries' ink had been sucked into his system and ran in his blood. He was still in the prime of life, but his mind was aged by that eager monotonous construction which comes of feverish excitement on a single topic and uses up the intellectual strength.

Merman had never been a rich man, but he was now conspicuously poor, and in need of the friends who had power or interest which he believed they could exert on his behalf. Their omitting or declining to give this help could not seem to him so clearly as to them an inevitable consequence of his having become impracticable, or at least of his passing for a man whose views were not likely to be safe and sober. Each friend in turn offended him, though unwillingly, and was suspected of wishing to shake him off. It was not altogether so; but poor Merman's society had undeniably ceased to be attractive, and it was difficult to help him. At last the pressure of want urged him to try for a post far beneath his earlier prospects, and he gained it. He holds it still, for he has no vices, and his domestic life has kept up a sweetening current of motive around and within him.

Nevertheless, the bitter flavour mingling itself with all topics, the premature weariness and withering, are irrevocably there. It is as if he had gone through a disease which alters what we call the constitution. He has long ceased to talk eagerly of the ideas which possess him, or to attempt making proselytes. The dial has moved onward, and he himself sees many of his former guesses in a new light. On the other hand, he has seen what he foreboded, that the main idea which was at the root of his too rash theorising has been adopted by Grampus and received with general respect, no reference being heard to the ridiculous figure this important conception made when ushered in by the incompetent 'Others.'

Now and then, on rare occasions, when a sympathetic *tête-à-tête* has restored some of his old expansiveness, he will tell a companion in a railway carriage, or other place of meeting favourable to autobiographical confidences, what has been the course of things in his particular case, as an example of the justice to be expected of the world. The companion usually allows for the bitterness of a disappointed man, and is secretly disinclined to believe that Grampus was to blame.

A MAN SURPRISED AT HIS ORIGINALITY

AMONG the many acute sayings of La Rochefoucauld, there is hardly one more acute than this: 'La plus grande ambition n'en a pas la moindre apparence lorsqu'elle se rencontre dans une impossibilité absolue d'arriver où elle aspire.'[1] Some of us might do well to use this hint in our treatment of acquaintances and friends from whom we are expecting gratitude because we are so very kind in thinking of them, inviting them, and even listening to what they say – considering how insignificant they must feel themselves to be. We are often fallaciously confident in supposing that our friend's state of mind is appropriate to our moderate estimate of his importance: almost as if we imagined the humble mollusc (so useful as an illustration) to have a sense of his own exceeding softness and low place in the scale of being.[2] Your mollusc, on the contrary, is inwardly objecting to every other grade of solid rather than to himself. Accustomed to observe what we think an unwarrantable conceit exhibiting itself in ridiculous pretensions and forwardness to play the lion's part, in obvious self-complacency and loud peremptoriness, we are not on the alert to detect the egoistic claims of a more exorbitant kind often hidden under an apparent neutrality or an acquiescence in being put out of the question.

Thoughts of this kind occurred to me yesterday when I saw the name of Lentulus[3] in the obituary. The majority of his acquaintances, I imagine, have always thought of him as a man justly unpretending and as nobody's rival; but some of them have perhaps been struck with surprise at his reserve in praising the works of his contemporaries, and have now and then felt

themselves in need of a key to his remarks on men of celebrity
in various departments. He was a man of fair position, deriving
his income from a business in which he did nothing, at leisure
to frequent clubs and at ease in giving dinners; well-looking,
polite, and generally acceptable in society as a part of what we
may call its bread-crumb – the neutral basis needful for the
plums and spice. Why, then, did he speak of the modern Maro
or the modern Flaccus[4] with a peculiarity in his tone of assent
to other people's praise which might almost have led you to
suppose that the eminent poet had borrowed money of him and
showed an indisposition to repay? He had no criticism to offer,
no sign of objection more specific than a slight cough, a scarcely
perceptible pause before assenting, and an air of self-control in
his utterance – as if certain considerations had determined him
not to inform against the so-called poet, who to his knowledge
was a mere versifier. If you had questioned him closely, he
would perhaps have confessed that he did think something
better might be done in the way of Eclogues and Georgics, or of
Odes and Epodes,[5] and that to his mind poetry was something
very different from what had hitherto been known under that
name.

For my own part, being of a superstitious nature, given
readily to imagine alarming causes, I immediately, on first
getting these mystic hints from Lentulus, concluded that he held
a number of entirely original poems, or at the very least a
revolutionary treatise on poetics, in that melancholy manuscript
state to which works excelling all that is ever printed are
necessarily condemned; and I was long timid in speaking of the
poets when he was present. For what might not Lentulus have
done, or be profoundly aware of, that would make my ignorant
impressions ridiculous? One cannot well be sure of the negative
in such a case, except through certain positives that bear witness
to it; and those witnesses are not always to be got hold of. But
time wearing on, I perceived that the attitude of Lentulus
towards the philosophers was essentially the same as his attitude
towards the poets; nay, there was something so much more
decided in his mode of closing his mouth after brief speech on

the former, there was such an air of rapt consciousness in his private hints as to his conviction that all thinking hitherto had been an elaborate mistake, and as to his own power of conceiving a sound basis for a lasting superstructure, that I began to believe less in the poetical stores, and to infer that the line of Lentulus lay rather in the rational criticism of our beliefs and in systematic construction. In this case I did not figure to myself the existence of formidable manuscripts ready for the press; for great thinkers are known to carry their theories growing within their minds long before committing them to paper, and the ideas which made a new passion for them when their locks were jet or auburn, remain perilously unwritten, an inwardly developing condition of their successive selves, until the locks are grey or scanty. I only meditated improvingly on the way in which a man of exceptional faculties, and even carrying within him some of that fierce refiner's fire which is to purge away the dross of human error,[6] may move about in society totally unrecognised, regarded as a person whose opinion is superfluous, and only rising into a power in emergencies of threatened black-balling. Imagine a Descartes or a Locke[7] being recognised for nothing more than a good fellow and a perfect gentleman – what a painful view does such a picture suggest of impenetrable dulness in the society around them!

I would at all times rather be reduced to a cheaper estimate of a particular person, if by that means I can get a more cheerful view of my fellow-men generally; and I confess that in a certain curiosity which led me to cultivate Lentulus's acquaintance, my hope leaned to the discovery that he was a less remarkable man than he had seemed to imply. It would have been a grief to discover that he was bitter or malicious, but by finding him to be neither a mighty poet, nor a revolutionary poetical critic, nor an epoch-making philosopher, my admiration for the poets and thinkers whom he rated so low would recover all its buoyancy, and I should not be left to trust to that very suspicious sort of merit which constitutes an exception in the history of mankind, and recommends itself as the total abolitionist of all previous claims on our confidence. You are not greatly surprised at the

infirm logic of the coachman who would persuade you to engage
him by insisting that any other would be sure to rob you in the
matter of hay and corn, thus demanding a difficult belief in him
as the sole exception from the frailties of his calling; but it is
rather astonishing that the wholesale decriers of mankind and its
performances should be even more unwary in their reasoning
than the coachman, since each of them not merely confides in
your regarding himself as an exception, but overlooks the almost
certain fact that you are wondering whether he inwardly ex-
cepts *you*. Now, conscious of entertaining some common opinions which seemed to fall under the mildly intimated but
sweeping ban of Lentulus, my self-complacency was a little
concerned.

Hence I deliberately attempted to draw out Lentulus in
private dialogue, for it is the reverse of injury to a man to offer
him that hearing which he seems to have found nowhere else.
And for whatever purposes silence may be equal to gold, it
cannot be safely taken as an indication of specific ideas. I sought
to know why Lentulus was more than indifferent to the poets,
and what was that new poetry which he had either written or,
as to its principles, distinctly conceived. But I presently found
that he knew very little of any particular poet, and had a general
notion of poetry as the use of artificial language to express
unreal sentiments: he instanced 'The Giaour,' 'Lalla Rookh,'
'The Pleasures of Hope,' and 'Ruin seize thee, ruthless King;'
adding, 'and plenty more.'[8] On my observing that he probably
preferred a larger, simpler style, he emphatically assented. 'Have
you not,' said I, 'written something of that order?' 'No; but I
often compose as I go along. I see how things might be written
as fine as Ossian,[9] only with true ideas. The world has no notion
what poetry will be.'

It was impossible to disprove this, and I am always glad to
believe that the poverty of our imagination is no measure of the
world's resources. Our posterity will no doubt get fuel in ways
that we are unable to devise for them. But what this conversation persuaded me of was, that the birth with which the mind
of Lentulus was pregnant could not be poetry, though I did not

question that he composed as he went along, and that the
exercise was accompanied with a great sense of power. This is a
frequent experience in dreams, and much of our waking experience is but a dream in the daylight. Nay, for what I saw, the
compositions might be fairly classed as Ossianic. But I was
satisfied that Lentulus could not disturb my grateful admiration
for the poets of all ages by eclipsing them, or by putting them
under a new electric light of criticism.

Still, he had himself thrown the chief emphasis of his
protest and his consciousness of corrective illumination on the
philosophic thinking of our race; and his tone in assuring me
that everything which had been done in that way was wrong —
that Plato, Robert Owen, and Dr Tuffle who wrote in the
'Regulator,'[10] were all equally mistaken — gave my superstitious nature a thrill of anxiety. After what had passed about
the poets, it did not seem likely that Lentulus had all systems by
heart; but who could say he had not seized that thread which
may somewhere hang out loosely from the web of things and be
the clue of unravelment? We need not go far to learn that a
prophet is not made by erudition. Lentulus at least had not the
bias of a school; and if it turned out that he was in agreement
with any celebrated thinker, ancient or modern, the agreement
would have the value of an undesigned coincidence not due to
forgotten reading. It was therefore with renewed curiosity that
I engaged him on this large subject — the universal erroneous-
ness of thinking up to the period when Lentulus began that
process. And here I found him more copious than on the theme
of poetry. He admitted that he did contemplate writing down
his thoughts, but his difficulty was their abundance. Apparently
he was like the woodcutter entering the thick forest and saying,
'Where shall I begin?' The same obstacle appeared in a minor
degree to cling about his verbal exposition, and accounted
perhaps for his rather helter-skelter choice of remarks bearing
on the number of unaddressed letters sent to the post-office; on
what logic really is, as tending to support the buoyancy of
human mediums and mahogany tables; on the probability of all
miracles under all religions when explained by hidden laws, and

my unreasonableness in supposing that their profuse occurrence
at half a guinea an hour in recent times was anything more than
a coincidence; on the haphazard way in which marriages are
determined – showing the baselessness of social and moral
schemes; and on his expectation that he should offend the
scientific world when he told them what he thought of elec-
tricity as an agent.

No man's appearance could be graver or more gentleman-like
than that of Lentulus as we walked along the Mall while he
delivered these observations, understood by himself to have a
regenerative bearing on human society. His wristbands and
black gloves, his hat and nicely clipped hair, his laudable moder-
ation in beard, and his evident discrimination in choosing his
tailor, all seemed to excuse the prevalent estimate of him as a
man untainted with heterodoxy, and likely to be so unencum-
bered with opinions that he would always be useful as an
assenting and admiring listener. Men of science seeing him at
their lectures doubtless flattered themselves that he came to
learn from them; the philosophic ornaments of our time, ex-
pounding some of their luminous ideas in the social circle, took
the meditative gaze of Lentulus for one of surprise not unmixed
with a just reverence at such close reasoning towards so novel a
conclusion; and those who are called men of the world considered him a good fellow who might be asked to vote for a friend
of their own and would have no troublesome notions to make
him unaccommodating. You perceive how very much they were
all mistaken, except in qualifying him as a good fellow.

This Lentulus certainly was, in the sense of being free from
envy, hatred, and malice;[11] and such freedom was all the more
remarkable an indication of native benignity, because of his
gaseous, illimitably expansive conceit. Yes, conceit; for that his
enormous and contentedly ignorant confidence in his own
rambling thoughts was usually clad in a decent silence, is no
reason why it should be less strictly called by the name directly
implying a complacent self-estimate unwarranted by performance. Nay, the total privacy in which he enjoyed his consciousness of inspiration was the very condition of its undisturbed

placid nourishment and gigantic growth. Your audibly arrogant man exposes himself to tests: in attempting to make an impression on others he may possibly (not always) be made to feel his own lack of definiteness; and the demand for definiteness is to all of us a needful check on vague depreciation of what others do, and vague ecstatic trust in our own superior ability. But Lentulus was at once so unreceptive, and so little gifted with the power of displaying his miscellaneous deficiency of information, that there was really nothing to hinder his astonishment at the spontaneous crop of ideas which his mind secretly yielded. If it occurred to him that there were more meanings than one for the word 'motive,' since it sometimes meant the end aimed at and sometimes the feeling that prompted the aiming, and that the word 'cause' was also of changeable import, he was naturally struck with the truth of his own perception, and was convinced that if this vein were well followed out much might be made of it. Men were evidently in the wrong about cause and effect, else why was society in the confused state we behold? And as to motive, Lentulus felt that when he came to write down his views he should look deeply into this kind of subject and show up thereby the anomalies of our social institutions; meanwhile the various aspects of 'motive' and 'cause' flitted about among the motley crowd of ideas which he regarded as original, and pregnant with reformative efficacy. For his unaffected goodwill made him regard all his insight as only valuable because it tended towards reform.

The respectable man had got into his illusory maze of discoveries by letting go that clue of conformity in his thinking which he had kept fast hold of in his tailoring and manners. He regarded heterodoxy as a power in itself, and took his inacquaintance with doctrines for a creative dissidence. But his epitaph needs not to be a melancholy one. His benevolent disposition was more effective for good than his silent presumption for harm. He might have been mischievous but for the lack of words: instead of being astonished at his inspirations in private, he might have clad his addled originalities, disjointed commonplaces, blind denials, and balloon-like conclusions, in

that mighty sort of language which would have made a new
Koran for a knot of followers. I mean no disrespect to the
ancient Koran, but one would not desire the roc to lay more
eggs and give us a whole wing-flapping brood to soar and make
twilight.[12]

Peace be with Lentulus, for he has left us in peace. Blessed is
the man who, having nothing to say, abstains from giving us
wordy evidence of the fact – from calling on us to look through
a heap of millet-seed in order to be sure that there is no pearl in
it.[13]

A TOO DEFERENTIAL MAN

A LITTLE unpremeditated insincerity must be indulged under the stress of social intercourse. The talk even of an honest man must often represent merely his wish to be inoffensive or agreeable rather than his genuine opinion or feeling on the matter in hand. His thought, if uttered, might be wounding; or he has not the ability to utter it with exactness and snatches at a loose paraphrase; or he has really no genuine thought on the question and is driven to fill up the vacancy by borrowing the remarks in vogue. These are the winds and currents we have all to steer amongst, and they are often too strong for our truthfulness or our wit. Let us not bear too hardly on each other for this common incidental frailty, or think that we rise superior to it by dropping all considerateness and deference.

But there are studious, deliberate forms of insincerity which it is fair to be impatient with: Hinze's,[1] for example. From his name you might suppose him to be German: in fact, his family is Alsatian, but has been settled in England for more than one generation. He is the superlatively deferential man, and walks about with murmured wonder at the wisdom and discernment of everybody who talks to him. He cultivates the low-toned *tête-à-tête*, keeping his hat carefully in his hand and often stroking it, while he smiles with downcast eyes, as if to relieve his feelings under the pressure of the remarkable conversation which it is his honour to enjoy at the present moment. I confess to some rage on hearing him yesterday talking to Felicia, who is certainly a clever woman, and, without any unusual desire to show her cleverness, occasionally says something of her own or makes an allusion which is not quite common. Still, it must happen to her as to every one else to speak of many subjects on which the best things were said long ago, and in conversation with a person who has been newly introduced those well-worn themes naturally recur as a further development of salutations and preliminary media of understanding, such as pipes, chocolate, or mastic-chewing,[2] which serve to confirm the impression that our new acquaintance is on a civilised footing and has enough regard for formulas to save us from shocking outbursts of individualism, to which we are always exposed with the tamest bear or baboon. Considered purely as a matter of information, it cannot any longer be important for us to learn that a British subject included in the last census holds Shakspere to be supreme in the presentation of character; still, it is as admissible for any one to make this statement about himself as to rub his hands and tell you that the air is brisk, if only he will let it fall as a matter of course, with a parenthetic lightness, and not announce his adhesion to a commonplace with an emphatic insistance, as if it were a proof of singular insight. We mortals should chiefly like to talk to each other out of goodwill and fellowship, not for the sake of hearing revelations or being stimulated by witticisms; and I have usually found that it is the rather dull person who appears to be disgusted with his contemporaries because they are not always strikingly original, and to satisfy whom the party at a country house should have included the prophet Isaiah, Plato, Francis Bacon, and Voltaire.[3] It is always your heaviest bore who is astonished at the tameness of modern celebrities: naturally; for a little of his company has reduced them to a state of flaccid fatigue. It is right and meet that there should be an abundant utterance of good sound commonplaces. Part of an agreeable talker's charm is that he lets them fall continually with no more than their due emphasis. Giving a pleasant voice to what we are all well assured of, makes a sort of wholesome air for more special and dubious remark to move in.

Hence it seemed to me far from unbecoming in Felicia that in her first dialogue with Hinze, previously quite a stranger to her, her observations were those of an ordinarily refined and well-educated woman on standard subjects, and might have been printed in a manual of polite topics and creditable opinions. She had no desire to astonish a man of whom she had heard nothing particular. It was all the more exasperating to see and hear Hinze's reception of her well-bred conformities. Felicia's acquaintances know her as the suitable wife of a distinguished man, a sensible, vivacious, kindly-disposed woman, helping her husband with graceful apologies written and spoken, and making her receptions agreeable to all comers. But you would have imagined that Hinze had been prepared by general report to regard this introduction to her as an opportunity comparable to an audience of the Delphic Sibyl.[4] When she had delivered herself on the changes in Italian travel, on the difficulty of reading Ariosto[5] in these busy times, on the want of equilibrium in French political affairs, and on the pre-eminence of German music, he would know what to think. Felicia was evidently embarrassed by his reverent wonder, and, in dread lest she should seem to be playing the oracle, became somewhat confused, stumbling on her answers rather than choosing them. But this made no difference to Hinze's rapt attention and subdued eagerness of inquiry. He continued to put large questions, bending his head slightly that his eyes might be a little lifted in awaiting her reply.

'What, may I ask, is your opinion as to the state of Art in England?'

'Oh,' said Felicia, with a light deprecatory laugh, 'I think it suffers from two diseases – bad taste in the patrons and want of inspiration in the artists.'

'That is true indeed,' said Hinze, in an undertone of deep conviction. 'You have put your finger with strict accuracy on the causes of decline. To a cultivated taste like yours this must be particularly painful.'

'I did not say there was actual decline,' said Felicia, with a touch of *brusquerie*. 'I don't set myself up as the great personage whom nothing can please.'

'That would be too severe a misfortune for others,' says my complimentary ape. 'You approve, perhaps, of Rosemary's

"Babes in the Wood,"[6] as something fresh and *naïve* in sculpture?'
  'I think it enchanting.'
  'Does he know that? Or *will* you permit me to tell him?'
  'Heaven forbid! It would be an impertinence in me to praise a work of his – to pronounce on its quality; and that I happen to like it can be of no consequence to him.'
  Here was an occasion for Hinze to smile down on his hat and stroke it – Felicia's ignorance that her praise was inestimable being peculiarly noteworthy to an observer of mankind. Presently he was quite sure that her favourite author was Shakspere, and wished to know what she thought of Hamlet's madness. When she had quoted Wilhelm Meister[7] on this point, and had afterwards testified that 'Lear' was beyond adequate presentation, that 'Julius Cæsar' was an effective acting play, and that a poet may know a good deal about human nature while knowing little of geography, Hinze appeared so impressed with the plenitude of these revelations that he recapitulated them, weaving them together with threads of compliment – 'As you very justly observed;' and – 'It is most true, as you say;' and – 'It were well if others noted what you have remarked.'
  Some listeners incautious in their epithets would have called Hinze an 'ass.' For my part I would never insult that intelligent and unpretending animal who no doubt brays with perfect simplicity and substantial meaning to those acquainted with his idiom, and if he feigns more submission than he feels, has weighty reasons for doing so – I would never, I say, insult that historic and ill-appreciated animal, the ass, by giving his name to a man whose continuous pretence is so shallow in its motive, so unexcused by any sharp appetite as this of Hinze's.
  But perhaps you would say that his adulatory manner was originally adopted under strong promptings of self-interest, and that his absurdly over-acted deference to persons from whom he expects no patronage is the unreflecting persistence of habit – just as those who live with the deaf will shout to everybody else.
  And you might indeed imagine that in talking to Tulpian, who has considerable interest at his disposal, Hinze had a desired appointment in his mind. Tulpian is appealed to on

innumerable subjects, and if he is unwilling to express himself on any one of them, says so with instructive copiousness: he is much listened to, and his utterances are registered and reported with more or less exactitude. But I think he has no other listener who comports himself as Hinze does – who, figuratively speaking, carries about a small spoon ready to pick up any dusty crumb of opinion that the eloquent man may have let drop. Tulpian, with reverence be it said, has some rather absurd notions, such as a mind of large discourse often finds room for: they slip about among his higher conceptions and multitudinous acquirements like disreputable characters at a national celebration in some vast cathedral, where to the ardent soul all is glorified by rainbow light and grand associations: any vulgar detective knows them for what they are. But Hinze is especially fervid in his desire to hear Tulpian dilate on his crotchets, and is rather troublesome to bystanders in asking them whether they have read the various fugitive writings in which these crotchets have been published.[8] If an expert is explaining some matter on which you desire to know the evidence, Hinze teases you with Tulpian's guesses, and asks the expert what he thinks of them.

In general, Hinze delights in the citation of opinions, and would hardly remark that the sun shone without an air of respectful appeal or fervid adhesion. The 'Iliad,' one sees, would impress him little if it were not for what Mr Fugleman[9] has lately said about it; and if you mention an image or sentiment in Chaucer he seems not to heed the bearing of your reference, but immediately tells you that Mr Hautboy,[10] too, regards Chaucer as a poet of the first order, and he is delighted to find that two such judges as you and Hautboy are at one.

What is the reason of all this subdued ecstasy, moving about, hat in hand, with well-dressed hair and attitudes of unimpeachable correctness? Some persons conscious of sagacity decide at once that Hinze knows what he is about in flattering Tulpian, and has a carefully appraised end to serve though they may not see it. They are misled by the common mistake of supposing that men's behaviour, whether habitual or occasional, is chiefly determined by a distinctly conceived motive, a definite object to be gained or a definite evil to be avoided. The truth is, that, the primitive wants of nature once tolerably satisfied, the majority of mankind, even in a civilised life full of solicitations, are with difficulty aroused to the distinct conception of an object towards which they will direct their actions with careful adaptation, and it is yet rarer to find one who can persist in the systematic pursuit of such an end. Few lives are shaped, few characters formed, by the contemplation of definite consequences seen from a distance and made the goal of continuous effort or the beacon of a constantly avoided danger: such control by foresight, such vivid picturing and practical logic are the distinction of exceptionally strong natures; but society is chiefly made up of human beings whose daily acts are all performed either in unreflecting obedience to custom and routine or from immediate promptings of thought or feeling to execute an immediate purpose. They pay their poor-rates, give their vote in affairs political or parochial, wear a certain amount of starch, hinder boys from tormenting the helpless, and spend money on tedious observances called pleasures, without mentally adjusting these practices to their own well-understood interest or to the general, ultimate welfare of the human race; and when they fall into ungraceful compliment, excessive smiling or other luckless efforts of complaisant behaviour, these are but the tricks or habits gradually formed under the successive promptings of a wish to be agreeable, stimulated day by day without any widening resources for gratifying the wish. It does not in the least follow that they are seeking by studied hypocrisy to get something for themselves. And so with Hinze's deferential bearing, complimentary parentheses, and worshipful tones, which seem to some like the over-acting of a part in a comedy. He expects no appointment or other appreciable gain through Tulpian's favour; he has no doubleness towards Felicia; there is no sneering or backbiting obverse to his ecstatic admiration. He is very well off in the world, and cherishes no unsatisfied ambition that could feed design and direct flattery. As you perceive, he has had the education and other advantages of a gentleman without being conscious of marked result, such as a decided preference for any particular ideas or functions: his mind is furnished as hotels are, with everything for occasional and transient use. But one cannot be an Englishman and gentleman in general: it is in the nature of things that one must have an individuality, though it may be of an often-repeated type. As Hinze in growing to maturity had grown into a particular form and expression of person, so he necessarily gathered a manner and frame of speech which made him additionally recognisable. His nature is not tuned to the pitch of a genuine direct admiration, only to an attitudinising deference which does not fatigue itself with the formation of real judgments. All human achievement must be wrought down to this spoon-meat — this mixture of other persons' washy opinions and his own flux of reverence for what is third-hand, before Hinze can find a relish for it.

He has no more leading characteristic than the desire to stand well with those who are justly distinguished; he has no base admirations, and you may know by his entire presentation of himself, from the management of his hat to the angle at which he keeps his right foot, that he aspires to correctness. Desiring to behave becomingly and also to make a figure in dialogue, he is only like the bad artist whose picture is a failure. We may pity these ill-gifted strivers, but not pretend that their works are pleasant to behold. A man is bound to know something of his own weight and muscular dexterity, and the puny athlete is called foolish before he is seen to be thrown. Hinze has not the stuff in him to be at once agreeably conversational and sincere, and he has got himself up to be at all events agreeably conversational. Notwithstanding this deliberateness of intention in his talk he is unconscious of falsity, for he has not enough of deep and lasting impression to find a contrast or diversity between his words and his thoughts. He is not fairly to be called a hypocrite, but I have already confessed to the more exasperation at his make-believe reverence, because it has no deep hunger to excuse it.

ONLY TEMPER

WHAT is temper? Its primary meaning, the proportion and mode in which qualities are mingled, is much neglected in popular speech, yet even here the word often carries a reference to an habitual state or general tendency of the organism in distinction from what are held to be specific virtues and vices. As people confess to bad memory without expecting to sink in mental reputation, so we hear a man declared to have a bad temper and yet glorified as the possessor of every high quality. When he errs or in any way commits himself, his temper is accused, not his character, and it is understood that but for a brutal bearish mood he is kindness itself. If he kicks small animals, swears violently at a servant who mistakes orders, or is grossly rude to his wife, it is remarked apologetically that these things mean nothing – they are all temper.

Certainly there is a limit to this form of apology, and the forgery of a bill, or the ordering of goods without any prospect of paying for them, has never been set down to an unfortunate habit of sulkiness or of irascibility. But on the whole there is a peculiar exercise of indulgence towards the manifestations of bad temper which tends to encourage them, so that we are in danger of having among us a number of virtuous persons who conduct themselves detestably, just as we have hysterical patients who, with sound organs, are apparently labouring under many sorts of organic disease. Let it be admitted, however, that a man may be 'a good fellow' and yet have a bad temper, so bad that we recognise his merits with reluctance, and are inclined to resent his occasionally amiable behaviour as an unfair demand on our admiration.

Touchwood[1] is that kind of good fellow. He is by turns insolent, quarrelsome, repulsively haughty to innocent people who approach him with respect, neglectful of his friends, angry in face of legitimate demands, procrastinating in the fulfilment of such demands, prompted to rude words and harsh looks by a moody disgust with his fellow-men in general – and yet, as everybody will assure you, the soul of honour, a steadfast friend, a defender of the oppressed, an affectionate-hearted creature. Pity that, after a certain experience of his moods, his intimacy becomes insupportable! A man who uses his balmorals[2] to tread on your toes with much frequency and an unmistakeable emphasis may prove a fast friend in adversity, but meanwhile your adversity has not arrived and your toes are tender. The daily sneer or growl at your remarks is not to be made amends for by a possible eulogy or defence of your understanding against depreciators who may not present themselves, and on an occasion which may never arise. I cannot submit to a chronic state of blue and green bruise as a form of insurance against an accident.

Touchwood's bad temper is of the contradicting pugnacious sort. He is the honourable gentleman in opposition, whatever proposal or proposition may be broached, and when others join him he secretly damns their superfluous agreement, quickly discovering that his way of stating the case is not exactly theirs. An invitation or any sign of expectation throws him into an attitude of refusal. Ask his concurrence in a benevolent measure: he will not decline to give it, because he has a real sympathy with good aims; but he complies resentfully, though where he is let alone he will do much more than any one would have thought of asking for. No man would shrink with greater sensitiveness from the imputation of not paying his debts, yet when a bill is sent in with any promptitude he is inclined to make the tradesman wait for the money he is in such a hurry to get. One sees that this antagonistic temper must be much relieved by finding a particular object, and that its worst moments must be those where the mood is that of vague resistance, there being nothing specific to oppose. Touchwood is never so

little engaging as when he comes down to breakfast with a cloud
on his brow, after parting from you the night before with an
affectionate effusiveness at the end of a confidential conversation which has assured you of mutual understanding. Impossible
that you can have committed any offence. If mice have disturbed him, that is not your fault; but, nevertheless, your
cheerful greeting had better not convey any reference to the
weather, else it will be met by a sneer which, taking you
unawares, may give you a crushing sense that you make a poor
figure with your cheerfulness, which was not asked for. Some
daring person perhaps introduces another topic, and uses the
delicate flattery of appealing to Touchwood for his opinion, the
topic being included in his favourite studies. An indistinct
muttering, with a look at the carving-knife in reply, teaches that
daring person how ill he has chosen a market for his deference.
If Touchwood's behaviour affects you very closely you had
better break your leg in the course of the day: his bad temper
will then vanish at once; he will take a painful journey on your
behalf; he will sit up with you night after night; he will do all the
work of your department so as to save you from any loss in
consequence of your accident; he will be even uniformly tender
to you till you are well on your legs again, when he will some
fine morning insult you without provocation, and make you
wish that his generous goodness to you had not closed your lips
against retort.

It is not always necessary that a friend should break his leg
for Touchwood to feel compunction and endeavour to make
amends for his bearishness or insolence. He becomes spontane-
ously conscious that he has misbehaved, and he is not only
ashamed of himself, but has the better prompting to try and heal
any wound he has inflicted. Unhappily the habit of being
offensive 'without meaning it' leads usually to a way of making
amends which the injured person cannot but regard as a being
amiable without meaning it. The kindnesses, the complimentary
indications or assurances, are apt to appear in the light of a
penance adjusted to the foregoing lapses, and by the very
contrast they offer call up a keener memory of the wrong they

atone for. They are not a spontaneous prompting of goodwill, but an elaborate compensation. And, in fact, Touchwood's[3] atoning friendliness has a ring of artificiality. Because he formerly disguised his good feeling towards you he now expresses more than he quite feels. It is in vain. Having made you extremely uncomfortable last week he has absolutely diminished his power of making you happy to-day: he struggles against this result by excessive effort, but he has taught you to observe his fitfulness rather than to be warmed by his episodic show of regard.

I suspect that many persons who have an uncertain, incalculable temper flatter themselves that it enhances their fascination; but perhaps they are under the prior mistake of exaggerating the charm which they suppose to be thus strengthened; in any case they will do well not to trust in the attractions of caprice and moodiness for a long continuance or for close intercourse. A pretty woman may fan the flame of distant adorers by harassing them, but if she lets one of them make her his wife, the point of view from which he will look at her poutings and tossings and mysterious inability to be pleased will be seriously altered. And if slavery to a pretty woman, which seems among the least conditional forms of abject service, will not bear too great a strain from her bad temper even though her beauty remain the same, it is clear that a man whose claims lie in his high character or high performances had need impress us very constantly with his peculiar value and indispensableness, if he is to test our patience by an uncertainty of temper which leaves us absolutely without grounds for guessing how he will receive our persons or humbly advanced opinions, or what line he will take on any but the most momentous occasions.

For it is among the repulsive effects of this bad temper, which is supposed to be compatible with shining virtues, that it is apt to determine a man's sudden adhesion to an opinion, whether on a personal or impersonal matter, without leaving him time to consider his grounds. The adhesion is sudden and momentary, but it either forms a precedent for his line of thought and action, or it is presently seen to have been inconsistent with his true mind. This determination of partisanship by temper has its worst effects in the career of the public man, who is always in danger of getting so enthralled by his own words that he looks into facts and questions not to get rectifying knowledge, but to get evidence that will justify his actual attitude which was assumed under an impulse dependent on something else than knowledge. There has been plenty of insistance on the evil of swearing by the words of a master, and having the judgment uniformly controlled by a 'He said it;' but a much worse woe to befall a man is to have every judgment controlled by an 'I said it' – to make a divinity of his own short-sightedness or passion-led aberration and explain the world in its honour. There is hardly a more pitiable degradation than this for a man of high gifts. Hence I cannot join with those who wish that Touchwood, being young enough to enter on public life, should get elected for Parliament and use his excellent abilities to serve his country in that conspicuous manner. For hitherto, in the less momentous incidents of private life, his capricious temper has only produced the minor evil of inconsistency, and he is even greatly at ease in contradicting himself, provided he can contradict you, and disappoint any smiling expectation you may have shown that the impressions you are uttering are likely to meet with his sympathy, considering that the day before he himself gave you the example which your mind is following. He is at least free from those fetters of self-justification which are the curse of parliamentary speaking, and what I rather desire for him is that he should produce the great book which he is generally pronounced capable of writing, and put his best self imperturbably on record for the advantage of society; because I should then have steady ground for bearing with his diurnal incalculableness, and could fix my gratitude as by a strong staple to that unvarying monumental service. Unhappily, Touch-wood's great powers have been only so far manifested as to be believed in, not demonstrated. Everybody rates them highly, and thinks that whatever he chose to do would be done in a first-rate manner. Is it his love of disappointing complacent expectancy which has gone so far as to keep up this lamentable negation, and made him resolve not to write the comprehensive work which he would have written if nobody had expected it of him?

One can see that if Touchwood were to become a public man and take to frequent speaking on platforms or from his seat in the House, it would hardly be possible for him to maintain much integrity of opinion, or to avoid courses of partisanship which a healthy public sentiment would stamp with discredit. Say that he were endowed with the purest honesty, it would inevitably be dragged captive by this mysterious, Protean bad temper. There would be the fatal public necessity of justifying oratorical Temper which had got on its legs in its bitter mood and made insulting imputations, or of keeping up some decent show of consistency with opinions vented out of Temper's contradictoriness. And words would have to be followed up by acts of adhesion.

Certainly if a bad-tempered man can be admirably virtuous, he must be so under extreme difficulties. I doubt the possibility that a high order of character can coexist with a temper like Touchwood's. For it is of the nature of such temper to interrupt the formation of healthy mental habits, which depend on a growing harmony between perception, conviction, and impulse. There may be good feelings, good deeds – for a human nature may pack endless varieties and blessed inconsistencies in its windings – but it is essential to what is worthy to be called high character, that it may be safely calculated on, and that its qualities shall have taken the form of principles or laws habit-ually, if not perfectly, obeyed.

If a man frequently passes unjust judgments, takes up false attitudes, intermits his acts of kindness with rude behaviour or cruel words, and falls into the consequent vulgar error of supposing that he can make amends by laboured agreeableness, I cannot consider such courses any the less ugly because they are ascribed to 'temper.' Especially I object to the assumption that his having a fundamentally good disposition is either an apology or a compensation for his bad behaviour. If his temper yesterday made him lash the horses, upset the curricle[4] and cause a breakage in my rib, I feel it no compensation that to-day he vows he will drive me anywhere in the gentlest manner any day as long as he lives. Yesterday was what it was, my rib is paining me, it is not a main object of my life to be driven by Touchwood – and I have no confidence in his lifelong gentleness. The utmost form of placability I am capable of is to try and remember his better deeds already performed, and, mindful of my own offences, to bear him no malice. But I cannot accept his amends.

If the bad-tempered man wants to apologise he had need to do it on a large public scale, make some beneficent discovery, produce some stimulating work of genius, invent some powerful process – prove himself such a good to contemporary multitudes and future generations, as to make the discomfort he causes his friends and acquaintances a vanishing quality, a trifle even in their own estimate.

A POLITICAL MOLECULE

THE most arrant denier must admit that a man often furthers larger ends than he is conscious of, and that while he is transacting his particular affairs with the narrow pertinacity of a respectable ant, he subserves an economy larger than any purpose of his own.[1] Society is happily not dependent for the growth of fellowship on the small minority already endowed with comprehensive sympathy: any molecule of the body politic working towards his own interest in an orderly way gets his understanding more or less penetrated with the fact that his interest is included in that of a large number. I have watched several political molecules being educated in this way by the nature of things into a faint feeling of fraternity. But at this moment I am thinking of Spike, an elector who voted on the side of Progress though he was not inwardly attached to it under that name. For abstractions are deities having many specific names, local habitations, and forms of activity, and so get a multitude of devout servants who care no more for them under their highest titles than the celebrated person who, putting with forcible brevity a view of human motives now much insisted on, asked what Posterity had done for him that he should care for Posterity?[2] To many minds even among the ancients (thought by some to have been invariably poetical) the goddess of wisdom was doubtless worshipped simply as the patroness of spinning and weaving.[3] Now spinning and weaving from a manufacturing, wholesale point of view, was the chief form under which Spike from early years had unconsciously been a devotee of Progress.

He was a political molecule of the most gentlemanlike appearance, not less than six feet high, and showing the utmost nicety in the care of his person and equipment. His umbrella was especially remarkable for its neatness, though perhaps he swung it unduly in walking. His complexion was fresh, his eyes small, bright, and twinkling. He was seen to great advantage in a hat and greatcoat – garments frequently fatal to the impressiveness of shorter figures; but when he was uncovered in the drawing-room, it was impossible not to observe that his head shelved off too rapidly from the eyebrows towards the crown, and that his length of limb seemed to have used up his mind so as to cause an air of abstraction from conversational topics. He appeared, indeed, to be preoccupied with a sense of his exquisite cleanliness, clapped his hands together and rubbed them frequently, straightened his back, and even opened his mouth and closed it again with a slight snap, apparently for no other purpose than the confirmation to himself of his own powers in that line. These are innocent exercises, but they are not such as give weight to a man's personality. Sometimes Spike's mind, emerging from its preoccupation, burst forth in a remark delivered with smiling zest; as, that he did like to see gravel walks well rolled, or that a lady should always wear the best jewellery, or that a bride was a most interesting object; but finding these ideas received rather coldly, he would relapse into abstraction, draw up his back, wrinkle his brows longitudinally, and seem to regard society, even including gravel walks, jewellery, and brides, as essentially a poor affair. Indeed his habit of mind was desponding, and he took melancholy views as to the possible extent of human pleasure and the value of existence. Especially after he had made his fortune in the cotton manufacture, and had thus attained the chief object of his ambition – the object which had engaged his talent for order and persevering application. For his easy leisure caused him much *ennui*. He was abstemious, and had none of those temptations to sensual excess which fill up a man's time first with indulgence and then with the process of getting well from its effects. He had not, indeed, exhausted the sources of knowledge, but here again his notions of human pleasure were narrowed by his want of appetite; for though he seemed rather surprised at the consideration that Alfred the Great was a Catholic,[4] or that apart from the Ten Commandments any conception of moral conduct had occurred to mankind, he was not stimulated to further inquiries on these remote matters. Yet he aspired to what he regarded as intellectual society, willingly entertained beneficed clergymen, and bought the books he heard spoken of, arranging them carefully on the shelves of what he called his library, and occasionally sitting alone in the same room with them. But some minds seem well glazed by nature against the admission of knowledge, and Spike's was one of them. It was not, however, entirely so with regard to politics. He had a strong opinion about the Reform Bill,[5] and saw clearly that the large trading towns ought to send members. Portraits of the Reform heroes hung framed and glazed in his library: he prided himself on being a Liberal. In this last particular, as well as in not giving benefactions and not making loans without interest, he showed unquestionable firmness. On the Repeal of the Corn Laws,[6] again, he was thoroughly convinced. His mind was expansive towards foreign markets, and his imagination could see that the people from whom we took corn might be able to take the cotton goods which they had hitherto dispensed with. On his conduct in these political concerns, his wife, otherwise influential as a woman who belonged to a family with a title in it, and who had condescended in marrying him, could gain no hold: she had to blush a little at what was called her husband's 'radicalism' – an epithet which was a very unfair impeachment of Spike, who never went to the root of anything. But he understood his own trading affairs, and in this way became a genuine, constant political element. If he had been born a little later he could have been accepted as an eligible member of Parliament, and if he had belonged to a high family he might have done for a member of the Government. Perhaps his indifference to 'views' would have passed for administrative judiciousness, and he would have been so generally silent that he must often have been silent in the right place. But this is empty speculation: there is no warrant

for saying what Spike would have been and known so as to have
made a calculable political element, if he had not been educated
by having to manage his trade. A small mind trained to useful
occupation for the satisfying of private need becomes a representative of genuine class-needs. Spike objected to certain items
of legislation because they hampered his own trade, but his
neighbours' trade was hampered by the same causes; and though
he would have been simply selfish in a question of light or water
between himself and a fellow-townsman, his need for a change
in legislation, being shared by all his neighbours in trade, ceased
to be simply selfish, and raised him to a sense of common injury
and common benefit. True, if the law could have been changed
for the benefit of his particular business, leaving the cotton trade
in general in a sorry condition while he prospered, Spike might
not have thought that result intolerably unjust; but the nature of
things did not allow of such a result being contemplated as
possible; it allowed of an enlarged market for Spike only
through the enlargement of his neighbours' market, and the
Possible is always the ultimate master of our efforts and desires.
Spike was obliged to contemplate a general benefit, and thus
became public-spirited in spite of himself. Or rather, the nature
of things transmuted his active egoism into a demand for a
public benefit.

Certainly if Spike had been born a marquis he could not have
had the same chance of being useful as a political element. But
he might have had the same appearance, have been equally null
in conversation, sceptical as to the reality of pleasure, and
destitute of historical knowledge; perhaps even dimly disliking
Jesuitism as a quality in Catholic minds, or regarding Bacon as
the inventor of physical science. The depths of middle-aged
gentlemen's ignorance will never be known, for want of public
examinations in this branch.

THE WATCH-DOG OF KNOWLEDGE[1]

MORDAX[2] is an admirable man, ardent in intellectual work, public-spirited, affectionate, and able to find the right words in conveying ingenious ideas or elevated feeling. Pity that to all these graces he cannot add what would give them the utmost finish – the occasional admission that he has been in the wrong, the occasional frank welcome of a new idea as something not before present to his mind! But no: Mordax's self-respect seems to be of that fiery quality which demands that none but the monarchs of thought shall have an advantage over him, and in the presence of contradiction or the threat of having his notions corrected, he becomes astonishingly unscrupulous and cruel for so kindly and conscientious a man.

'You are fond of attributing those fine qualities to Mordax,' said Acer,[3] the other day, 'but I have not much belief in virtues that are always requiring to be asserted in spite of appearances against them. True fairness and goodwill show themselves precisely where his are conspicuously absent. I mean, in recognising claims which the rest of the world are not likely to stand up for. It does not need much love of truth and justice in me to say that Aldebaran[4] is a bright star, or Isaac Newton the greatest of discoverers; nor much kindliness in me to want my notes to be heard above the rest in a chorus of hallelujahs to one already crowned. It is my way to apply tests. Does the man who has the ear of the public use his advantage tenderly towards poor fellows who may be hindered of their due if he treats their pretensions with scorn? That is my test of his justice and benevolence.'

My answer was, that his system of moral tests might be as delusive as what ignorant people take to be tests of intellect and learning. If the scholar or *savant* cannot answer their haphazard questions on the shortest notice, their belief in his capacity is shaken. But the better-informed have given up the Johnsonian theory of mind as a pair of legs able to walk east or west according to choice.[5] Intellect is no longer taken to be a ready-made dose of ability to attain eminence (or mediocrity) in all departments; it is even admitted that application in one line of study or practice has often a laming effect in other directions, and that an intellectual quality or special facility which is a furtherance in one medium of effort is a drag in another. We have convinced ourselves by this time that a man may be a sage in celestial physics and a poor creature in the purchase of seed-corn, or even in theorising about the affections; that he may be a mere fumbler in physiology and yet show a keen insight into human motives; that he may seem the 'poor Poll'[6] of the company in conversation and yet write with some humorous vigour. It is not true that a man's intellectual power is like the strength of a timber beam, to be measured by its weakest point.

Why should we any more apply that fallacious standard of what is called consistency to a man's moral nature, and argue against the existence of fine impulses or habits of feeling in relation to his actions generally, because those better movements are absent in a class of cases which act peculiarly on an irritable form of his egoism? The mistake might be corrected by our taking notice that the ungenerous words or acts which seem to us the most utterly incompatible with good dispositions in the offender, are those which offend ourselves. All other persons are able to draw a milder conclusion. Laniger,[7] who has a temper but no talent for repartee, having been run down in a fierce way by Mordax, is inwardly persuaded that the highly-lauded man is a wolf at heart: he is much tried by perceiving that his own friends seem to think no worse of the reckless assailant than they did before; and Corvus,[8] who has lately been flattered by some kindness from Mordax, is unmindful enough of Laniger's feeling to dwell on this instance of good-nature with admiring gratitude. There is a fable[9] that when the badger had been stung all over by bees, a bear consoled him by a rhapsodic account of how he himself had just breakfasted on their honey. The badger replied, peevishly, 'The stings are in my flesh, and the sweetness is on your muzzle.' The bear, it is said, was surprised at the badger's want of altruism.

But this difference of sensibility between Laniger and his friends only mirrors in a faint way the difference between his own point of view and that of the man who has injured him. If those neutral, perhaps even affectionate persons, form no lively conception of what Laniger suffers, how should Mordax have any such sympathetic imagination to check him in what he persuades himself is a scourging administered by the qualified man to the unqualified? Depend upon it, his conscience, though active enough in some relations, has never given him a twinge because of his polemical rudeness and even brutality. He would go from the room where he has been tiring himself through the watches of the night in lifting and turning a sick friend, and straightway write a reply or rejoinder in which he mercilessly pilloried a Laniger who had supposed that he could tell the world something else or more than had been sanctioned by the eminent Mordax – and what was worse, had sometimes really done so. Does this nullify the genuineness of motive which made him tender to his suffering friend? Not at all. It only proves that his arrogant egoism, set on fire, sends up smoke and flame[10] where just before there had been the dews of fellowship and pity. He is angry and equips himself accordingly – with a penknife to give the offender a *comprachico*[11] countenance, a mirror to show him the effect, and a pair of nailed boots to give him his dismissal. All this to teach him who the Romans really were, and to purge Inquiry of incompetent intrusion, so rendering an important service to mankind.

When a man is in a rage and wants to hurt another in consequence, he can always regard himself as the civil arm of a spiritual power, and all the more easily because there is real need to assert the righteous efficacy of indignation. I for my part feel with the Lanigers, and should object all the more to their or

my being lacerated and dressed with salt, if the administrator of
such torture alleged as a motive his care for Truth and posterity,
and got himself pictured with a halo in consequence. In transactions between fellow-men it is well to consider a little, in the
first place, what is fair and kind towards the person immediately
concerned, before we spit and roast him on behalf of the next
century but one. Wide-reaching motives, blessed and glorious as
they are, and of the highest sacramental virtue, have their
dangers, like all else that touches the mixed life of the earth.
They are archangels with awful brow and flaming sword, sum-
moning and encouraging us to do the right and the divinely
heroic, and we feel a beneficent tremor in their presence; but to
learn what it is they thus summon us to do, we have to consider
the mortals we are elbowing, who are of our own stature and
our own appetites. I cannot feel sure how my voting will affect
the condition of Central Asia in the coming ages, but I have
good reason to believe that the future populations there will be
none the worse off because I abstain from conjectural vilification
of my opponents during the present parliamentary session, and
I am very sure that I shall be less injurious to my contemporaries. On the whole, and in the vast majority of instances, the
action by which we can do the best for future ages is of the sort
which has a certain beneficence and grace for contemporaries. A
sour father may reform prisons, but considered in his sourness
he does harm. The deed of Judas has been attributed to far-
reaching views, and the wish to hasten his Master's declaration
of himself as the Messiah. Perhaps – I will not maintain the
contrary – Judas represented his motive in this way, and felt
justified in his traitorous kiss; but my belief that he deserved,
metaphorically speaking, to be where Dante saw him, at the
bottom of the Malebolge,[12] would not be the less strong because
he was not convinced that his action was detestable. I refuse to
accept a man who has the stomach for such treachery, as a hero
impatient for the redemption of mankind and for the beginning
of a reign when the kisses shall be those of peace and righteous-
ness.

All this is by the way, to show that my apology for Mordax

was not founded on his persuasion of superiority in his own motives, but on the compatibility of unfair, equivocal, and even cruel actions with a nature which, apart from special temptations, is kindly and generous; and also to enforce the need of checks from a fellow-feeling with those whom our acts immediately (not distantly) concern. Will any one be so hardy as to maintain that an otherwise worthy man cannot be vain and arrogant? I think most of us have some interest in arguing the contrary. And it is of the nature of vanity and arrogance, if unchecked, to become cruel and self-justifying. There are fierce beasts within: chain them, chain them, and let them learn to cower before the creature with wider reason. This is what one wishes for Mordax – that his heart and brain should restrain the outleap of roar and talons.

As to his unwillingness to admit that an idea which he has not discovered is novel to him, one is surprised that quick intellect and shrewd observation do not early gather reasons for being ashamed of a mental trick which makes one among the comic parts of that various actor Conceited Ignorance.

I have a sort of valet and factotum, an excellent, respectable servant, whose spelling is so unvitiated by non-phonetic superfluities that he writes *night* as *nit*. One day, looking over his accounts, I said to him jocosely, 'You are in the latest fashion with your spelling, Pummel: most people spell 'night' with a *gh* between the *i* and the *t*, but the greatest scholars now spell it as you do.' 'So I suppose, sir,' says Pummel; 'I've see it with a *gh*, but I've noways give into that myself.' You would never catch Pummel in an interjection of surprise. I have sometimes laid traps for his astonishment, but he has escaped them all, either by a respectful neutrality, as of one who would not appear to notice that his master had been taking too much wine, or else by that strong persuasion of his all-knowingness which makes it simply impossible for him to feel himself newly informed. If I tell him that the world is spinning round and along like a top, and that he is spinning with it, he says, 'Yes, I've heard a deal of that in my time, sir,' and lifts the horizontal lines of his brow a little higher, balancing his head from side to side as if it were too painfully full. Whether I tell him that they cook puppies in China, that there are ducks with fur coats in Australia, or that in some parts of the world it is the pink of politeness to put your tongue out on introduction to a respectable stranger, Pummel replies, 'So I suppose, sir,' with an air of resignation to hearing my poor version of well-known things, such as elders use in listening to lively boys lately presented with an anecdote book. His utmost concession is, that what you state is what he would have supplied if you had given him *carte blanche* instead of your needless instruction, and in this sense his favourite answer is, 'I should say.'

'Pummel,' I observed, a little irritated at not getting my coffee, 'if you were to carry your kettle and spirits of wine up a mountain of a morning, your water would boil there sooner.' 'I should say, sir.' 'Or, there are boiling springs in Iceland. Better go to Iceland.' 'That's what I've been thinking, sir.'

I have taken to asking him hard questions, and as I expected, he never admits his own inability to answer them without representing it as common to the human race. 'What is the cause of the tides, Pummel?' 'Well, sir, nobody rightly knows. Many gives their opinion, but if I was to give mine, it 'ud be different.'

But while he is never surprised himself, he is constantly imagining situations of surprise for others. His own conscious-ness is that of one so thoroughly soaked in knowledge that further absorption is impossible, but his neighbours appear to him to be in the state of thirsty sponges which it is a charity to besprinkle. His great interest in thinking of foreigners is that they must be surprised at what they see in England, and especially at the beef. He is often occupied with the surprise Adam must have felt at the sight of the assembled animals – 'for he was not like us, sir, used from a b'y to Wombwell's shows.'[13] He is fond of discoursing to the lad who acts as shoe-black and general subaltern, and I have overheard him saying to that small upstart, with some severity, 'Now don't you pretend to know, because the more you pretend the more I see your ignirance' – a lucidity on his part which has confirmed my impression that the thoroughly self-satisfied person is the only one fully to appreciate the charm of humility in others.

Your diffident self-suspecting mortal is not very angry that others should feel more comfortable about themselves, provided they are not otherwise offensive: he is rather like the chilly person, glad to sit next a warmer neighbour; or the timid, glad to have a courageous fellow-traveller. It cheers him to observe the store of small comforts that his fellow-creatures may find in their self-complacency, just as one is pleased to see poor old souls soothed by the tobacco and snuff for which one has neither nose nor stomach oneself.

But your arrogant man will not tolerate a presumption which he sees to be ill-founded. The service he regards society as most in need of is to put down the conceit which is so particularly rife around him that he is inclined to believe it the growing characteristic of the present age. In the schools of Magna Græcia,[14] or in the sixth century of our era, or even under Kublai Khan, he finds a comparative freedom from that presumption by which his contemporaries are stirring his able gall. The way people will now flaunt notions which are not his without appearing to mind that they are not his, strikes him as especially disgusting. It might seem surprising to us that one strongly convinced of his own value should prefer to exalt an age in which *he* did not flourish, if it were not for the reflection that the present age is the only one in which anybody has appeared to undervalue him.

A HALF-BREED

AN early deep-seated love to which we become faithless has its unfailing Nemesis,[1] if only in that division of soul which narrows all newer joys by the intrusion of regret and the established presentiment of change. I refer not merely to the love of a person, but to the love of ideas, practical beliefs, and social habits. And faithlessness here means not a gradual conversion dependent on enlarged knowledge, but a yielding to seductive circumstance; not a conviction that the original choice was a mistake, but a subjection to incidents that flatter a growing desire. In this sort of love it is the forsaker who has the melancholy lot; for an abandoned belief may be more effectively vengeful than Dido.[2] The child of a wandering tribe caught young and trained to polite life, if he feels an hereditary yearning can run away to the old wilds and get his nature into tune. But there is no such recovery possible to the man who remembers what he once believed without being convinced that he was in error, who feels within him unsatisfied stirrings towards old beloved habits and intimacies from which he has far receded without conscious justification or unwavering sense of superior attractiveness in the new. This involuntary renegade has his character hopelessly jangled and out of tune.[3] He is like an organ with its stops in the lawless condition of obtruding themselves without method, so that hearers are amazed by the most unexpected transitions – the trumpet breaking in on the flute, and the oboe confounding both.

Hence the lot of Mixtus affects me pathetically, notwithstanding that he spends his growing wealth with liberality and manifest enjoyment. To most observers he appears to be simply one of the fortunate and also sharp commercial men who began with meaning to be rich and have become what they meant to be: a man never taken to be well-born, but surprisingly better informed than the well-born usually are, and distinguished among ordinary commercial magnates by a personal kindness which prompts him not only to help the suffering in a material way through his wealth, but also by direct ministration of his own; yet with all this, diffusing, as it were, the odour of a man delightedly conscious of his wealth as an equivalent for the other social distinctions of rank and intellect which he can thus admire without envying. Hardly one among those superficial observers can suspect that he aims or has ever aimed at being a writer; still less can they imagine that his mind is often moved by strong currents of regret and of the most unworldly sympathies from the memories of a youthful time when his chosen associates were men and women whose only distinction was a religious, a philanthropic, or an intellectual enthusiasm, when the lady on whose words his attention most hung was a writer of minor religious literature, when he was a visitor and exhorter of the poor in the alleys of a great provincial town, and when he attended the lectures given specially to young men by Mr Apollos,[4] the eloquent congregational preacher, who had studied in Germany and had liberal advanced views then far beyond the ordinary teaching of his sect. At that time Mixtus thought himself a young man of socially reforming ideas, of religious principles and religious yearnings. It was within his prospects also to be rich, but he looked forward to a use of his riches chiefly for reforming and religious purposes. His opinions were of a strongly democratic stamp, except that even then, belonging to the class of employers, he was opposed to all demands in the employed that would restrict the expansiveness of trade. He was the most democratic in relation to the unreasonable privileges of the aristocracy and landed interest; and he had also a religious sense of brotherhood with the poor. Altogether, he was a sincerely benevolent young man, interested in ideas, and renoun-cing personal ease for the sake of study, religious communion, and

good works. If you had known him then you would have expected him to marry a highly serious and perhaps literary woman,
sharing his benevolent and religious habits, and likely to encourage his studies – a woman who along with himself would play a
distinguished part in one of the most enlightened religious circles
of a great provincial capital.

How is it that Mixtus finds himself in a London mansion, and
in society totally unlike that which made the ideal of his younger
years? And whom *did* he marry?

Why, he married Scintilla,[5] who fascinated him as she had
fascinated others, by her prettiness, her liveliness, and her music.
It is a common enough case, that of a man being suddenly captivated by a woman nearly the opposite of his ideal; or if not wholly
captivated, at least effectively captured by a combination of circumstances along with an unwarily manifested inclination which
might otherwise have been transient. Mixtus was captivated and
then captured on the worldly side of his disposition, which had
been always growing and flourishing side by side with his philanthropic and religious tastes. He had ability in business, and he had
early meant to be rich; also, he was getting rich, and the taste for
such success was naturally growing with the pleasure of rewarded
exertion. It was during a business sojourn in London that he met
Scintilla, who, though without fortune, associated with families
of Greek merchants living in a style of splendour, and with artists
patronised by such wealthy entertainers. Mixtus on this occasion
became familiar with a world in which wealth seemed the key to
a more brilliant sort of dominance than that of a religious patron
in the provincial circles of X. Would it not be possible to unite the
two kinds of sway? A man bent on the most useful ends might,
with a fortune large enough, make morality magnificent, and recom-
mend religious principle by showing it in combination with the
best kind of house and the most liberal of tables; also with a wife
whose graces, wit, and accomplishments gave a finish sometimes
lacking even to establishments got up with that unhesitating
worldliness to which high cost is a sufficient reason. Enough.

Mixtus married Scintilla. Now this lively lady knew nothing
of Nonconformists, except that they were unfashionable: she did

not distinguish one conventicle[6] from another, and Mr Apollos with his enlightened interpretations seemed to her as heavy a bore, if not quite so ridiculous, as Mr Johns could have been with his solemn twang at the Baptist chapel in the lowest suburbs, or as a local preacher among the Methodists. In general, people who appeared seriously to believe in any sort of doctrine, whether religious, social, or philosophical, seemed rather absurd to Scintilla. Ten to one these theoretic people pronounced oddly, had some reason or other for saying that the most agreeable things were wrong, wore objectionable clothes, and wanted you to subscribe to something. They were probably ignorant of art and music, did not understand *badinage*, and, in fact, could talk of nothing amusing. In Scintilla's eyes the majority of persons were ridiculous and deplorably wanting in that keen perception of what was good taste, with which she herself was blest by nature and education; but the people understood to be religious or otherwise theoretic, were the most ridiculous of all, without being proportionately amusing and invitable.

Did Mixtus not discover this view of Scintilla's before their marriage? Or did he allow her to remain in ignorance of habits and opinions which had made half the occupation of his youth?

When a man is inclined to marry a particular woman, and has made any committal of himself, this woman's opinions, however different from his own, are readily regarded as part of her pretty ways, especially if they are merely negative; as, for example, that she does not insist on the Trinity or on the rightfulness or expediency of church rates, but simply regards her lover's troubling himself in disputation on these heads as stuff and nonsense. The man feels his own superior strength, and is sure that marriage will make no difference to him on the subjects about which he is in earnest. And to laugh at men's affairs is a woman's privilege, tending to enliven the domestic hearth. If Scintilla had no liking for the best sort of nonconformity, she was without any troublesome bias towards Episcopacy, Anglicanism, and early sacraments, and was quite contented not to go to church.

As to Scintilla's acquaintance with her lover's tastes on these subjects, she was equally convinced on her side that a husband's

queer ways while he was a bachelor would be easily laughed out
of him when he had married an adroit woman. Mixtus, she felt,
was an excellent creature, quite likable, who was getting rich;
and Scintilla meant to have all the advantages of a rich man's
wife. She was not in the least a wicked woman; she was simply
a pretty animal of the ape kind, with an aptitude for certain
accomplishments which education had made the most of.

But we have seen what has been the result to poor Mixtus.
He has become richer even than he dreamed of being, has a little
palace in London, and entertains with splendour the half-
aristocratic, professional, and artistic society which he is proud
to think select. This society regards him as a clever fellow in his
particular branch, seeing that he has become a considerable
capitalist, and as a man desirable to have on the list of one's
acquaintance. But from every other point of view Mixtus finds
himself personally submerged: what he happens to think is not
felt by his esteemed guests to be of any consequence, and what
he used to think with the ardour of conviction he now hardly
ever expresses. He is transplanted, and the sap within him has
long been diverted into other than the old lines of vigorous
growth. How could he speak to the artist Crespi[7] or to Sir Hong
Kong Bantam about the enlarged doctrine of Mr Apollos? How
could he mention to them his former efforts towards evangelis-
ing the inhabitants of the X. alleys? And his references to his
historical and geographical studies towards a survey of possible
markets for English products are received with an air of ironical
suspicion by many of his political friends, who take his preten-
sion to give advice concerning the Amazon, the Euphrates, and
the Niger as equivalent to the currier's wide views on the
applicability of leather. He can only make a figure through his
genial hospitality. It is in vain that he buys the best pictures and
statues of the best artists. Nobody will call him a judge in art. If
his pictures and statues are well chosen it is generally thought
that Scintilla told him what to buy; and yet Scintilla in other
connections is spoken of as having only a superficial and often
questionable taste. Mixtus, it is decided, is a good fellow, not
ignorant – no, really having a good deal of knowledge as well as

sense, but not easy to classify otherwise than as a rich man. He has consequently become a little uncertain as to his own point of view, and in his most unreserved moments of friendly inter-course, even when speaking to listeners whom he thinks likely to sympathise with the earlier part of his career, he presents himself in all his various aspects and feels himself in turn what he has been, what he is, and what others take him to be (for this last status is what we must all more or less accept). He will recover with some glow of enthusiasm the vision of his old associates, the particular limit he was once accustomed to trace of freedom in religious speculation, and his old ideal of a worthy life; but he will presently pass to the argument that money is the only means by which you can get what is best worth having in the world, and will arrive at the exclamation 'Give me money!' with the tone and gesture of a man who both feels and knows. Then if one of his audience, not having money, remarks that a man may have made up his mind to do without money because he prefers something else, Mixtus is with him immediately, cordially concurring in the supreme value of mind and genius, which indeed make his own chief delight, in that he is able to entertain the admirable possessors of these attributes at his own table, though not himself reckoned among them. Yet, he will proceed to observe, there was a time when he sacrificed his sleep to study, and even now amid the press of business he from time to time thinks of taking up the manuscripts which he hopes some day to complete, and is always increasing his collection of valuable works bearing on his favourite topics. And it is true that he has read much in certain directions, and can remember what he has read; he knows the history and theories of colonisation and the social condition of countries that do not at present consume a sufficiently large share of our products and manufactures. He continues his early habit of regarding the spread of Christianity as a great result of our commercial intercourse with black, brown, and yellow populations; but this is an idea not spoken of in the sort of fashionable society that Scintilla collects round her husband's table, and Mixtus now philosophically reflects that the cause must come before the effect, and that the thing to be directly striven for is the commercial intercourse, not excluding a little war if that also should prove needful as a pioneer of Christianity. He has long been wont to feel bashful about his former religion; as if it were an old attachment having consequences which he did not abandon but kept in decent privacy, his avowed objects and actual position being incompatible with their public acknowledgment.

There is the same kind of fluctuation in his aspect towards social questions and duties. He has not lost the kindness that used to make him a benefactor and succourer of the needy, and he is still liberal in helping forward the clever and industrious; but in his active superintendence of commercial undertakings he has contracted more and more of the bitterness which capitalists and employers often feel to be a reasonable mood towards obstructive proletaries. Hence many who have occasionally met him when trade questions were being discussed, conclude him to be indistinguishable from the ordinary run of moneyed and money-getting men. Indeed, hardly any of his acquaintances know what Mixtus really is, considered as a whole – nor does Mixtus himself know it.

DEBASING THE MORAL CURRENCY[1]

'IL ne faut pas mettre un ridicule où il n'y en a point: c'est se gâter le goût, c'est corrompre son jugement et celui des autres. Mais le ridicule qui est quelque part, il faut l'y voir, l'en tirer avec grâce et d'une manière qui plaise et qui instruise.'[2]

I am fond of quoting this passage from La Bruyère, because the subject is one where I like to show a Frenchman on my side, to save my sentiments from being set down to my peculiar dulness and deficient sense of the ludicrous, and also that they may profit by that enhancement of ideas when presented in a foreign tongue, that glamour of unfamiliarity conferring a dignity on the foreign names of very common things, of which even a philosopher like Dugald Stewart[3] confesses the influence. I remember hearing a fervid woman attempt to recite in English the narrative of a begging Frenchman who described the violent death of his father in the July days.[4] The narrative had impressed her, through the mists of her flushed anxiety to understand it, as something quite grandly pathetic; but finding the facts turn out meagre, and her audience cold, she broke off, saying, 'It sounded so much finer in French − *j'ai vu le sang de mon père*, and so on − I wish I could repeat it in French.' This was a pardonable illusion in an old-fashioned lady who had not received the polyglot education of the present day; but I observe that even now much nonsense and bad taste win admiring acceptance solely by virtue of the French language, and one may fairly desire that what seems a just discrimination should profit by the fashionable prejudice in favour of La Bruyère's idiom. But I wish he had added that the habit of dragging the ludicrous into topics

where the chief interest is of a different or even opposite kind is
a sign not of endowment, but of deficiency. The art of spoiling
is within reach of the dullest faculty: the coarsest clown with a
hammer in his hand might chip the nose off every statue and
bust in the Vatican, and stand grinning at the effect of his work.
Because wit is an exquisite product of high powers, we are not
therefore forced to admit the sadly confused inference of the
monotonous jester that he is establishing his superiority over
every less facetious person, and over every topic on which he is
ignorant or insensible, by being uneasy until he has distorted it
in the small cracked mirror which he carries about with him as
a joking apparatus. Some high authority is needed to give many
worthy and timid persons the freedom of muscular repose
under the growing demand on them to laugh when they have no
other reason than the peril of being taken for dullards; still more
to inspire them with the courage to say that they object to the
theatrical spoiling for themselves and their children of all affecting themes, all the grander deeds and aims of men, by burlesque
associations adapted to the taste of rich fishmongers in the stalls
and their assistants in the gallery. The English people in the
present generation are falsely reputed to know Shakspere (as, by
some innocent persons, the Florentine mule-drivers are believed
to have known the *Divina Commedia*, not, perhaps, excluding all
the subtle discourses in the *Purgatorio* and *Paradiso*); but there
seems a clear prospect that in the coming generation he will be
known to them through burlesques, and that his plays will find
a new life as pantomimes. A bottle-nosed Lear will come on
with a monstrous corpulence from which he will frantically
dance himself free during the midnight storm; Rosalind and
Celia[5] will join in a grotesque ballet with shepherds and
shepherdesses; Ophelia in fleshings and a voluminous brevity of
grenadine will dance through the mad scene, finishing with the
famous 'attitude of the scissors'[6] in the arms of Laertes; and all
the speeches in 'Hamlet' will be so ingeniously parodied that the
originals will be reduced to a mere *memoria technica*[7] of the
improver's puns – premonitory signs of a hideous millennium,
in which the lion will have to lie down with the lascivious

monkeys whom (if we may trust Pliny)[8] his soul naturally abhors.

I have been amazed to find that some artists whose own works have the ideal stamp, are quite insensible to the damaging tendency of the burlesquing spirit which ranges to and fro and up and down on the earth, seeing no reason (except a precarious censorship) why it should not appropriate every sacred, heroic, and pathetic theme which serves to make up the treasure of human admiration, hope, and love.[9] One would have thought that their own half-despairing efforts to invest in worthy outward shape the vague inward impressions of sublimity, and the consciousness of an implicit ideal in the commonest scenes, might have made them susceptible of some disgust or alarm at a species of burlesque which is likely to render their compositions no better than a dissolving view,[10] where every noble form is seen melting into its preposterous caricature. It used to be imagined of the unhappy medieval Jews that they parodied Calvary by crucifying dogs; if they had been guilty they would at least have had the excuse of the hatred and rage begotten by persecution. Are we on the way to a parody which shall have no other excuse than the reckless search after fodder for degraded appetites – after the pay to be earned by pasturing Circe's herd[11] where they may defile every monument of that growing life which should have kept them human?

The world seems to me well supplied with what is genuinely ridiculous: wit and humour may play as harmlessly or beneficently round the changing facets of egoism, absurdity, and vice, as the sunshine over the rippling sea or the dewy meadows. Why should we make our delicious sense of the ludicrous, with its invigorating shocks of laughter and its irrepressible smiles which are the outglow of an inward radiation as gentle and cheering as the warmth of morning, flourish like a brigand on the robbery of our mental wealth? – or let it take its exercise as a madman might, if allowed a free nightly promenade, by drawing the populace with bonfires which leave some venerable structure a blackened ruin or send a scorching smoke across the portraits of the past, at which we once looked with a loving recognition of fellowship, and disfigure them into butts of mockery? – nay, worse – use it to degrade the healthy appetites and affections of our nature as they are seen to be degraded in insane patients whose system, all out of joint, finds matter for screaming laughter in mere topsy-turvy, makes every passion preposterous or obscene, and turns the hard-won order of life into a second chaos hideous enough to make one wail that the first was ever thrilled with light?

This is what I call debasing the moral currency: lowering the value of every inspiring fact and tradition so that it will command less and less of the spiritual products, the generous motives which sustain the charm and elevation of our social existence – the something besides bread by which man saves his soul alive.[12] The bread-winner of the family may demand more and more coppery shillings, or assignats, or greenbacks[13] for his day's work, and so get the needful quantum of food; but let that moral currency be emptied of its value – let a greedy buffoonery debase all historic beauty, majesty, and pathos, and the more you heap up the desecrated symbols the greater will be the lack of the ennobling emotions which subdue the tyranny of suffering, and make ambition one with social virtue.[14]

And yet, it seems, parents will put into the hands of their children ridiculous parodies (perhaps with more ridiculous 'illustrations') of the poems which stirred their own tenderness or filial piety, and carry them to make their first acquaintance with great men, great works, or solemn crises through the medium of some miscellaneous burlesque which, with its idiotic puns and farcical attitudes, will remain among their primary associations, and reduce them throughout their time of studious preparation for life to the moral imbecility of an inward giggle at what might have stimulated their high emulation or fed the fountains of compassion, trust, and constancy. One wonders where these parents have deposited that stock of morally educating stimuli which is to be independent of poetic tradition, and to subsist in spite of the finest images being degraded and the finest words of genius being poisoned as with some befooling drug.

Will fine wit, will exquisite humour prosper the more through this turning of all things indiscriminately into food for a gluttonous laughter, an idle craving without sense of flavours? On the contrary. That delightful power which La Bruyère points to – 'le ridicule qui est quelque part, il faut l'y voir, l'en tirer avec grâce et d'une manière qui plaise et qui instruise' – depends on a discrimination only compatible with the varied sensibilities which give sympathetic insight, and with the justice of perception which is another name for grave knowledge. Such a result is no more to be expected from faculties on the strain to find some small hook by which they may attach the lowest incongruity to the most momentous subject, than it is to be expected of a sharper, watching for gulls[15] in a great political assemblage, that he will notice the blundering logic of partisan speakers, or season his observation with the salt of historical parallels. But after all our psychological teaching, and in the midst of our zeal for education, we are still, most of us, at the stage of believing that mental powers and habits have somehow, not perhaps in the general statement, but in any particular case, a kind of spiritual glaze against conditions which we are continually applying to them. We soak our children in habits of contempt and exultant gibing, and yet are confident that – as Clarissa one day said to me – 'We can always teach them to be reverent in the right place, you know.' And doubtless if she were to take her boys to see a burlesque Socrates, with swollen legs, dying in the utterance of cockney puns, and were to hang up a sketch of this comic scene among their bedroom prints, she would think this preparation not at all to the prejudice of their emotions on hearing their tutor read that narrative of the *Apology*[16] which has been consecrated by the reverent gratitude of ages. This is the impoverishment that threatens our posterity: – a new Famine, a meagre fiend with lewd grin and clumsy hoof, is breathing a moral mildew over the harvest of our human sentiments. These are the most delicate elements of our too easily perishable civilisation. And here again I like to quote a French testimony. Sainte Beuve, referring to a time of insurrectionary disturbance, says: 'Rien de plus prompt à baisser que la civilisation dans des crises comme celle-ci; on perd en trois semaines le résultat de plusieurs siècles. La civilisation, la *vie* est une chose apprise et inventée, qu'on le sache bien: "*Inventas aut qui vitam excoluere per artes.*" Les hommes après quelques années de paix oublient trop cette verité: ils arrivent à croire que la *culture* est chose innée, qu'elle est la même chose que la *nature*. La sauvagerie est toujours là à deux pas, et, dès qu'on lâche pied, elle recommence.'[17] We have been severely enough taught (if we were willing to learn) that our civilisation, considered as a splendid material fabric, is helplessly in peril without the spiritual police of sentiments or ideal feelings. And it is this invisible police which we had need, as a community, strive to maintain in efficient force. How if a dangerous 'Swing'[18] were sometimes disguised in a versatile entertainer devoted to the amusement of mixed audiences? And I confess that sometimes when I see a certain style of young lady, who checks our tender admiration with rouge and henna and all the blazonry of an extravagant expenditure, with slang and bold *brusquerie* intended to signify her emancipated view of things, and with cynical mockery which she mistakes for penetration, I am sorely tempted to hiss out '*Pétroleuse!*'[19] It is a small matter to have our palaces set aflame compared with the misery of having our sense of a noble womanhood, which is the inspiration of a purifying shame, the promise of life-penetrating affection, stained and blotted out by images of repulsiveness. These things come – not of higher education, but – of dull ignorance fostered into pertness by the greedy vulgarity which reverses Peter's visionary lesson[20] and learns to call all things common and unclean. It comes of debasing the moral currency.

The Tirynthians, according to an ancient story reported by Athenæus,[21] becoming conscious that their trick of laughter at everything and nothing was making them unfit for the conduct of serious affairs, appealed to the Delphic oracle for some means of cure. The god prescribed a peculiar form of sacrifice, which would be effective if they could carry it through without laughing. They did their best; but the flimsy joke of a boy upset their unaccustomed gravity, and in this way the oracle taught them that even the gods could not prescribe a quick cure for a long vitiation, or give power and dignity to a people who in a crisis of the public wellbeing were at the mercy of a poor jest.

THE WASP CREDITED WITH
THE HONEYCOMB[1]

NO man, I imagine, would object more strongly than Euphorion[2] to communistic principles in relation to material property, but with regard to property in ideas he entertains such principles willingly, and is disposed to treat the distinction between Mine and Thine in original authorship as egoistic, narrowing, and low. I have known him, indeed, insist at some expense of erudition on the prior right of an ancient, a mediæval, or an eighteenth century writer to be credited with a view or statement lately advanced with some show of originality; and this championship seems to imply a nicety of conscience towards the dead. He is evidently unwilling that his neighbours should get more credit than is due to them, and in this way he appears to recognise a certain proprietorship even in spiritual production. But perhaps it is no real inconsistency that, with regard to many instances of modern origination, it is his habit to talk with a Gallic largeness and refer to the universe: he expatiates on the diffusive nature of intellectual products, free and all-embracing as the liberal air; on the infinitesimal smallness of individual origination compared with the massive inheritance of thought on which every new generation enters; on that growing preparation for every epoch through which certain ideas or modes of view are said to be in the air, and, still more metaphorically speaking, to be inevitably absorbed, so that every one may be excused for not knowing how he got them. Above all, he insists on the proper subordination of the irritable self, the mere vehicle of an idea or combination which, being produced by the sum total of the human race, must belong to that multiple entity, from the accomplished lecturer or popular-iser who transmits it, to the remotest generation of Fuegians or Hottentots,[3] however indifferent these may be to the superior-ity of their right above that of the eminently perishable dyspep-tic author.

One may admit that such considerations carry a profound truth to be even religiously contemplated, and yet object all the more to the mode in which Euphorion seems to apply them. I protest against the use of these majestic conceptions to do the dirty work of unscrupulosity and justify the non-payment of conscious debts which cannot be defined or enforced by the law. Especially since it is observable that the large views as to intellectual property which can apparently reconcile an able person to the use of lately borrowed ideas as if they were his own, when this spoliation is favoured by the public darkness, never hinder him from joining in the zealous tribute of recogni-tion and applause to those warriors of Truth whose triumphal arches are seen in the public ways, those conquerors whose battles and 'annexations' even the carpenters and bricklayers know by name. Surely the acknowledgment of a mental debt which will not be immediately detected, and may never be asserted, is a case to which the traditional susceptibility to 'debts of honour' would be suitably transferred. There is no massive public opinion that can be expected to tell on these relations of thinkers and investigators – relations to be thoroughly under-stood and felt only by those who are interested in the life of ideas and acquainted with their history. To lay false claim to an invention or discovery which has an immediate market value; to vamp up a professedly new book of reference by stealing from the pages of one already produced at the cost of much labour and material; to copy somebody else's poem and send the manuscript to a magazine, or hand it about among friends as an original 'effusion;' to deliver an elegant extract from a known writer as a piece of improvised eloquence: – these are the limits within which the dishonest pretence of originality is likely to get hissed or hooted and bring more or less shame on the culprit. It is not necessary to understand the merit of a performance, or even to spell with any comfortable confidence, in order to perceive at once that such pretences are not respectable. But the difference between these vulgar frauds, these devices of ridiculous jays whose ill-secured plumes are seen falling off them as they run, and the quiet appropriation of other people's philosophic or scientific ideas, can hardly be held to lie in their moral quality unless we take impunity as our criterion. The pitiable jays had no presumption in their favour and foolishly fronted an alert incredulity; but Euphorion, the accomplished theorist, has an audience who expect much of him, and take it as the most natural thing in the world that every unusual view which he presents anonymously should be due solely to his ingenuity. His borrowings are no incongruous feathers awkwardly stuck on; they have an appropriateness which makes them seem an answer to anticipation, like the return phrases of a melody. Certainly one cannot help the ignorant conclusions of polite society, and there are perhaps fashionable persons who, if a speaker has occasion to explain what the occiput[4] is, will consider that he has lately discovered that curiously named portion of the animal frame: one cannot give a genealogical introduction to every long-stored item of fact or conjecture that may happen to be a revelation for the large class of persons who are understood to judge soundly on a small basis of knowledge. But Euphorion would be very sorry to have it supposed that he is unacquainted with the history of ideas, and sometimes carries even into minutiæ the evidence of his exact registration of names in connection with quotable phrases or suggestions: I can therefore only explain the apparent infirmity of his memory in cases of larger 'conveyance' by supposing that he is accustomed by the very association of largeness to range them at once under those grand laws of the universe in the light of which Mine and Thine disappear and are resolved into Everybody's or Nobody's, and one man's particular obligations to another melt untraceably into the obligations of the earth to the solar system in general.

Euphorion himself, if a particular omission of acknowledgment

were brought home to him, would probably take a narrower
ground of explanation. It was a lapse of memory; or it did not
occur to him as necessary in this case to mention a name, the
source being well known – or (since this seems usually to act as
a strong reason for mention) he rather abstained from adducing
the name because it might injure the excellent matter advanced,
just as an obscure trade-mark casts discredit on a good com-
modity, and even on the retailer who has furnished himself from
a quarter not likely to be esteemed first-rate. No doubt this last
is a genuine and frequent reason for the non-acknowledgment
of indebtedness to what one may call impersonal as well as
personal sources: even an American editor of school classics
whose own English could not pass for more than a syntactical
shoddy of the cheapest sort, felt it unfavourable to his reputation for sound learning that he should be obliged to the Penny
Cyclopædia, and disguised his references to it under contrac-
tions in which *Us. Knowl.* took the place of the low word *Penny*.[5]
Works of this convenient stamp, easily obtained and well
nourished with matter, are felt to be like rich but unfashionable
relations who are visited and received in privacy, and whose
capital is used or inherited without any ostentatious insistance
on their names and places of abode. As to memory, it is known
that this frail faculty naturally lets drop the facts which are less
flattering to our self-love – when it does not retain them
carefully as subjects not to be approached, marshy spots with a
warning flag over them. But it is always interesting to bring
forward eminent names, such as Patricius or Scaliger, Euler or
Lagrange, Bopp or Humboldt.[6] To know exactly what has been
drawn from them is erudition and heightens our own influence,
which seems advantageous to mankind; whereas to cite an
author whose ideas may pass as higher currency under our own
signature can have no object except the contradictory one of
throwing the illumination over his figure when it is important to
be seen oneself. All these reasons must weigh considerably with
those speculative persons who have to ask themselves whether
or not Universal Utilitarianism[7] requires that in the particular
instance before them they should injure a man who has been of

service to them, and rob a fellow-workman of the credit which is due to him.

After all, however, it must be admitted that hardly any accusation is more difficult to prove, and more liable to be false, than that of a plagiarism which is the conscious theft of ideas and deliberate reproduction of them as original. The arguments on the side of acquittal are obvious and strong: – the inevitable coincidences of contemporary thinking; and our continual experience of finding notions turning up in our minds without any label on them to tell us whence they came; so that if we are in the habit of expecting much from our own capacity we accept them at once as a new inspiration. Then, in relation to the elder authors, there is the difficulty first of learning and then of remembering exactly what has been wrought into the backward tapestry of the world's history, together with the fact that ideas acquired long ago reappear as the sequence of an awakened interest or a line of inquiry which is really new in us, whence it is conceivable that if we were ancients some of us might be offering grateful hecatombs[8] by mistake, and proving our honesty in a ruinously expensive manner. On the other hand, the evidence on which plagiarism is concluded is often of a kind which, though much trusted in questions of erudition and historical criticism, is apt to lead us injuriously astray in our daily judgments, especially of the resentful, condemnatory sort. How Pythagoras came by his ideas, whether St Paul was acquainted with all the Greek poets, what Tacitus must have known by hearsay and systematically ignored,[9] are points on which a false persuasion of knowledge is less damaging to justice and charity than an erroneous confidence, supported by reasoning fundamentally similar, of my neighbour's blameworthy behaviour in a case where I am personally concerned. No premises require closer scrutiny than those which lead to the constantly echoed conclusion, 'He must have known,' or 'He must have read.' I marvel that this facility of belief on the side of knowledge can subsist under the daily demonstration that the easiest of all things to the human mind is *not* to know and *not* to read. To praise, to blame, to shout, grin, or hiss, where others shout, grin, or hiss

– these are native tendencies; but to know and to read are artificial, hard accomplishments, concerning which the only safe supposition is, that as little of them has been done as the case admits. An author, keenly conscious of having written, can hardly help imagining his condition of lively interest to be shared by others, just as we are all apt to suppose that the chill or heat we are conscious of must be general, or even to think that our sons and daughters, our pet schemes, and our quarrelling correspondence, are themes to which intelligent persons will listen long without weariness. But if the ardent author happen to be alive to practical teaching he will soon learn to divide the larger part of the enlightened public into those who have not read him and think it necessary to tell him so when they meet him in polite society, and those who have equally abstained from reading him, but wish to conceal this negation and speak of his 'incomparable works' with that trust in testimony which always has its cheering side.

Hence it is worse than foolish to entertain silent suspicions of plagiarism, still more to give them voice, when they are founded on a construction of probabilities which a little more attention to everyday occurrences as a guide in reasoning would show us to be really worthless, considered as proof. The length to which one man's memory can go in letting drop associations that are vital to another can hardly find a limit. It is not to be supposed that a person desirous to make an agreeable impression on you would deliberately choose to insist to you, with some rhetorical sharpness, on an argument which you were the first to elaborate in public; yet any one who listens may overhear such instances of obliviousness. You naturally remember your peculiar connection with your acquaintance's judicious views; but why should *he?* Your fatherhood, which is an intense feeling to you, is only an additional fact of meagre interest for him to remember; and a sense of obligation to the particular living fellow-struggler who has helped us in our thinking, is not yet a form of memory the want of which is felt to be disgraceful or derogatory, unless it is taken to be a want of polite instruction, or causes the missing of a cockade on a day of celebration. In our suspicions of plagiarism we must recognise as the first weighty probability, that what we who feel injured remember best is precisely what is least likely to enter lastingly into the memory of our neighbours. But it is fair to maintain that the neighbour who borrows your property, loses it for a while, and when it turns up again forgets your connection with it and counts it his own, shows himself so much the feebler in grasp and rectitude of mind. Some absent persons cannot remember the state of wear in their own hats and umbrellas, and have no mental check to tell them that they have carried home a fellow-visitor's more recent purchase: they may be excellent householders, far removed from the suspicion of low devices, but one wishes them a more correct perception, and a more wary sense that a neighbour's umbrella may be newer than their own.

True, some persons are so constituted that the very excellence of an idea seems to them a convincing reason that it must be, if not solely, yet especially theirs. It fits in so beautifully with their general wisdom, it lies implicitly in so many of their manifested opinions, that if they have not yet expressed it (because of preoccupation) it is clearly a part of their indigenous produce, and is proved by their immediate eloquent promulgation of it to belong more naturally and appropriately to them than to the person who seemed first to have alighted on it, and who sinks in their all-originating consciousness to that low kind of entity, a second cause. This is not lunacy, nor pretence, but a genuine state of mind very effective in practice, and often carrying the public with it, so that the poor Columbus is found to be a very faulty adventurer, and the continent is named after Amerigo.[10] Lighter examples of this instinctive appropriation are constantly met with among brilliant talkers. Aquila[11] is too agreeable and amusing for any one who is not himself bent on display to be angry at his conversational rapine – his habit of darting down on every morsel of booty that other birds may hold in their beaks, with an innocent air, as if it were all intended for his use, and honestly counted on by him as a tribute in kind. Hardly any man, I imagine, can have had less trouble in gathering a showy stock of information than Aquila.

On close inquiry you would probably find that he had not read one epoch-making book of modern times, for he has a career which obliges him to much correspondence and other official work, and he is too fond of being in company to spend his leisure moments in study; but to his quick eye, ear, and tongue, a few predatory excursions in conversation where there are instructed persons, gradually furnish surprisingly clever modes of statement and allusion on the dominant topic. When he first adopts a subject he necessarily falls into mistakes, and it is interesting to watch his gradual progress into fuller information and better nourished irony, without his ever needing to admit that he has made a blunder or to appear conscious of correction. Suppose, for example, he had incautiously founded some ingenious remarks on a hasty reckoning that nine thirteens made a hundred and two, and the insignificant Bantam, hitherto silent, seemed to spoil the flow of ideas by stating that the product could not be taken as less than a hundred and seventeen, Aquila would glide on in the most graceful manner from a repetition of his previous remark to the continuation – 'All this is on the supposition that a hundred and two were all that could be got out of nine thirteens; but as all the world knows that nine thirteens will yield,' &c. – proceeding straightway into a new train of ingenious consequences, and causing Bantam to be regarded by all present as one of those slow persons who take irony for ignorance, and who would warn the weasel to keep awake. How should a small-eyed, feebly crowing mortal like him be quicker in arithmetic than the keen-faced forcible Aquila, in whom universal knowledge is easily credible? Looked into closely, the conclusion from a man's profile, voice, and fluency to his certainty in multiplication beyond the twelves, seems to show a confused notion of the way in which very common things are connected; but it is on such false correlations that men found half their inferences about each other, and high places of trust may sometimes be held on no better foundation.

It is a commonplace that words, writings, measures, and performances in general, have qualities assigned them not by a direct judgment on the performances themselves, but by a presumption of what they are likely to be, considering who is the performer. We all notice in our neighbours this reference to names as guides in criticism, and all furnish illustrations of it in our own practice; for, check ourselves as we will, the first impression from any sort of work must depend on a previous attitude of mind, and this will constantly be determined by the influences of a name. But that our prior confidence or want of confidence in given names is made up of judgments just as hollow as the consequent praise or blame they are taken to warrant, is less commonly perceived, though there is a conspicuous indication of it in the surprise or disappointment often manifested in the disclosure of an authorship about which everybody has been making wrong guesses. No doubt if it had been discovered who wrote the 'Vestiges,'[12] many an ingenious structure of probabilities would have been spoiled, and some disgust might have been felt for a real author who made comparatively so shabby an appearance of likelihood. It is this foolish trust in prepossessions, founded on spurious evidence, which makes a medium of encouragement for those who, happening to have the ear of the public, give other people's ideas the advantage of appearing under their own well-received name, while any remonstrance from the real producer becomes an unwelcome disturbance of complacency with each person who has paid complimentary tributes in the wrong place.

Hardly any kind of false reasoning is more ludicrous than this on the probabilities of origination. It would be amusing to catechise the guessers as to their exact reasons for thinking their guess 'likely:' why Hoopoe of John's has fixed on Toucan of Magdalen;[13] why Shrike attributes its peculiar style to Buzzard, who has not hitherto been known as a writer; why the fair Columba thinks it must belong to the reverend Merula; and why they are all alike disturbed in their previous judgment of its value by finding that it really came from Skunk, whom they had either not thought of at all, or thought of as belonging to a species excluded by the nature of the case. Clearly they were all wrong in their notion of the specific conditions, which lay unexpectedly in the small Skunk, and in him alone – in spite of his education nobody knows where, in spite of somebody's knowing his uncles and cousins, and in spite of nobody's knowing that he was cleverer than they thought him.

Such guesses remind one of a fabulist's imaginary council of animals assembled to consider what sort of creature had constructed a honeycomb found and much tasted by Bruin and other epicures. The speakers all started from the probability that the maker was a bird, because this was the quarter from which a wondrous nest might be expected; for the animals at that time, knowing little of their own history, would have rejected as inconceivable the notion that a nest could be made by a fish; and as to the insects, they were not willingly received in society and their ways were little known. Several complimentary presumptions were expressed that the honeycomb was due to one or the other admired and popular bird, and there was much fluttering on the part of the Nightingale and Swallow, neither of whom gave a positive denial, their confusion perhaps extending to their sense of identity; but the Owl hissed at this folly, arguing from his particular knowledge that the animal which produced honey must be the Musk-rat, the wondrous nature of whose secretions required no proof; and, in the powerful logical procedure of the Owl, from musk to honey was but a step. Some disturbance arose hereupon, for the Musk-rat began to make himself obtrusive, believing in the Owl's opinion of his powers, and feeling that he could have produced the honey if he had thought of it; until an experimental Butcher-bird proposed to anatomise him as a help to decision. The hubbub increased, the opponents of the Musk-rat inquiring who his ancestors were; until a diversion was created by an able discourse of the Macaw on structures generally, which he classified so as to include the honeycomb, entering into so much admirable exposition that there was a prevalent sense of the honeycomb having probably been produced by one who understood it so well. But Bruin, who had probably eaten too much to listen with edification, grumbled in his low kind of language, that 'Fine words butter no parsnips,' by which he meant to say that there was no new honey forthcoming.

Perhaps the audience generally was beginning to tire, when the Fox entered with his snout dreadfully swollen, and reported that the beneficent originator in question was the Wasp, which he had found much smeared with undoubted honey, having applied his nose to it – whence indeed the able insect, perhaps justifiably irritated at what might seem a sign of scepticism, had stung him with some severity, an infliction Reynard could hardly regret, since the swelling of a snout normally so delicate would corroborate his statement and satisfy the assembly that he had really found the honey-creating genius.

The Fox's admitted acuteness, combined with the visible swelling, were taken as undeniable evidence, and the revelation undoubtedly met a general desire for information on a point of interest. Nevertheless, there was a murmur the reverse of delighted, and the feelings of some eminent animals were too strong for them: the Orang-outang's jaw dropped so as seriously to impair the vigour of his expression, the edifying Pelican screamed and flapped her wings, the Owl hissed again, the Macaw became loudly incoherent, and the Gibbon gave his hysterical laugh; while the Hyaena, after indulging in a more splenetic guffaw, agitated the question whether it would not be better to hush up the whole affair, instead of giving public recognition to an insect whose produce, it was now plain, had been much overestimated. But this narrow-spirited motion was negatived by the sweet-toothed majority. A complimentary deputation to the Wasp was resolved on, and there was a confident hope that this diplomatic measure would tell on the production of honey.

'SO YOUNG!'

GANYMEDE[1] was once a girlishly handsome precocious youth. That one cannot for any considerable number of years go on being youthful, girlishly handsome, and precocious, seems on consideration to be a statement as worthy of credit as the famous syllogistic conclusion, 'Socrates was mortal.' But many circumstances have conspired to keep up in Ganymede the illusion that he is surprisingly young. He was the last born of his family, and from his earliest memory was accustomed to be commended as such to the care of his elder brothers and sisters: he heard his mother speak of him as her youngest darling with a loving pathos in her tone, which naturally suffused his own view of himself, and gave him the habitual consciousness of being at once very young and very interesting. Then, the dis-closure of his tender years was a constant matter of astonish-ment to strangers who had had proof of his precocious talents, and the astonishment extended to what is called the world at large when he produced 'A Comparative Estimate of European Nations' before he was well out of his teens. All comers, on a first interview, told him that he was marvellously young, and some repeated the statement each time they saw him; all critics who wrote about him called attention to the same ground for wonder: his deficiencies and excesses were alike to be accounted for by the flattering fact of his youth, and his youth was the golden background which set off his many-hued endowments. Here was already enough to establish a strong association between his sense of identity and his sense of being unusually young. But after this he devised and founded an ingenious

organisation for consolidating the literary interests of all the
four continents (subsequently including Australasia and Poly-
nesia), he himself presiding in the central offfice, which thus
became a new theatre for the constantly repeated situation of an
astonished stranger in the presence of a boldly scheming administrator found to be remarkably young. If we imagine with due
charity the effect on Ganymede, we shall think it greatly to his
credit that he continued to feel the necessity of being something
more than young, and did not sink by rapid degrees into a
parallel of that melancholy object, a superannuated youthful
phenomenon. Happily he had enough of valid, active faculty to
save him from that tragic fate. He had not exhausted his
fountain of eloquent opinion in his 'Comparative Estimate,' so as
to feel himself, like some other juvenile celebrities, the sad
survivor of his own manifest destiny, or like one who has risen
too early in the morning, and finds all the solid day turned into
a fatigued afternoon. He has continued to be productive both of
schemes and writings, being perhaps helped by the fact that his
'Comparative Estimate' did not greatly affect the currents of
European thought, and left him with the stimulating hope that
he had not done his best, but might yet produce what would
make his youth more surprising than ever.

I saw something of him through his Antinous[2] period, the
time of rich chestnut locks, parted not by a visible white line, but
by a shadowed furrow from which they fell in massive ripples to
right and left. In these slim days he looked the younger for being
rather below the middle size, and though at last one perceived
him contracting an indefinable air of self-consciousness, a slight
exaggeration of the facial movements, the attitudes, the little
tricks, and the romance in shirt-collars, which must be expected
from one who, in spite of his knowledge, was so exceedingly
young, it was impossible to say that he was making any great
mistake about himself. He was only undergoing one form of a
common moral disease: being strongly mirrored for himself in
the remark of others, he was getting to see his real characteristics as a dramatic part, a type to which his doings were always
in correspondence. Owing to my absence on travel and to other

causes I had lost sight of him for several years, but such a
separation between two who have not missed each other seems
in this busy century only a pleasant reason, when they happen
to meet again in some old accustomed haunt, for the one who
has stayed at home to be more communicative about himself
than he can well be to those who have all along been in his
neighbourhood. He had married in the interval, and as if to keep
up his surprising youthfulness in all relations, he had taken a
wife considerably older than himself. It would probably have
seemed to him a disturbing inversion of the natural order that
any one very near to him should have been younger than he,
except his own children who, however young, would not necessarily hinder the normal surprise at the youthfulness of their
father. And if my glance had revealed my impression on first
seeing him again, he might have received a rather disagreeable
shock, which was far from my intention. My mind, having
retained a very exact image of his former appearance, took note
of unmistakeable changes such as a painter would certainly not
have made by way of flattering his subject. He had lost his
slimness, and that curved solidity which might have adorned a
taller man was a rather sarcastic threat to his short figure. The
English branch of the Teutonic race does not produce many fat
youths, and I have even heard an American lady say that she was
much 'disappointed' at the moderate number and size of our fat
men, considering their reputation in the United States; hence a
stranger would now have been apt to remark that Ganymede
was unusually plump for a distinguished writer, rather than
unusually young. But how was he to know this? Many long-
standing prepossessions are as hard to be corrected as a long-
standing mispronunciation, against which the direct experience
of eye and ear is often powerless. And I could perceive that
Ganymede's inwrought sense of his surprising youthfulness had
been stronger than the superficial reckoning of his years and the
merely optical phenomena of the looking-glass. He now held a
post under Government, and not only saw, like most subordin-
ate functionaries, how ill everything was managed, but also what
were the changes that a high constructive ability would dictate;

and in mentioning to me his own speeches and other efforts towards propagating reformatory views in his department, he concluded by changing his tone to a sentimental head voice and saying –

'But I am so young; people object to any prominence on my part; I can only get myself heard anonymously, and when some attention has been drawn the name is sure to creep out. The writer is known to be young, and things are none the forwarder.'

'Well,' said I, 'youth seems the only drawback that is sure to diminish. You and I have seven years less of it than when we last met.'

'Ah?' returned Ganymede, as lightly as possible, at the same time casting an observant glance over me, as if he were marking the effect of seven years on a person who had probably begun life with an old look, and even as an infant had given his countenance to that significant doctrine, the transmigration of ancient souls into modern bodies.

I left him on that occasion without any melancholy forecast that his illusion would be suddenly or painfully broken up. I saw that he was well victualled and defended against a ten years' siege from ruthless facts; and in the course of time observation convinced me that his resistance received considerable aid from without. Each of his written productions, as it came out, was still commented on as the work of a very young man. One critic, finding that he wanted solidity, charitably referred to his youth as an excuse. Another, dazzled by his brilliancy, seemed to regard his youth as so wondrous that all other authors appeared decrepit by comparison, and their style such as might be looked for from gentlemen of the old school. Able pens (according to a familiar metaphor) appeared to shake their heads good-humouredly, implying that Ganymede's crudities were pardonable in one so exceedingly young. Such unanimity amid diversity, which a distant posterity might take for evidence that on the point of age at least there could have been no mistake, was not really more difficult to account for than the prevalence of cotton in our fabrics. Ganymede had been first introduced into the

writing world as remarkably young, and it was no exceptional
consequence that the first deposit of information about him held
its ground against facts which, however open to observation,
were not necessarily thought of. It is not so easy, with our rates
and taxes and need for economy in all directions, to cast away
an epithet or remark that turns up cheaply, and to go in
expensive search after more genuine substitutes. There is high
Homeric precedent for keeping fast hold of an epithet under all
changes of circumstance, and so the precocious author of the
'Comparative Estimate' heard the echoes repeating 'Young
Ganymede' when an illiterate beholder at a railway station
would have given him forty years at least. Besides, important
elders, sachems of the clubs and public meetings, had a genuine
opinion of him as young enough to be checked for speech on
subjects which they had spoken mistakenly about when he was
in his cradle; and then, the midway parting of his crisp hair, not
common among English committee-men, formed a presumption
against the ripeness of his judgment which nothing but a speedy
baldness could have removed.

It is but fair to mention all these outward confirmations of
Ganymede's illusion, which shows no signs of leaving him. It is
true that he no longer hears expressions of surprise at his
youthfulness, on a first introduction to an admiring reader; but
this sort of external evidence has become an unnecessary crutch
to his habitual inward persuasion. His manners, his costume, his
suppositions of the impression he makes on others, have all their
former correspondence with the dramatic part of the young
genius. As to the incongruity of his contour and other little
accidents of *physique*, he is probably no more aware that they
will affect others as incongruities than Armida[3] is conscious how
much her rouge provokes our notice of her wrinkles, and causes
us to mention sarcastically that motherly age which we should
otherwise regard with affectionate reverence.

But let us be just enough to admit that there may be old-
young coxcombs as well as old-young coquettes.

HOW WE COME TO GIVE OURSELVES FALSE
TESTIMONIALS, AND BELIEVE IN THEM

IT is my way when I observe any instance of folly, any queer
habit, any absurd illusion, straightway to look for something of
the same type in myself, feeling sure that amid all differences
there will be a certain correspondence; just as there is more or
less correspondence in the natural history even of continents
widely apart, and of islands in opposite zones. No doubt men's
minds differ in what we may call their climate or share of solar
energy, and a feeling or tendency which is comparable to a
panther in one may have no more imposing aspect than that of
a weasel in another: some are like a tropical habitat in which
the very ferns cast a mighty shadow, and the grasses are a dry
ocean in which a hunter may be submerged; others like the
chilly latitudes in which your forest-tree, fit elsewhere to prop
a mine, is a pretty miniature suitable for fancy potting. The
eccentric man might be typified by the Australian fauna, refut-
ing half our judicious assumptions of what nature allows. Still,
whether fate commanded us to thatch our persons among the
Eskimos or to choose the latest thing in tattooing among the
Polynesian isles, our precious guide Comparison[1] would teach
us in the first place by likeness, and our clue to further knowledge would be resemblance to what we already know. Hence,
having a keen interest in the natural history of my inward self,
I pursue this plan I have mentioned of using my observation as
a clue or lantern by which I detect small herbage or lurking
life; or I take my neighbour in his least becoming tricks or
efforts as an opportunity for luminous deduction concerning

the figure the human genus makes in the specimen which I myself furnish.

Introspection which starts with the purpose of finding out one's own absurdities is not likely to be very mischievous, yet of course it is not free from dangers any more than breathing is, or the other functions that keep us alive and active. To judge of others by oneself is in its most innocent meaning the briefest expression for our only method of knowing mankind; yet, we perceive, it has come to mean in many cases either the vulgar mistake which reduces every man's value to the very low figure at which the valuer himself happens to stand; or else, the amiable illusion of the higher nature misled by a too generous construction of the lower. One cannot give a recipe for wise judgment: it resembles appropriate muscular action, which is attained by the myriad lessons in nicety of balance and of aim that only practice can give. The danger of the inverse procedure, judging of self by what one observes in others, if it is carried on with much impartiality and keenness of discernment, is that it has a laming effect, enfeebling the energies of indignation and scorn, which are the proper scourges of wrong-doing and meanness, and which should continually feed the wholesome restraining power of public opinion. I respect the horsewhip when applied to the back of Cruelty, and think that he who applies it is a more perfect human being because his out-leap of indignation is not checked by a too curious reflection on the nature of guilt – a more perfect human being because he more completely incorporates the best social life of the race, which can never be constituted by ideas that nullify action. This is the essence of Dante's sentiment (it is painful to think that he applies it very cruelly) –

'E cortesia fù, lui esser villano'[2]

and it is undeniable that a too intense consciousness of one's kinship with all frailties and vices undermines the active heroism which battles against wrong.

But certainly nature has taken care that this danger should

not at present be very threatening. One could not fairly describe the generality of one's neighbours as too lucidly aware of manifesting in their own persons the weaknesses which they observe in the rest of her Majesty's subjects; on the contrary, a hasty conclusion as to schemes of Providence might lead to the supposition that one man was intended to correct another by being most intolerant of the ugly quality or trick which he himself possesses. Doubtless philosophers will be able to explain how it must necessarily be so, but pending the full extension of the *à priori* method, which will show that only blockheads could expect anything to be otherwise, it does seem surprising that Heloisa should be disgusted at Laura's[3] attempts to disguise her age, attempts which she recognises so thoroughly because they enter into her own practice; that Semper,[4] who often responds at public dinners and proposes resolutions on platforms, though he has a trying gestation of every speech and a bad time for himself and others at every delivery, should yet remark pitilessly on the folly of precisely the same course of action in Ubique; that Aliquis, who lets no attack on himself pass unnoticed, and for every handful of gravel against his windows sends a stone in reply, should deplore the ill-advised retorts of Quispiam, who does not perceive that to show oneself angry with an adversary is to gratify him. To be unaware of our own little tricks of manner or our own mental blemishes and excesses is a comprehensible unconsciousness; the puzzling fact is that people should apparently take no account of their deliberate actions, and should expect them to be equally ignored by others. It is an inversion of the accepted order: *there* it is the phrases that are official and the conduct or privately manifested sentiment that is taken to be real; *here* it seems that the practice is taken to be official and entirely nullified by the verbal representation which contradicts it. The thief making a vow to heaven of full restitution and whispering some reservations, expecting to cheat Omniscience by an 'aside,' is hardly more ludicrous than the many ladies and gentlemen who have more belief, and expect others to have it, in their own statement about their habitual doings than in the contradictory fact which is patent in the daylight. One reason of the absurdity is that we are led by a tradition about ourselves, so that long after a man has practically departed from a rule or principle, he continues innocently to state it as a true description of his practice – just as he has a long tradition that he is not an old gentleman, and is startled when he is seventy at overhearing himself called by an epithet which he has only applied to others.

'A person with your tendency of constitution should take as little sugar as possible,' said Pilulus[5] to Bovis somewhere in the darker decades of this century. 'It has made a great difference to Avis since he took my advice in that matter: he used to consume half a pound a-day.'

'God bless me !' cries Bovis. 'I take very little sugar myself.'

'Twenty-six large lumps every day of your life, Mr Bovis,' says his wife.

'No such thing!' exclaims Bovis.

'You drop them into your tea, coffee, and whisky yourself, my dear, and I count them.'

'Nonsense!' laughs Bovis, turning to Pilulus, that they may exchange a glance of mutual amusement at a woman's inaccuracy.

But she happened to be right. Bovis had never said inwardly that he would take a large allowance of sugar, and he had the tradition about himself that he was a man of the most moderate habits; hence, with this conviction, he was naturally disgusted at the saccharine excesses of Avis.

I have sometimes thought that this facility of men in believing that they are still what they once meant to be – this undisturbed appropriation of a traditional character which is often but a melancholy relic of early resolutions, like the worn and soiled testimonial to soberness and honesty carried in the pocket of a tippler whom the need of a dram has driven into peculation – may sometimes diminish the turpitude of what seems a flat, barefaced falsehood. It is notorious that a man may go on uttering false assertions about his own acts till he at last believes in them: is it not possible that sometimes in the very first utterance there may be a shade of creed-reciting belief, a reproduction of a traditional self which is clung to against all evidence? There is no knowing all the disguises of the lying serpent.

When we come to examine in detail what is the sane mind in the sane body,[6] the final test of completeness seems to be a security of distinction between what we have professed and what we have done; what we have aimed at and what we have achieved; what we have invented and what we have witnessed or had evidenced to us; what we think and feel in the present and what we thought and felt in the past.

I know that there is a common prejudice which regards the habitual confusion of *now* and *then*, of *it was* and *it is*, of *it seemed so* and *I should like it to be so*, as a mark of high imaginative endowment, while the power of precise statement and description is rated lower, as the attitude of an everyday prosaic mind. High imagination is often assigned or claimed as if it were a ready activity in fabricating extravagances such as are presented by fevered dreams, or as if its possessors were in that state of inability to give credible testimony which would warrant their exclusion from the class of acceptable witnesses in a court of justice; so that a creative genius might fairly be subjected to the disability which some laws have stamped on dicers, slaves, and other classes whose position was held perverting to their sense of social responsibility.[7]

This endowment of mental confusion is often boasted of by persons whose imaginativeness would not otherwise be known, unless it were by the slow process of detecting that their descriptions and narratives were not to be trusted. Callista[8] is always ready to testify of herself that she is an imaginative person, and sometimes adds in illustration, that if she had taken a walk and seen an old heap of stones on her way, the account she would give on returning would include many pleasing particulars of her own invention, transforming the simple heap into an interesting castellated ruin. This creative freedom is all very well in the right place, but before I can grant it to be a sign of unusual mental power, I must inquire whether, on being requested to give a precise description of what she saw, she would be able to cast aside her arbitrary combinations and recover the objects she really perceived so as to make them recognisable by another person who passed the same way. Otherwise her glorifying imagination is not an addition to the fundamental power of strong, discerning perception, but a cheaper substitute. And, in fact, I find on listening to Callista's conversation, that she has a very lax conception even of common objects, and an equally lax memory of events. It seems of no consequence to her whether she shall say that a stone is overgrown with moss or with lichen, that a building is of sandstone or of granite, that Meliboeus[9] once forgot to put on his cravat or that he always appears without it; that everybody says so, or that one stock-broker's wife said so yesterday; that Philemon[10] praised Euphemia up to the skies, or that he denied knowing any particular evil of her. She is one of those respectable witnesses who would testify to the exact moment of an apparition, because any desirable moment will be as exact as another to her remembrance; or who would be the most worthy to witness the action of spirits on slates and tables[11] because the action of limbs would not probably arrest her attention. She would describe the surprising phenomena exhibited by the powerful Medium with the same freedom that she vaunted in relation to the old heap of stones. Her supposed imaginativeness is simply a very usual lack of discriminating perception, accompanied with a less usual activity of misrepresentation, which, if it had been a little more intense, or had been stimulated by circumstance, might have made her a profuse writer unchecked by the troublesome need of veracity.

These characteristics are the very opposite of such as yield a fine imagination, which is always based on a keen vision, a keen consciousness of what *is*, and carries the store of definite knowledge as material for the construction of its inward visions. Witness Dante, who is at once the most precise and homely in his reproduction of actual objects, and the most soaringly at large in his imaginative combinations. On a much lower level we distinguish the hyperbole and rapid development in descriptions of persons and events which are lit up by humorous intention in the speaker – we distinguish this charming play of intelligence which resembles musical improvisation on a given motive, where the farthest sweep of curve is looped into relevancy by an instinctive method, from the florid inaccuracy or helpless exaggeration which is really something commoner than the correct simplicity often depreciated as prosaic.

Even if high imagination were to be identified with illusion, there would be the same sort of difference between the imperial wealth of illusion which is informed by industrious submissive observation and the trumpery stage-property illusion which depends on the ill-defined impressions gathered by capricious inclination, as there is between a good and a bad picture of the Last Judgment. In both these the subject is a combination never actually witnessed, and in the good picture the general combination may be of surpassing boldness; but on examination it is seen that the separate elements have been closely studied from real objects. And even where we find the charm of ideal elevation with wrong drawing and fantastic colour, the charm is dependent on the selective sensibility of the painter to certain real delicacies of form which confer the expression he longed to render; for apart from this basis of an effect perceived in common, there could be no conveyance of æsthetic meaning by the painter to the beholder. In this sense it is as true to say of Fra Angelico's Coronation of the Virgin,[12] that it has a strain of reality, as to say so of a portrait by Rembrandt, which also has its strain of ideal elevation due to Rembrandt's virile selective sensibility.

To correct such self-flatterers as Callista, it is worth repeating that powerful imagination is not false outward vision, but intense inward representation, and a creative energy constantly fed by susceptibility to the veriest minutiæ of experience, which it reproduces and constructs in fresh and fresh wholes; not the habitual confusion of provable fact with the fictions of fancy and transient inclination, but a breadth of ideal association which informs every material object, every incidental fact with far-reaching memories and stored residues of passion, bringing into new light the less obvious relations of human existence. The illusion to which it is liable is not that of habitually taking duck-ponds for lilied pools, but of being more or less transiently and in varying degrees so absorbed in ideal vision as to lose the consciousness of surrounding objects or occurrences; and when that rapt condition is past, the sane genius discriminates clearly between what has been given in this parenthetic state of excitement, and what he has known, and may count on, in the ordinary world of experience. Dante seems to have expressed these conditions perfectly in that passage of the *Purgatorio* where, after a triple vision which has made him forget his surroundings, he says –

> 'Quando l'anima mia tornò di fuori
> Alle cose che son fuor di lei vere,
> Io riconobbi i miei non falsi errori.' – (c.xv.)[13]

He distinguishes the ideal truth of his entranced vision from the series of external facts to which his consciousness had returned. Isaiah gives us the date of his vision[14] in the Temple – 'the year that King Uzziah died' – and if afterwards the mighty-winged seraphim were present with him as he trod the street, he doubtless knew them for images of memory, and did not cry 'Look!' to the passers-by.

Certainly the seer, whether prophet, philosopher, scientific discoverer, or poet, may happen to be rather mad: his powers may have been used up, like Don Quixote's, in their visionary or theoretic constructions, so that the reports of common-sense fail to affect him, or the continuous strain of excitement may have robbed his mind of its elasticity. It is hard for our frail mortality to carry the burthen of greatness with steady gait and full alacrity of perception. But he is the strongest seer who can support the stress of creative energy and yet keep that sanity of expectation which consists in distinguishing, as Dante does, between the *cose che son vere* outside the individual mind, and the *non falsi errori* which are the revelations of true imaginative power.

THE TOO READY WRITER

ONE who talks too much, hindering the rest of the company from taking their turn, and apparently seeing no reason why they should not rather desire to know his opinion or experience in relation to all subjects, or at least to renounce the discussion of any topic where he can make no figure, has never been praised for this industrious monopoly of work which others would willingly have shared in. However various and brilliant his talk may be, we suspect him of impoverishing us by excluding the contributions of other minds, which attract our curiosity the more because he has shut them up in silence. Besides, we get tired of a 'manner' in conversation as in painting, when one theme after another is treated with the same lines and touches. I begin with a liking for an estimable master, but by the time he has stretched his interpretation of the world unbrokenly along a palatial gallery, I have had what the cautious Scotch mind would call 'enough' of him. There is monotony and narrowness already to spare in my own identity; what comes to me from without should be larger and more impartial than the judgment of any single interpreter. On this ground even a modest person, without power or will to shine in the conversation, may easily find the predominating talker a nuisance, while those who are full of matter on special topics are continually detecting miserably thin places in the web of that information which he will not desist from imparting. Nobody that I know of ever proposed a testimonial to a man for thus volunteering the whole expense of the conversation.

Why is there a different standard of judgment with regard to a writer who plays much the same part in literature as the excessive talker plays in what is traditionally called conversation? The busy Adrastus,[1] whose professional engagements might seem more than enough for the nervous energy of one man, and who yet finds time to print essays on the chief current subjects, from the tri-lingual inscriptions,[2] or the Idea of the Infinite among the prehistoric Lapps, to the Colorado beetle and the grape disease in the south of France, is generally praised if not admired for the breadth of his mental range and his gigantic powers of work. Poor Theron,[3] who has some original ideas on a subject to which he has given years of research and meditation, has been waiting anxiously from month to month to see whether his condensed exposition will find a place in the next advertised programme, but sees it, on the contrary, regularly excluded, and twice the space he asked for filled with the copious brew of Adrastus, whose name carries custom like a celebrated trade-mark. Why should the eager haste to tell what he thinks on the shortest notice, as if his opinion were a needed preliminary to discussion, get a man the reputation of being a conceited bore in conversation, when nobody blames the same tendency if it shows itself in print? The excessive talker can only be in one gathering at a time, and there is the comfort of thinking that everywhere else other fellow-citizens who have something to say may get a chance of delivering themselves; but the exorbitant writer can occupy space and spread over it the more or less agreeable flavour of his mind in four 'mediums' at once, and on subjects taken from the four winds. Such restless and versatile occupants of literary space and time should have lived earlier when the world wanted summaries of all extant knowledge, and this knowledge being small, there was the more room for commentary and conjecture. They might have played the part of an Isidor of Seville or a Vincent of Beauvais[4] brilliantly, and the willingness to write everything themselves would have been strictly in place. In the present day, the busy retailer of other people's knowledge which he has spoiled in the handling, the restless guesser and commentator, the importunate hawker of undesirable superfluities, the everlasting word-

compeller who rises early in the morning to praise what the
world has already glorified, or makes himself haggard at night in
writing out his dissent from what nobody ever believed, is not
simply 'gratis anhelans, multa agendo nihil agens'[5] − he is an
obstruction. Like an incompetent architect with too much
interest at his back, he obtrudes his ill-considered work where
place ought to have been left to better men.

Is it out of the question that we should entertain some
scruple about mixing our own flavour, as of the too cheap and
insistent nutmeg, with that of every great writer and every great
subject? − especially when our flavour is all we have to give, the
matter or knowledge having been already given by somebody
else. What if we were only like the Spanish wine-skins which
impress the innocent stranger with the notion that the Spanish
grape has naturally a taste of leather? One could wish that even
the greatest minds should leave some themes unhandled, or at
least leave us no more than a paragraph or two on them to show
how well they did in not being more lengthy.

Such entertainment of scruple can hardly be expected from
the young; but happily their readiness to mirror the universe
anew for the rest of mankind is not encouraged by easy public-
ity. In the vivacious Pepin[6] I have often seen the image of my
early youth, when it seemed to me astonishing that the philosophers had left so many difficulties unsolved, and that so many
great themes had raised no great poet to treat them. I had an
elated sense that I should find my brain full of theoretic clues
when I looked for them, and that wherever a poet had not done
what I expected, it was for want of my insight. Not knowing
what had been said about the play of Romeo and Juliet, I felt
myself capable of writing something original on its blemishes
and beauties. In relation to all subjects I had a joyous consciousness of that ability which is prior to knowledge, and of only
needing to apply myself in order to master any task − to
conciliate philosophers whose systems were at present but
dimly known to me, to estimate foreign poets whom I had not
yet read, to show up mistakes in an historical monograph that
roused my interest in an epoch which I had been hitherto

ignorant of, when I should once have had time to verify my views of probability by looking into an encyclopædia. So Pepin; save only that he is industrious while I was idle. Like the astronomer in Rasselas,[7] I swayed the universe in my consciousness without making any difference outside me; whereas Pepin, while feeling himself powerful with the stars in their courses, really raises some dust here below. He is no longer in his springtide, but having been always busy he has been obliged to use his first impressions as if they were deliberate opinions, and to range himself on the corresponding side in ignorance of much that he commits himself to; so that he retains some characteristics of a comparatively tender age, and among them a certain surprise that there have not been more persons equal to himself. Perhaps it is unfortunate for him that he early gained a hearing, or at least a place in print, and was thus encouraged in acquiring a fixed habit of writing, to the exclusion of any other breadwinning pursuit. He is already to be classed as a 'general writer,' corresponding to the comprehensive wants of the 'general reader,' and with this industry on his hands it is not enough for him to keep up the ingenuous self-reliance of youth: he finds himself under an obligation to be skilled in various methods of seeming to know; and having habitually expressed himself before he was convinced, his interest in all subjects is chiefly to ascertain that he has not made a mistake, and to feel his infallibility confirmed. That impulse to decide, that vague sense of being able to achieve the unattempted, that dream of aerial unlimited movement at will without feet or wings, which were once but the joyous mounting of young sap, are already taking shape as unalterable woody fibre: the impulse has hardened into 'style,' and into a pattern of peremptory sentences; the sense of ability in the presence of other men's failures is turning into the official arrogance of one who habitually issues directions which he has never himself been called on to execute; the dreamy buoyancy of the stripling has taken on a fatal sort of reality in written pretensions which carry consequences. He is on the way to become like the loud-buzzing, bouncing Bombus[8] who combines conceited illusions enough to supply several patients in a lunatic asylum with the freedom to show himself at large in various forms of print. If one who takes himself for the telegraphic centre of all American wires is to be confined as unfit to transact affairs, what shall we say to the man who believes himself in possession of the unexpressed motives and designs dwelling in the breasts of all sovereigns and all politicians? And I grieve to think that poor Pepin, though less political, may by-and-by manifest a persuasion hardly more sane, for he is beginning to explain people's writing by what he does not know about them. Yet he was once at the comparatively innocent stage which I have confessed to be that of my own early astonishment at my powerful originality; and copying the just humility of the old Puritan, I may say, 'But for the grace of discouragement, this coxcombry might have been mine.'

Pepin made for himself a necessity of writing (and getting printed) before he had considered whether he had the knowledge or belief that would furnish eligible matter. At first perhaps the necessity galled him a little, but it is now as easily borne, nay, is as irrepressible a habit as the outpouring of inconsiderate talk. He is gradually being condemned to have no genuine impressions, no direct consciousness of enjoyment or the reverse from the quality of what is before him: his perceptions are continually arranging themselves in forms suitable to a printed judgment, and hence they will often turn out to be as much to the purpose if they are written without any direct contemplation of the object, and are guided by a few external conditions which serve to classify it for him. In this way he is irrevocably losing the faculty of accurate mental vision: having bound himself to express judgments which will satisfy some other demands than that of veracity, he has blunted his perceptions by continual preoccupation. We cannot command veracity at will: the power of seeing and reporting truly is a form of health that has to be delicately guarded, and as an ancient Rabbi has solemnly said, 'The penalty of untruth is untruth.'[9] But Pepin is only a mild example of the fact that incessant writing with a view to printing carries internal consequences which have often the nature of disease. And however unpractical it may be held to consider whether we have anything to print which it is good for the world to read, or which has not been better said before, it will perhaps be allowed to be worth considering what effect the printing may have on ourselves. Clearly there is a sort of writing which helps to keep the writer in a ridiculously contented ignorance; raising in him continually the sense of having delivered himself effectively, so that the acquirement of more thorough knowledge seems as superfluous as the purchase of costume for a past occasion. He has invested his vanity (perhaps his hope of income) in his own shallownesses and mistakes, and must desire their prosperity. Like the professional prophet, he learns to be glad of the harm that keeps up his credit, and to be sorry for the good that contradicts him. It is hard enough for any of us, amid the changing winds of fortune and the hurly-burly of events, to keep quite clear of a gladness which is another's calamity; but one may choose not to enter on a course which will turn such gladness into a fixed habit of mind, committing ourselves to be continually pleased that others should appear to be wrong in order that we may have the air of being right.

In some cases, perhaps, it might be urged that Pepin has remained the more self-contented because he has *not* written everything he believed himself capable of. He once asked me to read a sort of programme of the species of romance which he should think it worth while to write – a species which he contrasted in strong terms with the productions of illustrious but overrated authors in this branch. Pepin's romance was to present the splendours of the Roman Empire at the culmination of its grandeur, when decadence was spiritually but not visibly imminent: it was to show the workings of human passion in the most pregnant and exalted of human circumstances, the designs of statesmen, the interfusion of philosophies, the rural relaxation and converse of immortal poets, the majestic triumphs of warriors, the mingling of the quaint and sublime in religious ceremony, the gorgeous delirium of gladiatorial shows, and under all the secretly working leaven of Christianity. Such a romance would not call the attention of society to the dialect of

stable-boys, the low habits of rustics, the vulgarity of small
schoolmasters, the manners of men in livery, or to any other
form of uneducated talk and sentiments: its characters would
have virtues and vices alike on the grand scale, and would
express themselves in an English representing the discourse of
the most powerful minds in the best Latin, or possibly Greek,
when there occurred a scene with a Greek philosopher on a visit
to Rome or resident there as a teacher. In this way Pepin would
do in fiction what had never been done before: something not at
all like 'Rienzi' or 'Notre Dame de Paris,'[10] or any other attempt
of that kind; but something at once more penetrating and more
magnificent, more passionate and more philosophical, more
panoramic yet more select: something that would present a
conception of a gigantic period; in short, something truly
Roman and world-historical.

When Pepin gave me this programme to read he was much
younger than at present. Some slight success in another vein
diverted him from the production of panoramic and select
romance, and the experience of not having tried to carry out his
programme has naturally made him more biting and sarcastic on
the failures of those who have actually written romances without apparently having had a glimpse of a conception equal to
his. Indeed, I am often comparing his rather touchingly inflated
naïveté, as of a small young person walking on tiptoe while he is
talking of elevated things, at the time when he felt himself the
author of that unwritten romance, with his present epigram-
matic curtness and affectation of power kept strictly in reserve.
His paragraphs now seem to have a bitter smile in them, from
the consciousness of a mind too penetrating to accept any other
man's ideas, and too equally competent in all directions to
seclude his power in any one form of creation, but rather fitted
to hang over them all as a lamp of guidance to the stumblers
below. You perceive how proud he is of not being indebted to
any writer: even with the dead he is on the creditor's side, for
he is doing them the service of letting the world know what
they meant better than those poor pre-Pepinians themselves had
any means of doing, and he treats the mighty shades very

cavalierly. Is this fellow-citizen of ours, considered simply in the light of a baptised Christian and tax-paying Englishman, really as madly conceited, as empty of reverential feeling, as unveracious and careless of justice, as full of catch-penny devices and stagey attitudinising as on examination his writing shows itself to be? By no means. He has arrived at his present pass in 'the literary calling' through the self-imposed obligation to give himself a manner which would convey the impression of superior knowledge and ability. He is much worthier and more admirable than his written productions, because the moral aspects exhibited in his writing are felt to be ridiculous or disgraceful in the personal relations of life. In blaming Pepin's writing we are accusing the public conscience, which is so lax and ill informed on the momentous bearings of authorship that it sanctions the total absence of scruple in undertaking and prosecuting what should be the best warranted of vocations.

Hence I still accept friendly relations with Pepin, for he has much private amiability, and though he probably thinks of me as a man of slender talents, without rapidity of *coup d'oeil* and with no compensatory penetration, he meets me very cordially, and would not, I am sure, willingly pain me in conversation by crudely declaring his low estimate of my capacity. Yet I have often known him to insult my betters and contribute (perhaps unreflectingly) to encourage injurious conceptions of them – but that was done in the course of his professional writing, and the public conscience still leaves such writing nearly on the level of the Merry-Andrew's dress,[11] which permits an impudent deportment and extraordinary gambols to one who in his ordinary clothing shows himself the decent father of a family.

DISEASES OF SMALL AUTHORSHIP

PARTICULAR callings, it is known, encourage particular diseases. There is a painter's colic: the Sheffield grinder falls a victim to the inhalation of steel dust: clergymen so often have a certain kind of sore throat that this otherwise secular ailment gets named after them. And perhaps, if we were to inquire, we should find a similar relation between certain moral ailments and these various occupations, though here in the case of clergymen there would be specific differences: the poor curate, equally with the rector, is liable to clergyman's sore throat, but he would probably be found free from the chronic moral ailments encouraged by the possession of glebe[1] and those higher chances of preferment which follow on having a good position already. On the other hand, the poor curate might have severe attacks of calculating expectancy concerning parishioners' turkeys, cheeses, and fat geese, or of uneasy rivalry for the donations of clerical charities.

Authors are so miscellaneous a class that their personified diseases, physical and moral, might include the whole procession of human disorders, led by dyspepsia and ending in madness – the awful Dumb Show of a world-historic tragedy. Take a large enough area of human life and all comedy melts into tragedy, like the Fool's part by the side of Lear. The chief scenes get filled with erring heroes, guileful usurpers, persecuted discoverers, dying deliverers: everywhere the protagonist has a part pregnant with doom. The comedy sinks to an accessory, and if there are loud laughs they seem a convulsive transition from sobs; or if the comedy is touched with a gentle lovingness, the panoramic scene is one where

'Sadness is a kind of mirth
So mingled as if mirth did make us sad
And sadness merry.'[2]

But I did not set out on the wide survey that would carry me
into tragedy, and in fact had nothing more serious in my mind
than certain small chronic ailments that come of small authorship. I was thinking principally of Vorticella,[3] who flourished in
my youth not only as a portly lady walking in silk attire, but also
as the authoress of a book entitled 'The Channel Islands, with
Notes and an Appendix.' I would by no means make it a
reproach to her that she wrote no more than one book; on the
contrary, her stopping there seems to me a laudable example.
What one would have wished, after experience, was that she
had refrained from producing even that single volume, and thus
from giving her self-importance a troublesome kind of double
incorporation which became oppressive to her acquaintances,
and set up in herself one of those slight chronic forms of disease
to which I have just referred. She lived in the considerable
provincial town of Pumpiter, which had its own newspaper
press, with the usual divisions of political partisanship and the
usual varieties of literary criticism – the florid and allusive, the
staccato and peremptory, the clairvoyant and prophetic, the safe
and pattern-phrased, or what one might call 'the many-a-long-
day style.'

Vorticella being the wife of an important townsman had
naturally the satisfaction of seeing 'The Channel Islands' re-
viewed by all the organs of Pumpiter opinion, and their articles
or paragraphs held as naturally the opening pages in the elegantly
bound album prepared by her for the reception of 'critical
opinions.' This ornamental volume lay on a special table in her
drawing-room close to the still more gorgeously bound work of
which it was the significant effect, and every guest was allowed
the privilege of reading what had been said of the authoress and
her work in the 'Pumpiter Gazette and Literary Watchman,' the
'Pumpshire Post,' the 'Church Clock,' the 'Independent Monitor,' and the lively but judicious publication known as the

'Medley Pie;' to be followed up, if he chose, by the instructive perusal of the strikingly confirmatory judgments, sometimes concurrent in the very phrases, of journals from the most distant counties; as the 'Latchgate Argus,' the 'Penllwy Universe,' the 'Cockaleekie Advertiser,' the 'Goodwin Sands Opinion,' and the 'Land's End Times.'

I had friends in Pumpiter and occasionally paid a long visit there. When I called on Vorticella, who had a cousinship with my hosts, she had to excuse herself because a message claimed her attention for eight or ten minutes, and handing me the album of critical opinions said, with a certain emphasis which, considering my youth, was highly complimentary, that she would really like me to read what I should find there. This seemed a permissive politeness which I could not feel to be an oppression, and I ran my eyes over the dozen pages, each with a strip or islet of newspaper in the centre, with that freedom of mind (in my case meaning freedom to forget) which would be a perilous way of preparing for examination. This *ad libitum* perusal had its interest for me. The private truth being that I had not read 'The Channel Islands,' I was amazed at the variety of matter which the volume must contain to have impressed these different judges with the writer's surpassing capacity to handle almost all branches of inquiry and all forms of presentation. In Jersey she had shown herself an historian, in Guernsey a poetess, in Alderney a political economist, and in Sark a humorist: there were sketches of character scattered through the pages which might put our 'fictionists' to the blush; the style was eloquent and racy, studded with gems of felicitous remark; and the moral spirit throughout was so superior that, said one, 'the recording angel' (who is not supposed to take account of literature as such) 'would assuredly set down the work as a deed of religion.' The force of this eulogy on the part of several reviewers was much heightened by the incidental evidence of their fastidious and severe taste, which seemed to suffer considerably from the imperfections of our chief writers, even the dead and canonised: one afflicted them with the smell of oil, another lacked erudition and attempted (though vainly) to dazzle them with trivial conceits, one wanted to be more philosophical than nature had made him, another in attempting to be comic produced the melancholy effect of a half-starved Merry-Andrew; while one and all, from the author of the 'Areopagitica'[4] downwards, had faults of style which must have made an able hand in the 'Latchgate Argus' shake the many-glanced head belonging thereto with a smile of compassionate disapproval. Not so the authoress of 'The Channel Islands:' Vorticella and Shakspere were allowed to be faultless. I gathered that no blemishes were observable in the work of this accomplished writer, and the repeated information that she was 'second to none' seemed after this superfluous. Her thick octavo – notes, appendix and all – was unflagging from beginning to end; and the 'Land's End Times,' using a rather dangerous rhetorical figure, recommended you not to take up the volume unless you had leisure to finish it at a sitting. It had given one writer more pleasure than he had had for many a long day – a sentence which had a melancholy resonance, suggesting a life of studious languor such as all previous achievements of the human mind failed to stimulate into enjoyment. I think the collection of critical opinions wound up with this sentence, and I had turned back to look at the lithographed sketch of the authoress which fronted the first page of the album, when the fair original re-entered and I laid down the volume on its appropriate table.

'Well, what do you think of them?' said Vorticella, with an emphasis which had some significance unperceived by me. 'I know you are a great student. Give me *your* opinion of these opinions.'

'They must be very gratifying to you,' I answered with a little confusion, for I perceived that I might easily mistake my footing, and I began to have a presentiment of an examination for which I was by no means crammed.

'On the whole – yes,' said Vorticella, in a tone of concession. 'A few of the notices are written with some pains, but not one of them has really grappled with the chief idea in the appendix. I don't know whether you have studied political economy, but you saw what I said on page 398 about the Jersey fisheries?'

I bowed – I confess it – with the mean hope that this movement in the nape of my neck would be taken as sufficient proof that I had read, marked, and learned. I do not forgive myself for this pantomimic falsehood, but I was young and morally timorous, and Vorticella's personality had an effect on me something like that of a powerful mesmeriser when he directs all his ten fingers towards your eyes, as unpleasantly visible ducts for the invisible stream. I felt a great power of contempt in her, if I did not come up to her expectations.

'Well,' she resumed, 'you observe that not one of them has taken up that argument. But I hope I convinced you about the dragnets?'

Here was a judgment on me. Orientally speaking, I had lifted up my foot on the steep descent of falsity and was compelled to set it down on a lower level. 'I should think you must be right,' said I, inwardly resolving that on the next topic I would tell the truth.

'I *know* that I am right,' said Vorticella. 'The fact is that no critic in this town is fit to meddle with such subjects, unless it be Volvox,[5] and he, with all his command of language, is very superficial. It is Volvox who writes in the "Monitor." I hope you noticed how he contradicts himself?'

My resolution, helped by the equivalence of dangers, stoutly prevailed, and I said, 'No.'

'No! I am surprised. He is the only one who finds fault with me. He is a Dissenter, you know. The "Monitor" is the Dissenters' organ, but my husband has been so useful to them in municipal affairs that they would not venture to run my book down; they feel obliged to tell the truth about me. Still Volvox betrays himself. After praising me for my penetration and accuracy, he presently says I have allowed myself to be imposed upon and have let my active imagination run away with me. That is like his dissenting impertinence. Active my imagination may be, but I have it under control. Little Vibrio,[6] who writes the playful notice in the "Medley Pie," has a clever hit at Volvox in that passage about the steeplechase of imagination, where the loser wants to make it appear that the winner was only run away with. But if you did not notice Volvox's self-contradiction you would not see the point,' added Vorticella, with rather a chilling intonation. 'Or perhaps you did not read the "Medley Pie" notice? That is a pity. Do take up the book again. Vibrio is a poor little tippling creature, but, as Mr Carlyle would say, he has an eye, and he is always lively.'

I did take up the book again, and read as demanded.

'It is very ingenious,' said I, really appreciating the difficulty of being lively in this connection: it seemed even more wonderful than that a Vibrio should have an eye. 'You are probably surprised to see no notices from the London press,' said Vorticella.' I have one – a very remarkable one. But I reserve it until the others have spoken, and then I shall introduce it to wind up. I shall have them reprinted, of course, and inserted in future copies. This from the "Candelabrum" is only eight lines in length, but full of venom. It calls my style dull and pompous. I think that will tell its own tale, placed after the other critiques.'

'People's impressions are so different,' said I. 'Some persons find "Don Quixote" dull.'

'Yes,' said Vorticella, in emphatic chest tones, 'dulness is a matter of opinion; but pompous! That I never was and never could be. Perhaps he means that my matter is too important for his taste; and I have no objection to *that*. I did not intend to be trivial. I should just like to read you that passage about the dragnets, because I could make it clearer to you.'

A second (less ornamental) copy was at her elbow and was already opened, when to my great relief another guest was announced, and I was able to take my leave without seeming to run away from 'The Channel Islands,' though not without being compelled to carry with me the loan of 'the marked copy,' which I was to find advantageous in a re-perusal of the appendix, and was only requested to return before my departure from Pumpiter. Looking into the volume now with some curiosity, I found it a very ordinary combination of the commonplace and ambitious, one of those books which one might imagine to have been written under the old Grub Street[7] coercion of hunger and thirst, if they were not known beforehand to be the gratuitous productions of ladies and gentlemen whose circumstances might be called altogether easy, but for an uneasy vanity that happened to have been directed towards authorship. Its importance was that of a polypus, tumour, fungus, or other erratic outgrowth, noxious and disfiguring in its effect on the individual organism which nourishes it. Poor Vorticella might not have been more wearisome on a visit than the majority of her neighbours, but for this disease of magnified self-importance belonging to small authorship. I understand that the chronic complaint of 'The Channel Islands' never left her. As the years went on and the publication tended to vanish in the distance for her neighbours' memory, she was still bent on dragging it to the foreground, and her chief interest in new acquaintances was the possibility of lending them her book, entering into all details concerning it, and requesting them to read her album of 'critical opinions.' This really made her more tiresome than Gregarina, whose distinction was that she had had cholera, and who did not feel herself in her true position with strangers until they knew it.

My experience with Vorticella led me for a time into the false supposition that this sort of fungous disfiguration, which makes Self disagreeably larger, was most common to the female sex; but I presently found that here too the male could assert his superiority and show a more vigorous boredom. I have known a man with a single pamphlet containing an assurance that somebody else was wrong, together with a few approved quotations, produce a more powerful effect of shuddering at his approach than ever Vorticella did with her varied octavo volume, including notes and appendix. Males of more than one nation recur to my memory who produced from their pocket on the slightest encouragement a small pink or buff duodecimo pamphlet, wrapped in silver paper, as a present held ready for an intelligent reader. 'A mode of propagandism,' you remark in excuse; 'they wished to spread some useful corrective doctrine.' Not necessarily: the indoctrination aimed at was perhaps to convince you of their own talents by the sample of an 'Ode on Shakspere's Birthday,' or a translation from Horace.

Vorticella may pair off with Monas,[8] who had also written his

one book – 'Here and There; or, a Trip from Truro to Tran-
sylvania' – and not only carried it in his portmanteau when he
went on visits, but took the earliest opportunity of depositing it
in the drawing-room, and afterwards would enter to look for it,
as if under pressure of a need for reference, begging the lady of
the house to tell him whether she had seen 'a small volume
bound in red.' One hostess at last ordered it to be carried into
his bedroom to save his time; but it presently reappeared in his
hands, and was again left with inserted slips of paper on the
drawing-room table.

Depend upon it, vanity is human, native alike to men and
women; only in the male it is of denser texture, less volatile, so
that it less immediately informs you of its presence, but is more
massive and capable of knocking you down if you come into
collision with it; while in women vanity lays by its small
revenges as in a needle-case always at hand. The difference is in
muscle and finger-tips, in traditional habits and mental perspective, rather than in the original appetite of vanity. It is an
approved method now to explain ourselves by a reference to the
races as little like us as possible, which leads me to observe that
in Fiji the men use the most elaborate hair-dressing, and that
wherever tattooing is in vogue the male expects to carry off the
prize of admiration for pattern and workmanship. Arguing
analogically, and looking for this tendency of the Fijian or
Hawaian male in the eminent European, we must suppose that
it exhibits itself under the forms of civilised apparel; and it
would be a great mistake to estimate passionate effort by the
effect it produces on our perception or understanding. It is
conceivable that a man may have concentrated no less will and
expectation on his wristbands, gaiters, and the shape of his hat-
brim, or an appearance which impresses you as that of the
modern 'swell,' than the Ojibbeway[9] on an ornamentation
which seems to us much more elaborate. In what concerns the
search for admiration at least, it is not true that the effect is
equal to the cause and resembles it. The cause of a flat curl on
the masculine forehead, such as might be seen when George the
Fourth was king,[10] must have been widely different in quality and

intensity from the impression made by that small scroll of hair on the organ of the beholder. Merely to maintain an attitude and gait which I notice in certain club men, and especially an inflation of the chest accompanying very small remarks, there goes, I am convinced, an expenditure of psychical energy little appreciated by the multitude – a mental vision of Self and deeply impressed beholders which is quite without antitype in what we call the effect produced by that hidden process.

No! there is no need to admit that women would carry away the prize of vanity in a competition where differences of custom were fairly considered. A man cannot show his vanity in a tight skirt which forces him to walk sideways down the staircase; but let the match be between the respective vanities of largest beard and tightest skirt, and here too the battle would be to the strong.

XVI

MORAL SWINDLERS

IT is a familiar example of irony in the degradation of words
that 'what a man is worth' has come to mean how much money
he possesses; but there seems a deeper and more melancholy
irony in the shrunken meaning that popular or polite speech
assigns to 'morality' and 'morals.' The poor part these words are
made to play recalls the fate of those pagan divinities who, after
being understood to rule the powers of the air and the destinies
of men, came down to the level of insignificant demons, or were
even made a farcical show for the amusement of the multitude.

Talking to Melissa[1] in a time of commercial trouble, I found
her disposed to speak pathetically of the disgrace which had
fallen on Sir Gavial Mantrap,[2] because of his conduct in relation
to the Eocene Mines, and to other companies ingeniously devised by him for the punishment of ignorance in people of small
means: a disgrace by which the poor titled gentleman was
actually reduced to live in comparative obscurity on his wife's
settlement of one or two hundred thousand in the consols.[3]

'Surely your pity is misapplied,' said I, rather dubiously, for I
like the comfort of trusting that a correct moral judgment is the
strong point in woman (seeing that she has a majority of about
a million in our islands), and I imagined that Melissa might have
some unexpressed grounds for her opinion. 'I should have
thought you would rather be sorry for Mantrap's victims – the
widows, spinsters, and hard-working fathers whom his unscrupulous haste to make himself rich has cheated of all their
savings, while he is eating well, lying softly, and after impudently
justifying himself before the public, is perhaps joining in the

General Confession with a sense that he is an acceptable object in the sight of God, though decent men refuse to meet him.'

'Oh, all that about the Companies, I know was most unfortunate. In commerce people are led to do so many things, and he might not know exactly how everything would turn out. But Sir Gavial made a good use of his money, and he is a thoroughly *moral* man.'

'What do you mean by a thoroughly moral man?' said I.

'Oh, I suppose every one means the same by that,' said Melissa, with a slight air of rebuke. 'Sir Gavial is an excellent family man – quite blameless there; and so charitable round his place at Tiptop. Very different from Mr Barabbas,[4] whose life, my husband tells me, is most objectionable, with actresses and that sort of thing. I think a man's morals should make a difference to us. I'm not sorry for Mr Barabbas, but I *am* sorry for Sir Gavial Mantrap.'

I will not repeat my answer to Melissa, for I fear it was offensively brusque, my opinion being that Sir Gavial was the more pernicious scoundrel of the two, since his name for virtue served as an effective part of a swindling apparatus; and perhaps I hinted that to call such a man moral showed rather a silly notion of human affairs. In fact, I had an angry wish to be instructive, and Melissa, as will sometimes happen, noticed my anger without appropriating my instruction, for I have since heard that she speaks of me as rather violent-tempered, and not over strict in my views of morality.

I wish that this narrow use of words which are wanted in their full meaning were confined to women like Melissa. Seeing that Morality and Morals under their *alias* of Ethics are the subject of voluminous discussion, and their true basis a pressing matter of dispute – seeing that the most famous book ever written on Ethics,[5] and forming a chief study in our colleges, allies ethical with political science or that which treats of the constitution and prosperity of States, one might expect that educated men would find reason to avoid a perversion of language which lends itself to no wider view of life than that of village gossips. Yet I find even respectable historians of our own

and of foreign countries, after showing that a king was treacherous, rapacious, and ready to sanction gross breaches in the
administration of justice, end by praising him for his pure moral
character, by which one must suppose them to mean that he
was not lewd nor debauched, not the European twin of the
typical Indian potentate whom Macaulay describes as passing his
life in chewing bang and fondling dancing-girls.[6] And since we
are sometimes told of such maleficent kings that they were
religious, we arrive at the curious result that the most serious
wide-reaching duties of man lie quite outside both Morality and
Religion – the one of these consisting in not keeping mistresses
(and perhaps not drinking too much), and the other in certain
ritual and spiritual transactions with God which can be carried
on equally well side by side with the basest conduct towards
men. With such a classification as this it is no wonder, considering the strong reaction of language on thought, that many
minds, dizzy with indigestion of recent science and philosophy,
are far to seek for the grounds of social duty, and without
entertaining any private intention of committing a perjury
which would ruin an innocent man, or seeking gain by supplying
bad preserved meats to our navy, feel themselves speculatively
obliged to inquire why they should not do so, and are inclined
to measure their intellectual subtlety by their dissatisfaction
with all answers to this 'Why?' It is of little use to theorise in
ethics while our habitual phraseology stamps the larger part of
our social duties as something that lies aloof from the deepest
needs and affections of our nature. The informal definitions of
popular language are the only medium through which theory
really affects the mass of minds even among the nominally
educated; and when a man whose business hours, the solid part
of every day, are spent in an unscrupulous course of public or
private action which has every calculable chance of causing
widespread injury and misery, can be called moral because he
comes home to dine with his wife and children and cherishes
the happiness of his own hearth, the augury is not good for the
use of high ethical and theological disputation.

Not for one moment would one willingly lose sight of the

truth that the relation of the sexes and the primary ties of kinship are the deepest roots of human wellbeing, but to make them by themselves the equivalent of morality is verbally to cut off the channels of feeling through which they are the feeders of that wellbeing. They are the original fountains of a sensibility to the claims of others, which is the bond of societies; but being necessarily in the first instance a private good, there is always the danger that individual selfishness will see in them only the best part of its own gain; just as knowledge, navigation, commerce, and all the conditions which are of a nature to awaken men's consciousness of their mutual dependence and to make the world one great society, are the occasions of selfish, unfair action, of war and oppression, so long as the public conscience or chief force of feeling and opinion is not uniform and strong enough in its insistence on what is demanded by the general welfare. And among the influences that must retard a right public judgment, the degradation of words which involve praise and blame will be reckoned worth protesting against by every mature observer. To rob words of half their meaning, while they retain their dignity as qualifications, is like allowing to men who have lost half their faculties the same high and perilous command which they won in their time of vigour; or like selling food and seeds after fraudulently abstracting their best virtues: in each case what ought to be beneficently strong is fatally enfeebled, if not empoisoned. Until we have altered our dictionaries and have found some other word than *morality* to stand in popular use for the duties of man to man, let us refuse to accept as moral the contractor who enriches himself by using large machinery to make pasteboard soles pass as leather for the feet of unhappy conscripts fighting at miserable odds against invaders: let us rather call him a miscreant, though he were the tenderest, most faithful of husbands, and contend that his own experience of home happiness makes his reckless infliction of suffering on others all the more atrocious. Let us refuse to accept as moral any political leader who should allow his conduct in relation to great issues to be determined by egoistic passion, and boldly say that he would be less immoral even though he were as lax in his personal habits as Sir Robert Walpole,[7] if at the same time his sense of the public welfare were supreme in his mind, quelling all pettier impulses beneath a magnanimous impartiality. And though we were to find among that class of journalists who live by recklessly reporting injurious rumours, insinuating the blackest motives in opponents, descanting at large and with an air of infallibility on dreams which they both find and interpret, and stimulating bad feeling between nations by abusive writing which is as empty of real conviction as the rage of a pantomime king, and would be ludicrous if its effects did not make it appear diabolical – though we were to find among these a man who was benignancy itself in his own circle, a healer of private differences, a soother in private calamities, let us pronounce him nevertheless flagrantly immoral, a root of hideous cancer in the commonwealth, turning the channels of instruction into feeders of social and political disease.[8]

In opposite ways one sees bad effects likely to be encouraged by this narrow use of the word *morals*, shutting out from its meaning half those actions of a man's life which tell momentously on the wellbeing of his fellow-citizens, and on the preparation of a future for the children growing up around him. Thoroughness of workmanship, care in the execution of every task undertaken, as if it were the acceptance of a trust which it would be a breach of faith not to discharge well, is a form of duty so momentous that if it were to die out from the feeling and practice of a people, all reforms of institutions would be helpless to create national prosperity and national happiness. Do we desire to see public spirit penetrating all classes of the community and affecting every man's conduct, so that he shall make neither the saving of his soul nor any other private saving an excuse for indifference to the general welfare? Well and good. But the sort of public spirit that scamps its bread-winning work, whether with the trowel, the pen, or the overseeing brain, that it may hurry to scenes of political or social agitation, would be as baleful a gift to our people as any malignant demon could devise. One best part of educational training is that which comes through special knowledge and manipulative or other skill, with its usual accompaniment of delight, in relation to work which is the daily bread-winning occupation – which is a man's contribution to the effective wealth of society in return for what he takes as his own share. But this duty of doing one's proper work well, and taking care that every product of one's labour shall be genuinely what it pretends to be, is not only left out of morals in popular speech, it is very little insisted on by public teachers, at least in the only effective way – by tracing the continuous effects of ill-done work. Some of them seem to be still hopeful that it will follow as a necessary consequence from week-day services, ecclesiastical decoration, and improved hymn-books; others apparently trust to descanting on self-culture in general, or to raising a general sense of faulty circumstances; and meanwhile lax, make-shift work, from the high conspicuous kind to the average and obscure, is allowed to pass unstamped with the disgrace of immorality, though there is not a member of society who is not daily suffering from it materially and spiritually, and though it is the fatal cause that must degrade our national rank and our commerce in spite of all open markets and discovery of available coal-seams.

I suppose one may take the popular misuse of the words Morality and Morals as some excuse for certain absurdities which are occasional fashions in speech and writing – certain old lay-figures, as ugly as the queerest Asiatic idol, which at different periods get propped into loftiness, and attired in magnificent Venetian drapery, so that whether they have a human face or not is of little consequence. One is, the notion that there is a radical, irreconcilable opposition between intellect and morality. I do not mean the simple statement of fact, which everybody knows, that remarkably able men have had very faulty morals, and have outraged public feeling even at its ordinary standard; but the supposition that the ablest intellect, the highest genius, will see through morality as a sort of twaddle for bibs and tuckers,[9] a doctrine of dulness, a mere incident in human stupidity. We begin to understand the acceptance of this foolishness by considering that we live in a society where we may hear a treacherous monarch, or a malignant and lying politician, or a man who uses either official or literary power as an instrument of his private partiality or hatred, or a manufacturer who devises the falsification of wares, or a trader who deals in virtueless seed-grains, praised or compassionated because of his excellent morals. Clearly if morality meant no more than such decencies as are practised by these poisonous members of society, it would be possible to say, without suspicion of light-headedness, that morality lay aloof from the grand stream of human affairs, as a small channel fed by the stream and not missed from it. While this form of nonsense is conveyed in the popular use of words, there must be plenty of well-dressed ignorance at leisure to run through a box of books, which will feel itself initiated in the freemasonry of intellect by a view of life which might take for a Shaksperian motto –

> 'Fair is foul and foul is fair,
> Hover through the fog and filthy air' –[10]

and will find itself easily provided with striking conversation by the rule of reversing all the judgments on good and evil which have come to be the calendar and clock-work of society. But let our habitual talk give morals their full meaning as the conduct which, in every human relation, would follow from the fullest knowledge and the fullest sympathy – a meaning perpetually corrected and enriched by a more thorough appreciation of dependence in things, and a finer sensibility to both physical and spiritual fact – and this ridiculous ascription of superlative power to minds which have no effective awe-inspiring vision of the human lot, no response of understanding to the connection between duty and the material processes by which the world is kept habitable for cultivated man, will be tacitly discredited without any need to cite the immortal names that all are obliged to take as the measure of intellectual rank and highly-charged genius.

Suppose a Frenchman – I mean no disrespect to the great French nation, for all nations are afflicted with their peculiar

parasitic growths, which are lazy, hungry forms, usually characterised by a disproportionate swallowing apparatus: suppose a
Parisian who should shuffle down the Boulevard with a soul
ignorant of the gravest cares and the deepest tenderness of
manhood, and a frame more or less fevered by debauchery,
mentally polishing into utmost refinement of phrase and rhythm
verses which were an enlargement on that Shaksperian motto,
and worthy of the most expensive title to be furnished by the
vendors of such antithetic ware as *Les marguerites de l'Enfer*, or *Les
délices de Béelzébuth*.[11] This supposed personage might probably
enough regard his negation of those moral sensibilities which
make half the warp and woof of human history, his indifference
to the hard thinking and hard handiwork of life, to which he
owed even his own gauzy mental garments with their spangles
of poor paradox, as the royalty of genius, for we are used to
witness such self-crowning in many forms of mental alienation;
but he would not, I think, be taken, even by his own generation,
as a living proof that there can exist such a combination as that
of moral stupidity and trivial emphasis of personal indulgence
with the large yet finely discriminating vision which marks the
intellectual masters of our kind. Doubtless there are many sorts
of transfiguration, and a man who has come to be worthy of all
gratitude and reverence may have had his swinish period, wal-
lowing in ugly places; but suppose it had been handed down to
us that Sophocles or Virgil had at one time made himself
scandalous in this way: the works which have consecrated their
memory for our admiration and gratitude are not a glorifying of
swinishness, but an artistic incorporation of the highest sentiment known to their age.

All these may seem to be wide reasons for objecting to
Melissa's pity for Sir Gavial Mantrap on the ground of his good
morals; but their connection will not be obscure to any one who
has taken pains to observe the links uniting the scattered signs
of our social development.

SHADOWS OF THE COMING RACE[1]

MY friend Trost,[2] who is no optimist as to the state of the universe hitherto, but is confident that at some future period within the duration of the solar system, ours will be the best of all possible worlds[3] – a hope which I always honour as a sign of beneficent qualities – my friend Trost always tries to keep up my spirits under the sight of the extremely unpleasant and disfiguring work by which many of our fellow-creatures have to get their bread, with the assurance that 'all this will soon be done by machinery.' But he sometimes neutralises the consolation by extending it over so large an area of human labour, and insisting so impressively on the quantity of energy which will thus be set free for loftier purposes, that I am tempted to desire an occasional famine of invention in the coming ages, lest the humbler kinds of work should be entirely nullified while there are still left some men and women who are not fit for the highest.

Especially, when one considers the perfunctory way in which some of the most exalted tasks are already executed by those who are understood to be educated for them, there rises a fearful vision of the human race evolving machinery which will by-and-by throw itself fatally out of work. When, in the Bank of England, I see a wondrously delicate machine for testing sovereigns, a shrewd implacable little steel Rhadamanthus[4] that, once the coins are delivered up to it, lifts and balances each in turn for the fraction of an instant, finds it wanting or sufficient, and dismisses it to right or left with rigorous justice; when I am told of micrometers and thermopiles and tasimeters which deal physically with the invisible, the impalpable, and the unimaginable; of cunning wires and wheels and pointing needles which will register your and my quickness so as to exclude flattering opinion; of a machine for drawing the right conclusion, which will doubtless by-and-by be improved into an automaton for finding true premises; of a microphone which detects the cadence of the fly's foot on the ceiling, and may be expected presently to discriminate the noises of our various follies as they soliloquise or converse in our brains – my mind seeming too small for these things, I get a little out of it, like an unfortunate savage too suddenly brought face to face with civilisation, and I exclaim –

'Am I already in the shadow of the Coming Race? and will the creatures who are to transcend and finally supersede us be steely organisms, giving out the effluvia of the laboratory, and performing with infallible exactness more than everything that we have performed with a slovenly approximativeness and self-defeating inaccuracy?'

'But,' says Trost, treating me with cautious mildness on hearing me vent this raving notion, 'you forget that these wonder-workers are the slaves of our race, need our tendance and regulation, obey the mandates of our consciousness, and are only deaf and dumb bringers of reports which we decipher and make use of. They are simply extensions of the human organism, so to speak, limbs immeasurably more powerful, ever more subtle finger-tips, ever more mastery over the invisibly great and the invisibly small. Each new machine needs a new appliance of human skill to construct it, new devices to feed it with material, and often keener-edged faculties to note its registrations or performances. How then can machines supersede us? – they depend upon us. When we cease, they cease.'

'I am not so sure of that,' said I, getting back into my mind, and becoming rather wilful in consequence. 'If, as I have heard you contend, machines as they are more and more perfected will require less and less of tendance, how do I know that they may not be ultimately made to carry, or may not in themselves evolve, conditions of self-supply, self-repair, and reproduction, and not only do all the mighty and subtle work possible on this planet better than we could do it, but with the immense advantage of banishing from the earth's atmosphere screaming consciousnesses which, in our comparatively clumsy race, make an intolerable noise and fuss to each other about every petty ant-like performance, looking on at all work only as it were to spring a rattle here or blow a trumpet there, with a ridiculous sense of being effective? I for my part cannot see any reason why a sufficiently penetrating thinker, who can see his way through a thousand years or so, should not conceive a parliament of machines, in which the manners were excellent and the motions infallible in logic: one honourable instrument, a remote descendant of the Voltaic family, might discharge a powerful current (entirely without animosity) on an honourable instrument opposite, of more upstart origin, but belonging to the ancient edge-tool race which we already at Sheffield see paring thick iron as if it were mellow cheese – by this unerringly directed discharge operating on movements corresponding to what we call Estimates, and by necessary mechanical consequence on movements corresponding to what we call the Funds, which with a vain analogy we sometimes speak of as 'sensitive.' For every machine would be perfectly educated, that is to say, would have the suitable molecular adjustments, which would act not the less infallibly for being free from the fussy accompaniment of that consciousness to which our prejudice gives a supreme governing rank, when in truth it is an idle parasite on the grand sequence of things.'

'Nothing of the sort!' returned Trost, getting angry, and judging it kind to treat me with some severity; 'what you have heard me say is, that our race will and must act as a nervous centre to the utmost development of mechanical processes: the subtly refined powers of machines will react in producing more subtly refined thinking processes which will occupy the minds set free from grosser labour. Say, for example, that all the scavengers' work of London were done, so far as human atten-tion is concerned, by the occasional pressure of a brass button (as in the ringing of an electric bell), you will then have a

multitude of brains set free for the exquisite enjoyment of
dealing with the exact sequences and high speculations supplied
and prompted by the delicate machines which yield a response
to the fixed stars, and give readings of the spiral vortices
fundamentally concerned in the production of epic poems or
great judicial harangues. So far from mankind being thrown out
of work according to your notion,' concluded Trost, with a
peculiar nasal note of scorn, 'if it were not for your incurable
dilettanteism in science as in all other things – if you had once
understood the action of any delicate machine – you would
perceive that the sequences it carries throughout the realm of
phenomena would require many generations, perhaps æons, of
understandings considerably stronger than yours, to exhaust the
store of work it lays open.'

'Precisely,' said I, with a meekness which I felt was praise-
worthy; 'it is the feebleness of my capacity, bringing me nearer
than you to the human average, that perhaps enables me to
imagine certain results better than you can. Doubtless the very
fishes of our rivers, gullible as they look, and slow as they are to
be rightly convinced in another order of facts, form fewer false
expectations about each other than we should form about them
if we were in a position of somewhat fuller intercourse with
their species; for even as it is we have continually to be surprised
that they do not rise to our carefully selected bait. Take me then
as a sort of reflective and experienced carp; but do not estimate
the justice of my ideas by my facial expression.'

'Pooh!' says Trost. (We are on very intimate terms.)

'Naturally,' I persisted, 'it is less easy to you than to me to
imagine our race transcended and superseded, since the more
energy a being is possessed of, the harder it must be for him to
conceive his own death. But I, from the point of view of a
reflective carp, can easily imagine myself and my congeners[5]
dispensed with in the frame of things and giving way not only to
a superior but a vastly different kind of Entity. What I would
ask you is, to show me why, since each new invention casts a
new light along the pathway of discovery, and each new combination or structure brings into play more conditions than its

inventor foresaw, there should not at length be a machine of such high mechanical and chemical powers that it would find and assimilate the material to supply its own waste, and then by a further evolution of internal molecular movements reproduce itself by some process of fission or budding. This last stage having been reached, either by man's contrivance or as an unforeseen result, one sees that the process of natural selection must drive men altogether out of the field; for they will long before have begun to sink into the miserable condition of those unhappy characters in fable who, having demons or djinns at their beck, and being obliged to supply them with work, found too much of everything done in too short a time. What demons so potent as molecular movements, none the less tremendously potent for not carrying the futile cargo of a consciousness screeching irrelevantly, like a fowl tied head downmost to the saddle of a swift horseman? Under such uncomfortable circumstances our race will have diminished with the diminishing call on their energies, and by the time that the self-repairing and reproducing machines arise, all but a few of the rare inventors, calculators, and speculators will have become pale, pulpy, and cretinous from fatty or other degeneration, and behold around them a scanty hydrocephalous offspring. As to the breed of the ingenious and intellectual, their nervous systems will at last have been overwrought in following the molecular revelations of the immensely powerful unconscious race, and they will naturally, as the less energetic combinations of movement, subside like the flame of a candle in the sunlight. Thus the feebler race, whose corporeal adjustments happened to be accompanied with a maniacal consciousness which imagined itself moving its mover,[6] will have vanished, as all less adapted existences do before the fittest – *i.e.*, the existence composed of the most persistent groups of movements and the most capable of incorporating new groups in harmonious relation. Who – if our consciousness is, as I have been given to understand, a mere stumbling of our organisms on their way to unconscious perfection – who shall say that those fittest existences will not be found along the track of what we call inorganic combinations, which will carry on the most elaborate processes as mutely and painlessly as we are now told that the minerals are metamorphosing themselves continually in the dark laboratory of the earth's crust? Thus this planet may be filled with beings who will be blind and deaf as the inmost rock, yet will execute changes as delicate and complicated as those of human language and all the intricate web of what we call its effects, without sensitive impression, without sensitive impulse: there may be, let us say, mute orations, mute rhapsodies, mute discussions, and no consciousness there even to enjoy the silence.'

'Absurd!' grumbled Trost.

'The supposition is logical,' said I. 'It is well argued from the premises.'

'Whose premises?' cried Trost, turning on me with some fierceness. 'You don't mean to call them mine, I hope.'

'Heaven forbid! They seem to be flying about in the air with other germs, and have found a sort of nidus[7] among my melancholy fancies. Nobody really holds them. They bear the same relation to real belief as walking on the head for a show does to running away from an explosion or walking fast to catch the train.'

THE MODERN HEP! HEP! HEP![1]

TO discern likeness amidst diversity, it is well known, does not require so fine a mental edge as the discerning of diversity amidst general sameness. The primary rough classification depends on the prominent resemblances of things: the progress is towards finer and finer discrimination according to minute differences.

Yet even at this stage of European culture one's attention is continually drawn to the prevalence of that grosser mental sloth which makes people dull to the most ordinary prompting of comparison – the bringing things together because of their likeness. The same motives, the same ideas, the same practices, are alternately admired and abhorred, lauded and denounced, according to their association with superficial differences, historical or actually social: even learned writers treating of great subjects often show an attitude of mind not greatly superior in its logic to that of the frivolous fine lady who is indignant at the frivolity of her maid.

To take only the subject of the Jews: it would be difficult to find a form of bad reasoning about them which has not been heard in conversation or been admitted to the dignity of print; but the neglect of resemblances is a common property of dulness which unites all the various points of view – the prejudiced, the puerile, the spiteful, and the abysmally ignorant.

That the preservation of national memories is an element and a means of national greatness, that their revival is a sign of reviving nationality, that every heroic defender, every patriotic restorer, has been inspired by such memories and has made them his watchword, that even such a corporate existence as that of a Roman legion or an English regiment has been made valorous by memorial standards, – these are the glorious commonplaces of historic teaching at our public schools and universities, being happily ingrained in Greek and Latin classics. They have also been impressed on the world by conspicuous modern instances. That there is a free modern Greece is due – through all infiltration of other than Greek blood – to the presence of ancient Greece in the consciousness of European men; and every speaker would feel his point safe if he were to praise Byron's devotion[2] to a cause made glorious by ideal identification with the past; hardly so, if he were to insist that the Greeks were not to be helped further because their history shows that they were anciently unsurpassed in treachery and lying, and that many modern Greeks are highly disreputable characters, while others are disposed to grasp too large a share of our commerce. The same with Italy: the pathos of his country's lot pierced the youthful soul of Mazzini,[3] because, like Dante's, his blood was fraught with the kinship of Italian greatness, his imagination filled with a majestic past that wrought itself into a majestic future. Half a century ago, what was Italy? An idling-place of dilettanteism or of itinerant motiveless wealth, a territory parcelled out for papal sustenance, dynastic convenience, and the profit of an alien Government.[4] What were the Italians? No people, no voice in European counsels, no massive power in European affairs: a race thought of in English and French society as chiefly adapted to the operatic stage, or to serve as models for painters; disposed to smile gratefully at the reception of halfpence; and by the more historical remembered to be rather polite than truthful, in all probability a combination of Machiavelli, Rubini, and Masaniello.[5] Thanks chiefly to the divine gift of a memory which inspires the moments with a past, a present, and a future, and gives the sense of corporate existence that raises man above the otherwise more respectable and innocent brute, all that, or most of it, is changed.

Again, one of our living historians[6] finds just sympathy in his vigorous insistence on our true ancestry, on our being the

strongly marked heritors in language and genius of those old
English seamen who, beholding a rich country with a most
convenient seaboard, came, doubtless with a sense of divine
warrant, and settled themselves on this or the other side of
fertilising streams, gradually conquering more and more of the
pleasant land from the natives who knew nothing of Odin,[7] and
finally making unusually clean work in ridding themselves of
those prior occupants. 'Let us,' he virtually says, 'let us know
who were our forefathers, who it was that won the soil for us,
and brought the good seed of those institutions through which
we should not arrogantly but gratefully feel ourselves distinguished among the nations as possessors of long-inherited freedom; let us not keep up an ignorant kind of naming which
disguises our true affinities of blood and language, but let us see
thoroughly what sort of notions and traditions our forefathers
had, and what sort of song inspired them. Let the poetic
fragments which breathe forth their fierce bravery in battle and
their trust in fierce gods who helped them, be treasured with
affectionate reverence. These seafaring, invading, self-asserting
men were the English of old time, and were our fathers who did
rough work by which we are profiting. They had virtues which
incorporated themselves in wholesome usages to which we trace
our own political blessings. Let us know and acknowledge our
common relationship to them, and be thankful that over and
above the affections and duties which spring from our manhood,
we have the closer and more constantly guiding duties which
belong to us as Englishmen.'

To this view of our nationality most persons who have feeling
and understanding enough to be conscious of the connection
between the patriotic affection and every other affection which
lifts us above emigrating rats and free-loving baboons, will be
disposed to say Amen. True, we are not indebted to those
ancestors for our religion: we are rather proud of having got
that illumination from elsewhere. The men who planted our
nation were not Christians, though they began their work
centuries after Christ; and they had a decided objection to
Christianity when it was first proposed to them: they were not

monotheists, and their religion was the reverse of spiritual. But since we have been fortunate enough to keep the island-home they won for us, and have been on the whole a prosperous people, rather continuing the plan of invading and spoiling other lands than being forced to beg for shelter in them, nobody has reproached us because our fathers thirteen hundred years ago worshiped Odin, massacred Britons, and were with difficulty persuaded to accept Christianity, knowing nothing of Hebrew history and the reasons why Christ should be received as the Saviour of mankind. The Red Indians, not liking us when we settled among them, might have been willing to fling such facts in our faces, but they were too ignorant, and besides, their opinions did not signify, because we were able, if we liked, to exterminate them. The Hindoos also have doubtless had their rancours against us and still entertain enough ill-will to make unfavourable remarks on our character, especially as to our historic rapacity and arrogant notions of our own superiority; they perhaps do not admire the usual English profile, and they are not converted to our way of feeding: but though we are a small number of an alien race profiting by the territory and produce of these prejudiced people, they are unable to turn us out; at least, when they tried we showed them their mistake.[8] We do not call ourselves a dispersed and a punished people: we are a colonising people, and it is we who have punished others.

Still the historian guides us rightly in urging us to dwell on the virtues of our ancestors with emulation, and to cherish our sense of a common descent as a bond of obligation. The eminence, the nobleness of a people depends on its capability of being stirred by memories, and of striving for what we call spiritual ends – ends which consist not in immediate material possession, but in the satisfaction of a great feeling that animates the collective body as with one soul. A people having the seed of worthiness in it must feel an answering thrill when it is adjured by the deaths of its heroes who died to preserve its national existence; when it is reminded of its small beginnings and gradual growth through past labours and struggles, such as are still demanded of it in order that the freedom and wellbeing thus inherited may be transmitted unimpaired to children and children's children; when an appeal against the permission of injustice is made to great precedents in its history and to the better genius breathing in its institutions. It is this living force of sentiment in common which makes a national consciousness. Nations so moved will resist conquest with the very breasts of their women, will pay their millions and their blood to abolish slavery, will share privation in famine and all calamity, will produce poets to sing 'some great story of a man,' and thinkers whose theories will bear the test of action. An individual man, to be harmoniously great, must belong to a nation of this order, if not in actual existence yet existing in the past, in memory, as a departed, invisible, beloved ideal, once a reality, and perhaps to be restored. A common humanity is not yet enough to feed the rich blood of various activity which makes a complete man. The time is not come for cosmopolitanism to be highly virtuous, any more than for communism to suffice for social energy. I am not bound to feel for a Chinaman as I feel for my fellow-countryman: I am bound not to demoralise him with opium, not to compel him to my will by destroying or plundering the fruits of his labour on the alleged ground that he is not cosmopolitan enough, and not to insult him for his want of my tailoring and religion when he appears as a peaceable visitor on the London pavement. It is admirable in a Briton with a good purpose to learn Chinese, but it would not be a proof of fine intellect in him to taste Chinese poetry in the original more than he tastes the poetry of his own tongue. Affection, intelligence, duty, radiate from a centre, and nature has decided that for us English folk that centre can be neither China nor Peru. Most of us feel this unreflectingly; for the affectation of undervaluing every-thing native, and being too fine for one's own country, belongs only to a few minds of no dangerous leverage. What is wanting is, that we should recognise a corresponding attachment to nationality as legitimate in every other people, and understand that its absence is a privation of the greatest good.

For, to repeat, not only the nobleness of a nation depends on the presence of this national consciousness, but also the nobleness

of each individual citizen. Our dignity and rectitude are pro-
portioned to our sense of relationship with something great,
admirable, pregnant with high possibilities, worthy of sacrifice,
a continual inspiration to self-repression and discipline by the
presentation of aims larger and more attractive to our generous
part than the securing of personal ease or prosperity. And a
people possessing this good should surely feel not only a ready
sympathy with the effort of those who, having lost the good,
strive to regain it, but a profound pity for any degradation
resulting from its loss; nay, something more than pity when
happier nationalities have made victims of the unfortunate
whose memories nevertheless are the very fountain to which the
persecutors trace their most vaunted blessings.

   These notions are familiar: few will deny them in the abstract, and many are found loudly asserting them in relation to
this or the other particular case. But here as elsewhere, in the
ardent application of ideas, there is a notable lack of simple
comparison or sensibility to resemblance. The European world
has long been used to consider the Jews as altogether exceptional, and it has followed naturally enough that they have been
excepted from the rules of justice and mercy, which are based
on human likeness. But to consider a people whose ideas have
determined the religion of half the world, and that the more
cultivated half, and who made the most eminent struggle against
the power of Rome, as a purely exceptional race, is a demoralising
offence against rational knowledge, a stultifying inconsistency in
historical interpretation. Every nation of forcible character – *i.e.*,
of strongly marked characteristics, is so far exceptional. The
distinctive note of each bird-species is in this sense exceptional,
but the necessary ground of such distinction is a deeper likeness.
The superlative peculiarity in the Jews admitted, our afffinity
with them is only the more apparent when the elements of their
peculiarity are discerned.

   From whatever point of view the writings of the Old Testament may be regarded, the picture they present of a national
development is of high interest and speciality, nor can their
historic momentousness be much affected by any varieties of

theory as to the relation they bear to the New Testament or to the rise and constitution of Christianity. Whether we accept the canonical Hebrew books as a revelation or simply as part of an ancient literature, makes no difference to the fact that we find there the strongly characterised portraiture of a people educated from an earlier or later period to a sense of separateness unique in its intensity, a people taught by many concurrent influences to identify faithfulness to its national traditions with the highest social and religious blessings. Our too scanty sources of Jewish history, from the return under Ezra to the beginning of the desperate resistance against Rome,[9] show us the heroic and triumphant struggle of the Maccabees, which rescued the religion and independence of the nation from the corrupting sway of the Syrian Greeks,[10] adding to the glorious sum of its memorials, and stimulating continuous efforts of a more peaceful sort to maintain and develop that national life which the heroes had fought and died for, by internal measures of legal administration and public teaching. Thenceforth the virtuous elements of the Jewish life were engaged, as they had been with varying aspects during the long and changeful prophetic period and the restoration under Ezra, on the side of preserving the specific national character against a demoralising fusion with that of foreigners whose religion and ritual were idolatrous and often obscene. There was always a Foreign party reviling the National party as narrow, and sometimes manifesting their own breadth in extensive views of advancement or profit to themselves by flattery of a foreign power. Such internal conflict naturally tightened the bands of conservatism, which needed to be strong if it were to rescue the sacred ark, the vital spirit of a small nation – 'the smallest of the nations' – whose territory lay on the highway between three continents; and when the dread and hatred of foreign sway had condensed itself into dread and hatred of the Romans, many Conservatives became Zealots,[11] whose chief mark was that they advocated resistance to the death against the submergence of their nationality. Much might be said on this point towards distinguishing the desperate struggle against a conquest which is regarded as degradation and corruption, from rash, hopeless insurrection against an established native government; and for my part (if that were of any consequence) I share the spirit of the Zealots. I take the spectacle of the Jewish people defying the Roman edict, and preferring death by starvation or the sword to the introduction of Caligula's deified statue[12] into the temple, as a sublime type of steadfastness. But all that need be noticed here is the continuity of that national education (by outward and inward circumstance) which created in the Jews a feeling of race, a sense of corporate existence, unique in its intensity.

But not, before the dispersion, unique in essential qualities. There is more likeness than contrast between the way we English got our island and the way the Israelites got Canaan. We have not been noted for forming a low estimate of ourselves in comparison with foreigners, or for admitting that our institutions are equalled by those of any other people under the sun. Many of us have thought that our sea-wall is a specially divine arrangement to make and keep us a nation of sea-kings after the manner of our forefathers, secure against invasion and able to invade other lands when we need them, though they may lie on the other side of the ocean. Again, it has been held that we have a peculiar destiny as a Protestant people, not only able to bruise the head of an idolatrous Christianity in the midst of us, but fitted as possessors of the most truth and the most tonnage to carry our purer religion over the world and convert mankind to our way of thinking. The Puritans, asserting their liberty to restrain tyrants, found the Hebrew history closely symbolical of their feelings and purpose; and it can hardly be correct to cast the blame of their less laudable doings on the writings they invoked, since their opponents made use of the same writings for different ends, finding there a strong warrant for the divine right of kings[13] and the denunciation of those who, like Korah, Dathan, and Abiram,[14] took on themselves the office of the priesthood which belonged of right solely to Aaron and his sons, or, in other words, to men ordained by the English bishops. We must rather refer the passionate use of the Hebrew writings to affinities of disposition between our own race and the Jewish. Is it true that the arrogance of a Jew was so immeasurably beyond that of a Calvinist? And the just sympathy and admiration which we give to the ancestors who resisted the oppressive acts of our native kings, and by resisting rescued or won for us the best part of our civil and religious liberties – is it justly to be withheld from those brave and steadfast men of Jewish race who fought and died, or strove by wise administration to resist, the oppression and corrupting influences of foreign tyrants, and by resisting rescued the nationality which was the very hearth of our own religion? At any rate, seeing that the Jews were more specifically than any other nation educated into a sense of their supreme moral value, the chief matter of surprise is that any other nation is found to rival them in this form of self-confidence.

More exceptional – less like the course of our own history – has been their dispersion and their subsistence as a separate people through ages in which for the most part they were regarded and treated very much as beasts hunted for the sake of their skins, or of a valuable secretion peculiar to their species. The Jews showed a talent for accumulating what was an object of more immediate desire to Christians than animal oils or well-furred skins, and their cupidity and avarice were found at once particularly hateful and particularly useful: hateful when seen as a reason for punishing them by mulcting[15] or robbery, useful when this retributive process could be successfully carried forward. Kings and emperors naturally were more alive to the usefulness of subjects who could gather and yield money; but edicts issued to protect 'the King's Jews'[16] equally with the King's game from being harassed and hunted by the commonalty were only slight mitigations to the deplorable lot of a race held to be under the divine curse, and had little force after the Crusades began. As the slave-holders in the United States counted the curse on Ham[17] a justification of negro slavery, so the curse on the Jews was counted a justification for hindering them from pursuing agriculture and handicrafts; for marking them out as execrable figures by a peculiar dress; for torturing them to make them part with their gains, or for more gratuitously

spitting at them and pelting them; for taking it as certain that
they killed and ate babies, poisoned the wells, and took pains to
spread the plague; for putting it to them whether they would be
baptised or burned, and not failing to burn and massacre them
when they were obstinate; but also for suspecting them of
disliking the baptism when they had got it, and then burning
them in punishment of their insincerity; finally, for hounding
them by tens on tens of thousands from the homes where they
had found shelter for centuries, and inflicting on them the
horrors of a new exile and a new dispersion. All this to avenge
the Saviour of mankind, or else to compel these stiff-necked
people to acknowledge a Master whose servants showed such
beneficent effects of His teaching.

   With a people so treated one of two issues was possible:
either from being of feebler nature than their persecutors, and
caring more for ease than for the sentiments and ideas which
constituted their distinctive character, they would everywhere
give way to pressure and get rapidly merged in the populations
around them; or, being endowed with uncommon tenacity,
physical and mental, feeling peculiarly the ties of inheritance
both in blood and faith, remembering national glories, trusting
in their recovery, abhorring apostasy, able to bear all things and
hope all things with the consciousness of being steadfast to
spiritual obligations, the kernel of their number would harden
into an inflexibility more and more insured by motive and habit.
They would cherish all differences that marked them off from
their hated oppressors, all memories that consoled them with a
sense of virtual though unrecognised superiority; and the separateness which was made their badge of ignominy would be
their inward pride, their source of fortifying defiance. Doubtless
such a people would get confirmed in vices. An oppressive
government and a persecuting religion, while breeding vices in
those who hold power, are well known to breed answering vices
in those who are powerless and suffering. What more direct
plan than the course presented by European history could have
been pursued in order to give the Jews a spirit of bitter isolation,
of scorn for the wolfish hypocrisy that made victims of them, of

triumph in prospering at the expense of the blunderers who stoned them away from the open paths of industry? – or, on the other hand, to encourage in the less defiant a lying conformity, a pretence of conversion for the sake of the social advantages attached to baptism, an outward renunciation of their hereditary ties with the lack of real love towards the society and creed which exacted this galling tribute? – or again, in the most unhappy specimens of the race, to rear transcendent examples of odious vice, reckless instruments of rich men with bad propensities, unscrupulous grinders of the alien people who wanted to grind *them*?

No wonder the Jews have their vices: no wonder if it were proved (which it has not hitherto appeared to be) that some of them have a bad pre-eminence in evil, an unrivalled superfluity of naughtiness. It would be more plausible to make a wonder of the virtues which have prospered among them under the shadow of oppression. But instead of dwelling on these, or treating as admitted what any hardy or ignorant person may deny, let us found simply on the loud assertions of the hostile. The Jews, it is said, resisted the expansion of their own religion into Christianity; they were in the habit of spitting on the cross; they have held the name of Christ to be *Anathema*. Who taught them that? The men who made Christianity a curse to them: the men who made the name of Christ a symbol for the spirit of vengeance, and, what was worse, made the execution of the vengeance a pretext for satisfying their own savageness, greed, and envy: the men who sanctioned with the name of Christ a barbaric and blundering copy of pagan fatalism in taking the words 'His blood be upon us and on our children'[18] as a divinely appointed verbal warrant for wreaking cruelty from generation to generation on the people from whose sacred writings Christ drew His teaching. Strange retrogression in the professors of an expanded religion, boasting an illumination beyond the spiritual doctrine of Hebrew prophets! For Hebrew prophets proclaimed a God who demanded mercy rather than sacrifices. The Christians also believed that God delighted not in the blood of rams and of bulls, but they apparently conceived Him as requiring for His satisfaction the sighs and groans, the blood and roasted flesh of men whose forefathers had misunderstood the metaphorical character of prophecies which spoke of spiritual pre-eminence under the figure of a material kingdom. Was this the method by which Christ desired His title to the Messiahship to be com-mended to the hearts and understandings of the nation in which He was born? Many of His sayings bear the stamp of that patriotism which places fellow-countrymen in the inner circle of affection and duty. And did the words 'Father, forgive them, they know not what they do,'[19] refer only to the centurion and his band, a tacit exception being made of every Hebrew there present from the mercy of the Father and the compassion of the Son? – nay, more, of every Hebrew yet to come who remained unconverted after hearing of His claim to the Messiahship, not from His own lips or those of His native apostles, but from the lips of alien men whom cross, creed, and baptism had left cruel, rapacious, and debauched? It is more reverent to Christ to believe that He must have approved the Jewish martyrs who deliberately chose to be burned or massacred rather than be guilty of a blaspheming lie, more than He approved the rabble of crusaders who robbed and murdered them in His name.

But these remonstrances seem to have no direct application to personages who take up the attitude of philosophic thinkers and discriminating critics, professedly accepting Christianity from a rational point of view as a vehicle of the highest religious and moral truth, and condemning the Jews on the ground that they are obstinate adherents of an outworn creed, maintain themselves in moral alienation from the peoples with whom they share citizenship, and are destitute of real interest in the welfare of the community and state with which they are thus identified. These anti-Judaic advocates usually belong to a party[20] which has felt itself glorified in winning for Jews, as well as Dissenters and Catholics, the full privileges of citizenship, laying open to them every path to distinction. At one time the voice of this party urged that differences of creed were made dangerous only by the denial of citizenship – that you must make a man a citizen before he could feel like one. At present, apparently, this confidence has been succeeded by a sense of mistake: there is a regret that no limiting clauses were insisted on, such as would have hindered the Jews from coming too far and in too large proportion along those opened pathways; and the Roumanians are thought to have shown an enviable wisdom in giving them as little chance as possible.[21] But then, the reflection occurring that some of the most objectionable Jews are baptised Christians, it is obvious that such clauses would have been insufficient, and the doctrine that you can turn a Jew into a good Christian is emphatically retracted. But clearly, these liberal gentlemen, too late enlightened by disagreeable events, must yield the palm of wise foresight to those who argued against them long ago; and it is a striking spectacle to witness minds so panting for advancement in some directions that they are ready to force it on an unwilling society, in this instance despairingly recurring to mediæval types of thinking – insisting that the Jews are made viciously cosmopolitan by holding the world's money-bag, that for them all national interests are resolved into the algebra of loans, that they have suffered an inward degradation stamping them as morally inferior, and – 'serve them right,' since they rejected Christianity. All which is mirrored in an analogy, namely, that of the Irish, also a servile race, who have rejected Protestantism though it has been repeatedly urged on them by fire and sword and penal laws, and whose place in the moral scale may be judged by our advertisements, where the clause, 'No Irish need apply,' parallels the sentence which for many polite persons sums up the question of Judaism – 'I never *did* like the Jews.'

It is certainly worth considering whether an expatriated, denationalised race, used for ages to live among antipathetic populations, must not inevitably lack some conditions of nobleness. If they drop that separateness which is made their reproach, they may be in danger of lapsing into a cosmopolitan indifference equivalent to cynicism, and of missing that inward identification with the nationality immediately around them which might make some amends for their inherited privation. No dispassionate observer can deny this danger. Why, our own

countrymen who take to living abroad without purpose or
function to keep up their sense of fellowship in the affairs of
their own land are rarely good specimens of moral healthiness;
still, the consciousness of having a native country, the birthplace
of common memories and habits of mind, existing like a paren-
tal hearth quitted but beloved; the dignity of being included in
a people which has a part in the comity of nations and the
growing federation of the world; that sense of special belonging
which is the root of human virtues, both public and private, –
all these spiritual links may preserve migratory Englishmen from
the worst consequences of their voluntary dispersion. Unques-
tionably the Jews, having been more than any other race exposed to the adverse moral influences of alienism, must, both in
individuals and in groups, have suffered some corresponding
moral degradation; but in fact they have escaped with less of
abjectness and less of hard hostility towards the nations whose
hand has been against them, than could have happened in the
case of a people who had neither their adhesion to a separate
religion founded on historic memories, nor their characteristic
family affectionateness. Tortured, flogged, spit upon, the *corpus
vile*[22] on which rage or wantonness vented themselves with
impunity, their name flung at them as an opprobrium by
superstition, hatred, and contempt, they have remained proud
of their origin. Does any one call this an evil pride? Perhaps he
belongs to that order of man who, while he has a democratic
dislike to dukes and earls, wants to make believe that his father
was an idle gentleman, when in fact he was an honourable
artisan, or who would feel flattered to be taken for other than
an Englishman. It is possible to be too arrogant about our blood
or our calling, but that arrogance is virtue compared with such
mean pretence. The pride which identifies us with a great
historic body is a humanising, elevating habit of mind, inspiring
sacrifices of individual comfort, gain, or other selfish ambition,
for the sake of that ideal whole; and no man swayed by such a
sentiment can become completely abject. That a Jew of Smyrna,[23]
where a whip is carried by passengers ready to flog off the too
officious specimens of his race, can still be proud to say, 'I am a

Jew,' is surely a fact to awaken admiration in a mind capable of understanding what we may call the ideal forces in human history. And again, a varied, impartial observation of the Jews in different countries tends to the impression that they have a predominant kindliness which must have been deeply ingrained in the constitution of their race to have outlasted the ages of persecution and oppression. The concentration of their joys in domestic life has kept up in them the capacity of tenderness: the pity for the fatherless and the widow, the care for the women and the little ones, blent intimately with their religion, is a well of mercy that cannot long or widely be pent up by exclusiveness. And the kindliness of the Jew overflows the line of division between him and the Gentile. On the whole, one of the most remarkable phenomena in the history of this scattered people, made for ages 'a scorn and a hissing' is, that after being subjected to this process, which might have been expected to be in every sense deteriorating and vitiating, they have come out of it (in any estimate which allows for numerical proportion) rivalling the nations of all European countries in healthiness and beauty of *physique*, in practical ability, in scientific and artistic aptitude, and in some forms of ethical value. A significant indication of their natural rank is seen in the fact that at this moment, the leader of the Liberal party in Germany is a Jew, the leader of the Republican party in France is a Jew, and the head of the Conservative ministry in England is a Jew.[24]

And here it is that we find the ground for the obvious jealousy which is now stimulating the revived expression of old antipathies. 'The Jews,' it is felt, 'have a dangerous tendency to get the uppermost places not only in commerce but in political life. Their monetary hold on governments is tending to perpetuate in leading Jews a spirit of universal alienism (euphemistically called cosmopolitanism), even where the West has given them a full share in civil and political rights. A people with oriental sunlight in their blood, yet capable of being everywhere acclimatised, they have a force and toughness which enables them to carry off the best prizes; and their wealth is likely to put half the seats in Parliament at their disposal.'

There is truth in these views of Jewish social and political relations. But it is rather too late for liberal pleaders to urge them in a merely vituperative sense. Do they propose as a remedy for the impending danger of our healthier national influences getting overridden by Jewish predominance, that we should repeal our emancipatory laws? Not all the Germanic immigrants who have been settling among us for generations, and are still pouring in to settle, are Jews, but thoroughly Teutonic and more or less Christian craftsmen, mechanicians, or skilled and erudite functionaries; and the Semitic Christians who swarm among us are dangerously like their unconverted brethren in complexion, persistence, and wealth. Then there are the Greeks who, by the help of Phœnician blood or otherwise, are objectionably strong in the city. Some judges think that the Scotch are more numerous and prosperous here in the South than is quite for the good of us Southerners; and the early inconvenience felt under the Stuarts[25] of being quartered upon by a hungry, hard-working people with a distinctive accent and form of religion, and higher cheek-bones than English taste requires, has not yet been quite neutralised. As for the Irish, it is felt in high quarters that we have always been too lenient towards them; – at least, if they had been harried a little more there might not have been so many of them on the English press, of which they divide the power with the Scotch, thus driving many Englishmen to honest and ineloquent labour.

So far shall we be carried if we go in search of devices to hinder people of other blood than our own from getting the advantage of dwelling among us.

Let it be admitted that it is a calamity to the English, as to any other great historic people, to undergo a premature fusion with immigrants of alien blood; that its distinctive national characteristics should be in danger of obliteration by the predominating quality of foreign settlers. I not only admit this, I am ready to unite in groaning over the threatened danger. To one who loves his native language, who would delight to keep our rich and harmonious English undefiled by foreign accent, foreign intonation, and those foreign tinctures of verbal meaning which tend to confuse all writing and discourse, it is an affliction as harassing as the climate, that on our stage, in our studios, at our public and private gatherings, in our offices, warehouses, and workshops, we must expect to hear our beloved English with its words clipped, its vowels stretched and twisted, its phrases of acquiescence and politeness, of cordiality, dissidence or argument, delivered always in the wrong tones, like ill-rendered melodies, marred beyond recognition; that there should be a general ambition to speak every language except our mother English, which persons 'of style' are not ashamed of corrupting with slang, false foreign equivalents, and a pronunciation that crushes out all colour from the vowels and jams them between jostling consonants. An ancient Greek might not like to be resuscitated for the sake of hearing Homer read in our universities, still he would at least find more instructive marvels in other developments to be witnessed at those institutions; but a modern Englishman is invited from his after-dinner repose to hear Shakspere delivered under circumstances which offer no other novelty than some novelty of false intonation, some new distribution of strong emphasis on prepositions, some new misconception of a familiar idiom. Well! it is our inertness that is in fault, our carelessness of excellence, our willing ignorance of the treasures that lie in our national heritage, while we are agape after what is foreign, though it may be only a vile imitation of what is native.

This marring of our speech, however, is a minor evil compared with what must follow from the predominance of wealth-acquiring immigrants, whose appreciation of our political and social life must often be as approximative or fatally erroneous as their delivery of our language. But take the worst issues – what can we do to hinder them? Are we to adopt the exclusiveness for which we have punished the Chinese? Are we to tear the glorious flag of hospitality which has made our freedom the world-wide blessing of the oppressed? It is not agreeable to find foreign accents and stumbling locutions passing from the piquant exception to the general rule of discourse. But to urge on that account that we should spike away the peaceful foreigner, would be a view of international relations not in the long-run favourable to the interests of our fellow-countrymen; for we are at least equal to the races we call obtrusive in the disposition to settle wherever money is to be made and cheaply idle living to be found. In meeting the national evils which are brought upon us by the onward course of the world, there is often no more immediate hope or resource than that of striving after fuller national excellence, which must consist in the moulding of more excellent individual natives. The tendency of things is towards the quicker or slower fusion of races. It is impossible to arrest this tendency: all we can do is to moderate its course so as to hinder it from degrading the moral status of societies by a too rapid effacement of those national traditions and customs which are the language of the national genius – the deep suckers of healthy sentiment. Such moderating and guidance of inevitable movement is worthy of all effort. And it is in this sense that the modern insistence on the idea of Nationalities has value. That any people at once distinct and coherent enough to form a state should be held in subjection by an alien antipathetic government has been becoming more and more a ground of sympathetic indignation; and in virtue of this, at least one great State has been added to European councils.[26] Nobody now complains of the result in this case, though far-sighted persons see the need to limit analogy by discrimination. We have to consider who are the stifled people and who the stiflers before we can be sure of our ground. The only point in this connection on which Englishmen are agreed is, that England itself shall not be subject to foreign rule. The fiery resolve to resist invasion, though with an improvised array of pitchforks, is felt to be virtuous, and to be worthy of a historic people. Why? Because there is a national life in our veins. Because there is something specifically English which we feel to be supremely worth striving for, worth dying for, rather than living to renounce it. Because we too have our share – perhaps a principal share – in that spirit of separateness which has not yet done its work in the education of mankind, which has created the varying genius of nations, and, like the Muses, is the offspring of memory.

Here, as everywhere else, the human task seems to be the

discerning and adjustment of opposite claims. But the end can hardly be achieved by urging contradictory reproaches, and instead of labouring after discernment as a preliminary to intervention, letting our zeal burst forth according to a capricious selection, first determined accidentally and afterwards justified by personal predilection. Not only John Gilpin and his wife, or Edwin and Angelina,[27] seem to be of opinion that their preference or dislike of Russians, Servians, or Greeks, consequent, perhaps, on hotel adventures, has something to do with the merits of the Eastern Question;[28] even in a higher range of intellect and enthusiasm we find a distribution of sympathy or pity for sufferers of different blood or votaries of differing religions, strangely unaccountable on any other ground than a fortuitous direction of study or trivial circumstances of travel. With some even admirable persons, one is never quite sure of any particular being included under a general term. A provincial physician, it is said, once ordering a lady patient not to eat salad, was asked pleadingly by the affectionate husband whether she might eat lettuce, or cresses, or radishes. The physician had too rashly believed in the comprehensiveness of the word 'salad,' just as we, if not enlightened by experience, might believe in the all-embracing breadth of 'sympathy with the injured and oppressed.' What mind can exhaust the grounds of exception which lie in each particular case? There is understood to be a peculiar odour from the negro body, and we know that some persons, too rationalistic to feel bound by the curse on Ham, used to hint very strongly that this odour determined the question on the side of negro slavery.

And this is the usual level of thinking in polite society concerning the Jews. Apart from theological purposes, it seems to be held surprising that anybody should take an interest in the history of a people whose literature has furnished all our devotional language; and if any reference is made to their past or future destinies some hearer is sure to state as a relevant fact which may assist our judgment, that she, for her part, is not fond of them, having known a Mr Jacobson who was very unpleasant, or that he, for his part, thinks meanly of them as a

race, though on inquiry you find that he is so little acquainted
with their characteristics that he is astonished to learn how
many persons whom he has blindly admired and applauded are
Jews to the backbone. Again, men who consider themselves in
the very van of modern advancement, knowing history and the
latest philosophies of history, indicate their contemptuous surprise that any one should entertain the destiny of the Jews as a
worthy subject, by referring to Moloch and their own agreement with the theory that the religion of Jehovah was merely a
transformed Moloch-worship,[29] while in the same breath they
are glorifying 'civilisation' as a transformed tribal existence of
which some lineaments are traceable in grim marriage customs
of the native Australians. Are these erudite persons prepared to
insist that the name 'Father' should no longer have any sanctity
for us, because in their view of likelihood our Aryan ancestors
were mere improvers on a state of things in which nobody knew
his own father?[30]

For less theoretic men, ambitious to be regarded as practical
politicians, the value of the Hebrew race has been measured by
their unfavourable opinion of a prime minister who is a Jew by
lineage. But it is possible to form a very ugly opinion as to the
scrupulousness of Walpole or of Chatham;[31] and in any case I
think Englishmen would refuse to accept the character and
doings of those eighteenth century statesmen as the standard of
value for the English people and the part they have to play in
the fortunes of mankind.

If we are to consider the future of the Jews at all, it seems
reasonable to take as a preliminary question: Are they destined
to complete fusion with the peoples among whom they are
dispersed, losing every remnant of a distinctive consciousness as
Jews; or, are there in the breadth and intensity with which the
feeling of separateness, or what we may call the organised
memory of a national consciousness, actually exists in the
world-wide Jewish communities – the seven millions scattered
from east to west – and again, are there in the political relations
of the world, the conditions present or approaching for the
restoration of a Jewish state planted on the old ground as a

centre of national feeling, a source of dignifying protection, a special channel for special energies which may contribute some added form of national genius, and an added voice in the councils of the world?

They are among us everywhere: it is useless to say we are not fond of them. Perhaps we are not fond of proletaries and their tendency to form Unions, but the world is not therefore to be rid of them. If we wish to free ourselves from the inconveniences that we have to complain of, whether in proletaries or in Jews, our best course is to encourage all means of improving these neighbours who elbow us in a thickening crowd, and of sending their incommodious energies into beneficent channels. Why are we so eager for the dignity of certain populations of whom perhaps we have never seen a single specimen, and of whose history, legend, or literature we have been contentedly ignorant for ages, while we sneer at the notion of a renovated national dignity for the Jews, whose ways of thinking and whose very verbal forms are on our lips in every prayer which we end with an Amen? Some of us consider this question dismissed when they have said that the wealthiest Jews have no desire to forsake their European palaces, and go to live in Jerusalem. But in a return from exile, in the restoration of a people, the question is not whether certain rich men will choose to remain behind, but whether there will be found worthy men who will choose to lead the return. Plenty of prosperous Jews remained in Babylon when Ezra marshalled his band of forty thousand and began a new glorious epoch in the history of his race, making the preparation for that epoch in the history of the world which has been held glorious enough to be dated from for evermore. The hinge of possibility is simply the existence of an adequate community of feeling as well as widespread need in the Jewish race, and the hope that among its finer specimens there may arise some men of instruction and ardent public spirit, some new Ezras, some modern Maccabees, who will know how to use all favouring outward conditions, how to triumph by heroic example, over the indifference of their fellows and the scorn of their foes, and will steadfastly set their faces towards making their people once more one among the nations.

Formerly, evangelical orthodoxy was prone to dwell on the fulfilment of prophecy in the 'restoration of the Jews.' Such interpretation of the prophets is less in vogue now. The dominant mode is to insist on a Christianity that disowns its origin, that is not a substantial growth having a genealogy, but is a vaporous reflex of modern notions. The Christ of Matthew had the heart of a Jew – 'Go ye first to the lost sheep of the house of Israel.'[32] The Apostle of the Gentiles had the heart of a Jew: 'For I could wish that myself were accursed from Christ for my brethren, my kinsmen according to the flesh: who are Israelites; to whom pertaineth the adoption, and the glory, and the covenants, and the giving of the law, and the service of God, and the promises; whose are the fathers, and of whom as concerning the flesh Christ came.'[33] Modern apostles, extolling Christianity, are found using a different tone: they prefer the mediæval cry translated into modern phrase. But the mediæval cry too was in substance very ancient – more ancient than the days of Augustus.[34] Pagans in successive ages said, 'These people are unlike us, and refuse to be made like us: let us punish them.' The Jews were steadfast in their separateness, and through that separateness Christianity was born. A modern book on Liberty[35] has maintained that from the freedom of individual men to persist in idiosyncrasies the world may be enriched. Why should we not apply this argument to the idiosyncrasy of a nation, and pause in our haste to hoot it down? There is still a great function for the steadfastness of the Jew: not that he should shut out the utmost illumination which knowledge can throw on his national history, but that he should cherish the store of inheritance which that history has left him. Every Jew should be conscious that he is one of a multitude possessing common objects of piety in the immortal achievements and immortal sorrows of ancestors who have transmitted to them a physical and mental type strong enough, eminent enough in faculties, pregnant enough with peculiar promise, to constitute a new beneficent individuality among the nations, and, by confuting the traditions of scorn, nobly avenge the wrongs done to their Fathers.

There is a sense in which the worthy child of a nation that

has brought forth illustrious prophets, high and unique among the poets of the world, is bound by their visions.

Is bound?

Yes, for the effective bond of human action is feeling, and the worthy child of a people owning the triple name of Hebrew, Israelite, and Jew, feels his kinship with the glories and the sorrows, the degradation and the possible renovation of his national family.

Will any one teach the nullification of this feeling and call his doctrine a philosophy? He will teach a blinding superstition – the superstition that a theory of human wellbeing can be constructed in disregard of the influences which have made us human.

We distinguish the hyperbole and rapid development in descriptions of faces or persons which is lit up by humorous consciousness in the speaker and might at will be replaced by a simply truthful statement from the fluid inaccuracy or helpless exaggeration which is really something commoner than the correct simplicity often called prosaic. I think the greatest works in the world have come from that thoroughly sane imagination which constantly distinguishes between its real experience and its ideal creations. And the supremely poetic mind is characterized not so much by the transformation of material fact as by the breadth of imaginative association which informs every material fact with memories and emotions – which sees the plain of Marathon[2] exactly as it is, when standing on it today, but feels too the presence of the sublime struggle of which it was once the scene – less in concrete images hard outline than in a rush of impressions which must use some brief symbol of passionate words.

As to the sanity of the greatest poets – leaving out the question of the Homeric mind. Here is Lucretius, at once lofty and minute; Virgil supremely real – ideal in the georgics; Dante, as before said; Spencer; Shakspeare; Milton; Goethe: thorough sanity is the strong stamp by which they are all akin and of the royal race. By sanity I mean a consciousness able to compass and sustain a proportionate conception of the mood as it is in the average experience of mankind, so that the mind shall not be under the continual sway of something exceptional in ourselves and circumstances. The sane genius with a deformed spine will know better than another how to present the peculiar experience consequent on that misfortune; but he will also know how to distinguish the bias given by his own pain from the fairly balanced estimate of the human lot in all its varieties. The lack of such sanity inevitably throws him into the monotonous shallowness of an overweening egoism which no splendour of expression and no search after scenic variety can make lastingly satisfactory to the growing consensus of society. His value will be that of an individual type for the museum. He will be studied as an instance, not taken as a representative of our common human nature. If one can without folly say anything about that vaguely conceived attribute called genius, a less futile remark than usual is that its degrees are best measured by the power it manifests of regarding and presenting life from a higher point of view than that of its own individual lot. And this is the reason why the dramatic is placed above the cynical – the presentation of many-mooded man above the utterance of mere moods.

Here is but a development of what I said about Celestina. The fundamental power, the basis of the best preeminence is that of seeing and observing things as they are in the ordinary experience of our kind. And the highest imagination is that in which, while it is intensely reflective, working towards an ideal effect, includes the largest amount of real life-like elements. For to imagine arbitrarily from slack observation is a feeble effort compared with the registration of clear perceptions and the reproducing of them by accurately suggestive touches in newly combined wholes.

For my part, until I can be assured that our language has another popular word instead of Morals to express right conduct in all our relations, I will never praise the morals of a king whose arrogance, obstinacy, and dulness to questions of justice as simple as addition or subtraction, were a cause of war to maintain oppression, and made him resist when he could not hinder every good measure for the relief of subjects at home or the victims of slavery abroad, however frugally he might dine, and though he might completely abstain from sowing 'his Maker's image o'er the land'[2] in the shape of illegitimate dukes. To distinguish between public and private duties (though they are essentially united) is not to call either order by itself the whole of morality. Charles the Second[3] led a grossly licentious life, and would have been an immoral man even if he had not been a bad king, one whose public acts are continually directed by a contemptibly or odiously false balance of motives or false estimate of value in results, can under no condition, except a change in our stock of words, be rightly called moral. For a continually false judgement in human affairs is not due to that supposed intellectual narrowness which is imagined as capable of coexisting with the finest rectitude and most generous sympathy: over the larger number of practical questions rectitude and generosity are themselves the light which widens the intellectual area. To define the boundaries of the emotional and intellectual in relation to human life is as hard a problem as that which frustrated Shylock.[4]

NOTES

Motto

[1] Phaedrus, *Fabulae* (Prologue to Bk. III:45–50):

> If someone will let his suspicions wander,
> Snatching as his own what applies to all,
> He will foolishly expose his guilty conscience.
> I should like to be excused no less than he,
> For I have no mind to brand any individual person,
> But rather truly to show life itself and the habits of men.

Chapter I

[1] Literally, Lippus means bleary-eyed. Metaphorically, it has been used, in Horace for example, to mean blind to one's own faults.

[2] From Shakespeare's *Hamlet*. Preparing the players for the dumb show, Hamlet says: 'for in the very torrent, tempest, and as I may say, whirlwind of your passion, you must acquire and beget a temperance that may give it smoothness' (3. 3. 5–7). All references are to *The Complete Works of Shakespeare*, ed. David Bevington (HarperCollins Publishers Inc., 1992)

[3] Jean Jacques Rousseau (1712–78), French philosopher whose *Confessions* (1781;1788) provide a model of introspective autobiography.

[4] Marcus Minutius Felix (also Minucius, c. 200–300) was a Christian apologist. In his dialogue *Octavius*, the title character tells Minucius Felix that the writings of the Jews reveal that 'their present lot they have deserved through their own wickedness and that no one thing has befallen them which was not foretold to them, should they persist in this stiff-necked arrogance.' See *The Octavius of Marcus Minucius Felix*, trans. G. W. Clarke (New York: Newman Press, 1974) 33:114.

[5] In the early nineteenth century, the Cherokee scholar, Sequoya (1770–1843), devised a written alphabet representing syllables of the Cherokee language. The Cherokee Syllabary facilitated translations between Cherokee and English, thus distinguishing the Cherokee from other Native American tribes.

[6] *Hamlet*, 3. 2. 19–22: 'For anything so o'erdone is from the purpose of playing, whose end, both at the first and now, was and is to hold as 'twere the mirror up to nature. . .'

[7] In ancient Greece and Rome, the name for former slaves. 'Our' free people seems to refer to the descendants of English peasants once bound to the land of a rural manor.

[8] The Hapsburgs, principal royal family of Austria and other European countries from the fifteenth to the nineteenth centuries, were distinguished by an exaggerated, protruding lower lip.

[9] 'You may judge of Hercules from his foot', meaning the whole of anything may be determined from one of its parts. This proverb derives from a story about Pythagoras attributed to Plutarch in Aulus Gellius's *The Attic Nights*.

[10] Glycera ('Sweet One'), the reputed mistress of the Attic poet and author of New Comedy plays, Menander (342–292 BC), who was a pupil of Theophrastus at the Peripatetic School. Glycera is a major character in one of Menander's plays, *Periceiromene*, which survives only in fragments.

[11] In John Bunyan's *The Pilgrim's Progress* (Part I, 1678), the Delectable Mountain is the site from which the pilgrim can see the Celestial City.

[12] The 'true version' carries a very different meaning: 'Therefore, whatsoever ye would that men should do to you, do ye even so to them. . . ' (Matthew 7:12. See also Luke 6:31). All references are to the King James Version.

Chapter II

[1] This passage traces time backwards from the Italian Renaissance (Leonardo da Vinci 1452–1519) to the Golden Age of Athens under Pericles (460–429 BC) to the Aeolic lyrists of Lesbos (birthplace of Theophrastus), including the poet Sappho, mentioned later, whose native Mitylene was the capital of Lesbos (c. 610–580 BC).

[2] William Pitt, The Younger (1759–1806), youngest Prime Minister at the age of 24, noted for reforms but later overtaken by the continuation of the post-revolutionary war against France.

[3] Sir Thomas Lawrence (1769–1830), English painter known especially for his portraits of the aristocracy.

[4] An heretical sect of medieval Christians who scourged themselves to atone for sins.

[5] David Garrick (1717–79), acclaimed as the greatest Shakespearean actor of his time, performed in his own contemporary dress rather than in the historically accurate costume subsequently familiar to nineteenth-century audiences.

[6] The fever caused by a wasting disease.

[7] Untrained military recruits.

[8] Philip II (382–336 BC) and his son Alexander the Great (356–323 BC) were Kings of Macedonia, where the Strymon river is located.

[9] The philosopher Theophrastus wrote a treatise 'On Odours'.

[10] Outer garment worn by the ancient Greeks, a cloth wrapped around the body, draped over the left shoulder and reaching to the ankles.

[11] From Shakespeare's Sonnet 107.

[12] *Hamlet*, 4. 4. 37–40:
    'Sure he that made us with such large discourse,
    Looking before and after, gave us not
    That capability and godlike reason
    To fust in us unused'

[13] Hesiod (c. 800 BC), Greek historian and poet, author of *Theogony* and *Works*

and Days, who lamented the decline of the times and looked back to an earlier, greater age.

[14] The inheritors of the Romantic literary tradition initiated by Sir Walter Scott (1771–1832) and William Wordsworth (1770–1850), are among those idealisers of the past Theophrastus criticises in this essay.

[15] The Tithes Commutation Act (1836) converted the payment of tithes from one-tenth of the land's produce into rent charges based on varying grain prices. A modus is the money payment in lieu of tithe.

[16] The type of a humble, rustic, devoted couple.

[17] Short prayers beginning the Anglican service, which vary on an annual basis.

[18] 'Quarterings', in heraldry, refer to the coat of arms in each of the divisions of a shield. The second 'quarterings' refer to a more general division into portions – in this case emphasising the stratification of English society.

[19] Michael Faraday (1791–1867), renowned English scientist whose humble origins were emphasised in biographies following his death.

[20] First of many references to the destructive consequences of the French Revolution. Napoleon combined revolutionary and imperial rhetoric in his conquests of Europe, which Theophrastus compares to the devastating campaigns of Attila the Hun (434–53).

[21] Arthur Wellesley, later Duke of Wellington (1769–1852), British general and Tory Prime Minister (1828–30). He resisted proposed reforms to the House of Commons, eliminating the 'saleable borroughs' and other inequities mentioned below. Such reforms were finally implemented under the Reform Bill of 1832. Despite his anti-reform politics, he supported Catholic emancipation, which was achieved in 1829.

[22] Rustic dancers who travelled the English countryside after about 1350.

[23] The Apennines is a mountain range along the length of Italy. Frequently figuring in histories of Rome and Italy, it here represents modern changes.

[24] Probably an allusion to Percy Bysshe Shelley's sonnet 'Ozymandias' (1818).

[25] Literally, land near a manor house kept for the use of the lord, used figuratively here to speak of a collective, national inheritance.

[26] A column of smoke seen symbolically as typifying the steam engine, a modern parallel to the pennons flown by medieval knights.

[27] Title of an 1834 essay by Thomas De Quincey, describing the sensual effects experienced upon approaching the city of London.

[28] Supposed Indo-European ancestors of the modern English. 'Uncles and no fathers' recalls the scene in *Daniel Deronda* (II. xvi. 149) in which the young Daniel, moved by Sismondi's *History of the Italian Republics* (1807–18), asks why 'the popes and cardinals always had so many nephews'. He is told: 'their own children were called nephews', an explanation which troubles Daniel with respect to his own apparent status as Sir Hugo Mallinger's nephew. All references are to George Eliot, *Daniel Deronda*, ed. Graham Handley (Oxford: Clarendon Press, 1984).

[29] Psalm 121: 'I will lift up mine eyes unto the hills, from whence cometh my help.'

Chapter III

[1] A Merman is a sea creature with the head and upper body of a man and lower body of a fish or sea mammal (cetacean), the male counterpart of a mermaid.

[2] One who deals in the legal transfer of property.

[3] Aaron's rod blossoms and bears almonds as a sign of God's power, but God turns it back into a rod as a warning to the rebels who murmur against him (Numbers 17:8–10).

[4] Each of the nineteenth-century debates alluded to here involves the determination of origins – literary, linguistic, scientific, historical – by means of unprovable theories. Merman has a position on whether there was a poet called Homer who wrote the works attributed to him, on the accuracy of the chronology of Egyptian dynasties established by the Egyptian priest Manetho (third century BC), and other scholarly controversies of the time.

[5] Laputa is the 'flying island' in Jonathan Swift's *Gulliver's Travels* (Book III), whose inhabitants are preoccupied with abstract and impractical theoretical knowledge.

[6] Merman's antagonists are all cetaceans: Grampus (Greenland whale), Narwhal (corpse whale or sea unicorn), Butzkopf (German for Grampus), Dugong (sea cow), Cachalot (sperm whale), Ziphius (bottle-nosed dolphin).

[7] Proteus is the name of a sea god who could assume different shapes.

[8] Proteus and Julia are characters in Shakespeare's *Two Gentlemen of Verona* (c. 1592). Julia stays true to her Proteus even after he has forsaken her.

[9] Names made up to sound like the exotic subjects of early anthropological inquiry. Magicodumbras suggests 'magical shadows'.

[10] 'Oh ruddier than the cherry', a song from 'Acis and Galatea' (1720), a musical masque by Georg Friedrich Handel with text from John Gay's poem.

[11] *Infrequently Appearing Monthly Journal.*

[12] One who has superficial knowledge.

[13] Drums were social gatherings in private homes popular in the late eighteenth and early nineteenth century. The pun on 'drums and clubs' suggests a comparison between primitive ritual and the men's clubs which are a major part of upper class social life in London.

[14] 'The Orient viewed from the present'; 'An almost-French view'; 'Who deserves to be known'.

[15] An allusion to Dante's *Inferno* (iv. 131). The same phrase is used to describe Klesmer in *Daniel Deronda* (Ch. 23).

[16] 'Preface'; 'The meaning of the Egyptian Labyrinths'.

[17] Literally, a loligo is a cuttle fish and a catulus is a young animal, in this case a shark pup.

[18] The language in which the canonical texts of Buddhism are written.

Chapter IV

[1] 'The greatest ambition appears the least like ambition when it encounters the absolute impossibility of achieving its goal.' From the *Maximes* (XCI, 1665) of the French philosopher François de La Rochefoucauld (1630–80).

[2] See George Henry Lewes's *Sea-side Studies* (1858): 'I have no doubt the mollusc is a moral individual, but you cannot consider him greatly impassioned' (51). George Eliot also wrote about molluscs in her *Ilfracombe Journals* from the same period.

[3] Literally, Lentulus means 'rather slow'. Lucius Cornelius Lentulus was a Roman consul (49 BC) whose character was disparaged by Cicero and others.

[4] Publius Vergilius Maro, or Virgil (70–19 BC) and Quintus Horatius Flaccus, or Horace (65–8 BC).

[5] The *Eclogues* and *Georgics* are poetic works by Virgil; the *Odes* and *Epodes* are poetic works by Horace.

[6] Malachi 3:2: 'for he is like a refiner's fire, and like a fuller's soap.'

[7] The French philosopher René Descartes (1596–1650) and the English philosopher John Locke (1632–1704).

[8] 'The Giaour' (1813) by Byron; 'Lalla Rookh' (1817) by Thomas Moore; 'The Bard' (1757) by Thomas Gray; 'The Pleasures of Hope' (1799) by Thomas Campbell.

[9] In 1762–3, James Macpherson published two epic poems he claimed to have discovered and translated. He attributed authorship to the legendary third-century Gaelic poet Ossian. Although the poems caused a sensation and appealed to Scottish nationalist sentiments, there was always suspicion about their authenticity, and in 1805 Macpherson's sources were exposed as forgeries.

[10] A descending scale of respectability in philosophic thinkers from the Greek philosopher Plato to Robert Owen (1771–1858), Welsh socialist who founded several socialist communities, and 'Dr Tuffle', representing popular, journalistic philosophy.

[11] 'Envy, hatred, and malice, and all uncharitableness. ' (The Litany, *The Book of Common Prayer*).

[12] The roc (rukh) is a bird so large it blocks the sun over Sinbad, who is mystified by the huge white dome of its egg. See 'The Second Voyage of Es-Sindibad of the Sea' in *The Thousand and One Nights*.

[13] From 'The Cock and the Pearl', an Aesopic fable. In La Fontaine's version, a cock finds a pearl and says 'le moindre grain de mil/ Seroit bien mieux mon affaire. ' (the least bit of millet seed would have suited me much better). In Phaedrus and La Fontaine, the pearl is taken as a metaphor for an unappreciated book.

Chapter V

[1] Hinze is a German name for Everyman. 'Hinze and Kunze' are names used like 'Tom, Dick, and Harry'.

[2] Chewing gum.

[3] The Old Testament prophet Isaiah, Francis Bacon (1561–1626) English scientist and essayist, and Voltaire (1694–1778), French satirist, philosopher, and poet.

[4] Prophetess consulted at the Oracle of Delphi.

[5] Italian epic poet Ludovico Ariosto (1474–1533), best known for his *Orlando Furioso* (1532).

[6] 'Babes in the Wood' is a traditional ballad which was popularised on stage and in a variety of other forms during the eighteenth and nineteenth centuries.

[7] Goethe's *Wilhelm Meister's Apprenticeship* (1795–6). See Bks. IV–V.

[8] Cracking the code of Tulpian's name reveals some brash punning by Theophrastus. Tulpian is 'much listened to' as he 'dilates' on his 'crotchets'. This portrait of Tulpian is drawn from Rembrandt's 'The Anatomy Lesson of Dr. Tulp' (1632) in which the doctor, a Dutch anatomist, distends (dilates) the muscles in the arm of a cadaver while he lectures (dilates) to a group of exaggeratedly attentive students (Tulpian is much listened to). The instrument with which he displays the body's muscle tissue is a 'crotchet', a kind of hook used in surgery.

[9] One who sets the standards of popular opinion.

[10] Literally, 'oboe', from the French 'hautbois' (high wood).

Chapter VI

[1] George Eliot originally gave this character the Roman name 'Cassius' (cf. Shakespeare's *Julius Caesar*), then the Greek name 'Dion' (tyrant of Syracuse assassinated in 354 BC), and finally settled on the English 'Touchwood', meaning old wood used for tinder and suggesting the possibility of a spontaneous combustion.

[2] Walking shoes.

[3] The First and Cabinet Editions mistakenly have 'Dion' for 'Touchwood' here.

[4] Horse carriage.

Chapter VII

[1] In this chapter, Theophrastus is engaging the philosophy expressed by Adam Smith in his *The Wealth of Nations* (1776). Smith claimed that every individual 'intends only his own gain, and he is in this, as in many other cases, led by an invisible hand to promote an end which was no part of his intention. . . . By pursuing his own interest he frequently promotes that of the society more effectually than when he really intends to promote it. I have never known much good done by those who affected to trade for the public good. ' (IV. ii). This chapter plays with Smith's idea of a 'natural law' by describing the capitalist as molecule educated by the nature of things into a 'faint feeling of fraternity'.

[2] From the *Spectator* (no. 583). In an essay on working and planting, Mr Spectator quotes 'an old fellow of a college': '"We are always doing" (says

he) "something for posterity, but I would fain see posterity do something for us."'

[3] The Goddess of Wisdom is Minerva. Spike's profession was 'tape and webbing' in the first draft of this chapter, but George Eliot changed this in the MS to 'spinning and weaving', perhaps to reflect the relationship between cotton manufacturers and Reform politics. Robert Peel (1788–1850), instrumental in early nineteenth century reform politics, was the son of one of the first cotton manufacturers in England.

[4] Alfred the Great (849–99) the Anglo-Saxon king. Spike wrongly assumes that because he is a hero of English history he was an Anglican.

[5] The First Reform Bill (1832) reallocated the seats in the House of Commons to reflect the changing population due to the growth of industrial towns in the north of England.

[6] The Corn Laws regulated the import and export of grain for the production of the home-producers at the expense of the home-consumer. After a long and bitter struggle they were abolished in 1846.

Chapter VIII

[1] The Greek Theophrastus describes 'The Patron of Rascals', who will defend a bad man, calling him 'the watchdog of the people' (170–73). All references are to *The Characters of Theophrastus*, ed. and trans. R. C. Jebb (London: Macmillan, 1870).

[2] In Latin the name means 'given to biting or snappishness', also dog-like.

[3] In Latin, the name means sharp or cutting.

[4] A red star in the eye of Tarus (usually Aldebarah).

[5] This reference to a conversation reported by Boswell follows from the reference to Isaac Newton above. Dr Johnson argues that Isaac Newton, had he applied himself, might have done anything with his genius, including write a fine epic poem: 'Sir, the man who has vigour, may walk to the east, just as well as to the west, if he happens to turn his head that way.' See Boswell's *Life of Johnson*, ed. G. B. Hill, rev. L. F. Powell (Oxford, 1934–64), V:35.

[6] This description of 'poor Poll' seems to fit Theophrastus, and, since George Eliot's nickname was 'Polly', represents another playful attempt to associate and confuse author and character.

[7] In Latin, Laniger means bearing or producing wool.

[8] In Latin, crow or raven.

[9] A tale from Native American folklore.

[10] By defending Mordax the 'watchdog' Theophrastus himself becomes, according to the definition of the *Characters*, a 'Patron of Rascals'. According to Diogenes Laertius, the Greek Theophrastus had a servant who was reputed to be a philosopher.

[11] *Comprachico*, literally 'vendor of children', refers to the disfiguring or deforming of children for the purposes of making them saleable as beggars.

[12] Malebolge is the pit inhabited by the fraudulent in the *Inferno* (Cantos

XVIII–XXXI). At the bottom of the pit, Judas Iscariot, punished for his betrayal of Jesus, writhes in the mouth of one of Satan's three heads.

[13] George Wombwell (1778–1850), founder of Wombwell's Menageries, the largest travelling collection of animals in the nineteenth century.

[14] Cities of southern Greece which at one time had their own schools of philosophy but began to decline in power after c. 500 BC.

Chapter IX

[1] One of the daughters of the night in Greek mythology, who brought down mortals hardened by hubris (excessive pride).

[2] In Virgil's *Aeneid*, Dido is the queen and founder of Carthage who falls in love with and is forsaken by Aeneas. She takes her own life in consequence.

[3] *Hamlet*, 3. 1. 158–62. Ophelia speaks of Hamlet:
    'And I, of ladies most deject and wretched,
    That sucked the honey of his music vows,
    Now see that noble and most sovereign reason
    Like sweet bells jangled out of tune and harsh. . .'

[4] Apollos was an Alexandrian Jew who became an eloquent preacher of the teachings of Jesus, attracting his own group of followers in Corinth (Acts 18:24–19:1). Paul preached against such factionalism among Christians (I Corinthians 3:4–9).

[5] Literally, a spark, or trace of something.

[6] Secret gathering for religious worship, esp. of Dissenters.

[7] Perhaps an allusion to the Italian painter Guiseppe Maria Crespi (1665–1747).

Chapter X

[1] The title is taken from a story about Diogenes of Sinope, the Cynic. Told by an oracle to 'alter the political currency', he misunderstood and 'adulterated the state coinage', for which he was exiled (See Diogenes Laertius, II:23). The Cynic, like the modern Sceptic invoked by the quotation from Wordsworth's *The Excursion* (see n. 9), is unable to appreciate the non-material needs of a community.

[2] 'The ridiculous must not be found where it does not exist: that is to spoil taste, it is to corrupt one's judgment and that of others. But the ridiculous must be seen where it exists, and some of it pointed out with grace and in a manner which pleases and instructs. ' La Bruyère, 'Des Ouvrages de l'esprit', *Caractères de Théophrast, Précedes d'une notice de Sainte-Beuve.* (Paris: Garnier Freres, 1872) p. 84. The quotation in this edition reads 'Il ne faut point' rather than 'il ne faut pas'. Note that Charles Augustin Sainte-Beuve wrote the introductory essay on La Bruyère for this edition (see n. 16 below).

[3] Scottish 'common sense' philosopher (1753–1820).

[4] Given the time frame of the book, the July Days most likely refers to a period of street violence in Paris in July 1830, after which Charles X abdicated the throne and Louis Phillipe replaced him.

[5] These characters from Shakespeare's *As You Like It* (1601) are superior to the shepherds and shepherdesses who also people this pastoral play, hence the absurdity of the image.

[6] A ballet position in which the legs move like scissors, a gesture grossly inappropriate to a tragedy like *Hamlet*, as are fleshings and grenadine.

[7] The 'art of memory', a form of ancient rhetoric in which signs or objects trigger the memory of the speaker. The technique was practiced in various forms through the nineteenth century, when it was used by spiritualists and other deceivers of the public.

[8] In Isaiah, the millennium is foretold as a time when 'The wolf shall also dwell with the lamb, and the leopard shall lie down with the kid; and the calf and the young lion and the fatling together; and a little child shall lead them.' (11:6) Pliny's *The Natural History* tells that a lion who has not been eating can be provoked by monkeys and will regain its appetite when it tastes their blood. (8:19) In Medieval and later Christian iconology, the monkey was associated with lasciviousness.

[9] From Wordsworth's *The Excursion* (1814: 4. 763): 'We live by Admiration, Hope, and Love.' The Sceptic replies 'Love, Hope, and Admiration – are they not / Mad Fancy's favourite vassals?' (4. 768–9).

[10] The effect created by a magic lantern show, in which one view fades and another gradually replaces it.

[11] The sorceress Circe turned the men of Odysseus's crew into swine (*Odyssey*, Bk. 10).

[12] 'When the wicked man turneth away from his wickedness that he hath committed, and doeth that which is lawful and right, he shall save his soul alive' (Ezekiel 28:27). Also: 'Man doth not live by bread only but by every word that proceedeth out of the mouth of the Lord doth man live' (Deuteronomy 8:3).

[13] Examples of debased currencies – English, French and American.

[14] Shakespeare's *Othello* (3. 3. 365–6): 'Farewell the plumed troops and the long wars/That makes ambition virtue'.

[15] A sharper is a cheater and a gull is a person easily cheated.

[16] Plato's *Apology*, in which Socrates explains how the people were slowly habituated to accept false opinions about him.

[17] The source for this quotation is 'De la Question des Théâtres et du Théâtre-Français en Particulier', *Les Causeries du lundi* (I, 1849) by the influential cultural critic Sainte-Beuve (1804–69). However, Theophrastus, like the 'old-fashioned lady', cannot get the French right. Sainte-Beuve's text reads: 'Nothing falls apart more quickly than civilisation in crises like this one; in three weeks the result of many centuries is lost. Civilisation, life is a thing learned and invented, let it be well-remembered: "Or who ennobled life by arts discovered". Men after several years of peace forget all this truth: they come to believe that culture is innate, that it is the same thing as nature. Savagery is always there at two paces, and, as soon as one runs off, it starts again.' The revolutionary disturbance is the Revolution of 1848 in Paris and the Latin quotation is from Virgil's *Aeneid* (6. 663).

[18] The 'Swing Riots' of 1830, during which unemployed agricultural workers destroyed farm machinery, takes its name from a mythical revolutionary called 'Captain Swing'.

[19] *Petroleuse* was the name given in the press to working class women who set fire to buildings during the Paris Commune of 1871.

[20] 'What God hath cleansed that call not thou common' (Acts 10:10–12). A reversal of this would be to call all revered things common, as in the example from Athenaeus which follows.

[21] Athenaeus of Naucratis, Egypt (c. AD 200). Greek grammarian and author. The *Deipnosophistae* (Banquet of the Learned), a compendious collection of anecdotes, extracts, and quotations, cites Theophrastus as an authority on many topics, and cites his treatise *On Comedy* as the source for this story. Theophrastus's work *On Comedy* does not survive.

Chapter XI

[1] The fable from which the title and the story within the chapter derive has historically taken a variety of forms from Aesop ('The Bees, the Drones, and the Wasp') to Phaedrus ('*Apes et Fuci Vespa Judice*' or 'The Bees and the Drones Judged by the Wasp') through La Fontaine ('*Les Frelons et les Mouches a Miel*', or 'The Hornets and the Honeybees'). In each case the issue is the origination of a work (the honeycomb) and the assignment of an authorship to it in the absence of irrefutable proof. Eliot's version of the fable, in this essay on plagiarism and literary property, reverses the traditional moral, and has the council of animals err in their judgment about who made the honeycomb.

[2] Third-century BC Greek poet who wrote *Epyllia* and other eclectic poems. Also a figure of Greek myth, the son of Achilles and Helen of Troy, transformed by Goethe in *Faust*, Part II (1832) into a character representing Byron. See Lewes's *The Life of Goethe* (1855, Ch. VII).

[3] Fuegians are native inhabitants of Tierra del Fuego, at the southern most tip of South America, and Hottentots are native inhabitants of South Africa. In Victorian England, as in this case, they become types of the most primitive human beings.

[4] The back part of the skull.

[5] The 'Society for the Diffusion of Useful Knowledge' published the *Penny Cyclopaedia* (1833–46). The former apparently sounds more respectable for a scholar citing sources. Lewes contributed a number of articles to the *Penny Cyclopaedia* (1841–2).

[6] These are all respected scholars who would not necessarily be known to popular audiences. Patricius, Latin name of the scholar Francesco Patrizi (1529–97); Italian scholar Julius Caesar Scaliger (1484–1558); Swiss mathematician Leonhard Euler (1707–83); French mathematician Joseph-Louis Lagrange (1736–1813); German philologist Franz Bopp (1791–1867); and German naturalist and explorer, Alexander von Humboldt (1769–1859).

[7] The doctrine of Utilitarianism holds that moral value is identical with prudence. One form of Utilitarianism, the one referred to by Theophrastus as Universal Utilitarianism, claims that the moral value of any particular

action is calculable solely in terms of the consequences of the act. By narrowing the terms of utilitarian calculation, however, it is possible to qualify certain actions as moral which would generally be thought of as immoral.

[8] In ancient Greece, a mass sacrifice to the Gods, literally an offering of one hundred oxen.

[9] Pythagoras (c. 580–500 BC), Greek philosopher and mathematician and Cornelius Tacitus (c. AD 55–117) Roman historian. Because St Paul wrote in Greek in the early Christian era, scholars wondered about his knowledge of the Greek tragedies in the fifth century BC.

[10] Amerigo Vespucci (1451–1512) was the Italian navigator who made several exploratory voyages to the New World and whose name was somewhat arbitrarily given to it. His first voyage was 1499–1500, after Columbus had already 'discovered' North America.

[11] *Aquila* means eagle in Latin.

[12] *Vestiges of the Natural History of Creation*, influential in popularising early evolutionary theories, was published anonymously in 1844. Not until 1884 was its author revealed to be Robert Chambers (1802–71), Scottish publisher and author.

[13] Theophrastus's parliament of fowls includes Hoopoe of Johns and Toucan of Magdalen (referring to Oxford Colleges), Shrike (butcherbird), Columba (dove), Merula (blackbird), and Bantam (rooster).

Chapter XII

[1] Cupbearer to Zeus, Greek ideal of male beauty.

[2] Roman ideal of male beauty, companion of Roman Emperor Hadrian.

[3] In Torquato Tasso's *Jerusalem Delivered* (1575), Armida is the beautiful sorceress with whom Rinaldo falls in love.

Chapter XIII

[1] The precious guide Comparison may allude to Virgil, Dante's guide through the *Inferno* and *Purgatorio* as well as to the extended similes used by Virgil and Dante.

[2] *Inferno*, xxx.ii.150 [GE's note]. In Cocytus in the ninth circle of Hell, where those who have been treacherous to guests are punished, Dante's pilgrim refuses to keep his promise to open the iced-over eyes of Fra Alberigo, saying 'To be rude to him was courtesy'.

[3] Characters whose names recall medieval lovers: Heloisa (c. 1098–1164) was the lover of Abelard. Their letters have been read as exemplifying medieval romance. Laura is the lady to whom Petrarch (1304–74) addresses his love poetry, on the model of Dante's poetry to Beatrice.

[4] The following characters bear Latin names resembling those in a medieval allegory, but rather than particularising, these names universalise without moralising: Semper (forever), Ubique (everywhere), Aliquis (anything), Quispiam (anyone).

[5] The Latin names of these characters: Pilulus (covered with hair), Bovis (ox), Avis (bird) give this episode, set 'somewhere in the darker ages of this century', the aspect of fable.

[6] Perhaps the allusion is to Juvanal's *Satires* (X:356) '*Orandum est ut sit mens sana in corpore sano*' (Your prayer must be that you may have a sound mind in a sound body).

[7] See Appendix I for material deleted at this point from an early draft of this chapter.

[8] George Eliot initially called this character 'Celestina'. *La Celestina* is the popular title of *La tragicomedia de Calisto y Melibea* (anonymous, 1499). Theophrastus turns Callisto (the male lover) into Callista, and connects her with the female lover Callisto of Callisto and Melibea in Edmund Spenser's *The Shepearde's Calender* (1579). The deleted passage reveals some of the authors George Eliot was weaving into her chapter, including Virgil and Spenser.

[9] The allusions to Medieval allegory continue with Meliboeus (or Melibee) who, in addition to being the name of a shepherd in Virgil's First Eclogue is also a character in Chaucer's *Canterbury Tales*.

[10] Philemon (c. 368–267 BC) was a New Comedy Poet in Athens and rival of Menander, here speaking to a character with a name reminiscent of New Comedies, Euphemia (well-speaking). But Philemon is also a character in Spenser's *The Faerie Queene* (1590; 1596). The couple Philemon and Baucis turn up in Goethe's *Faust*, Part II.

[11] Phenomena of spiritual communications, popularised in mid-nineteenth century England by American spiritualists. Eliot attended some seances and read articles on spiritualism, but remained unimpressed.

[12] Italian painter (1387–1455). 'Coronation of the Virgin' (1435).

[13] Canto xv [GE's note]. 'When my soul returned without to the things that are real outside of it, I recognised my not false errors' (115–118). Dante's pilgrim experiences a 'visione estatica', but returns to the material world, a necessary condition for his writing the poem.

[14] Isaiah 6:1. Uzziah was the tenth king of Judah after the split of the monarchy. His long reign (c. 781–40 BC) was characterised by increasing prosperity and luxury in Jerusalem about which prophets like Isaiah complained. Isaiah has a vision of god on a throne in the Temple surrounded by six-winged seraphim.

Chapter XIV

[1] See Atheneaus, *Deipnosophistae*, XV:637:

> 'And Hephaestion proved to be the same thieving sort in the case of our noble Adrastus. For Adrastus had published five books *On Questions of History and Style in the Morals of Theophrastus*, and a sixth book *On the Nicomachean Ethics of Aristotle*, abundantly setting forth ideas on the character of Plexippus in the play of Antiphon the tragic poet, as well as saying a very great deal about Antiphon himself; but Hephaestion appropriated this also and wrote a book entitled *On the Antiphon of Xenophon's Memorabilia*,

although he had discovered nothing additional of his own, any more than he had in his work *On the Wreath of Withes.*'

[2] The Rosetta Stone.

[3] Perhaps a reference to the Tyrant of Acragas in Sicily (488–472 BC).

[4] Spanish scholastic Isidor of Seville (c. 560–636), author of the encyclopedic *Etymologiae* and French scholastic Vincent of Beauvais (c. 1190–1264), who attempted a compendium of universal knowledge.

[5] 'Out of breath about nothing, with much ado doing nothing' (Phaedrus, *Fables* II:5).

[6] Frankish king, Pepin III (c. 714–768) began the conquest of the Saxons completed by his son Charlemagne.

[7] Unnamed character in Samuel Johnson's philosophical romance, *Rasselas* (1759), who takes his belief in the superiority of rationality over passion too far, becoming deluded about his own scientific powers.

[8] Literally, booming or buzzing.

[9] Perhaps Ben Azzai: 'for the reward of precept is precept, and the reward of transgression is transgression.' See *Sayings of the Jewish Fathers*, ed. Charles Taylor (Cambridge, 1877) IV. 5, a book owned by George Eliot. Mordecai quotes Ben Azzai in *Deronda*: '*the reward of one duty is the power to fulfill another*' (VI. xlvi. 536).

[10] *Rienzi, the Last of the Tribunes* (1835), an historical romance by Edward Bulwer-Lytton about Cola di Rienzi (1313–54). 'Notre Dame de Paris'. Or, *The Hunchback of Notre Dame* (1831) by Victor Hugo, an historical romance of medieval France.

[11] Clown's dress.

Chapter XV

[1] Land belonging to a parish church.

[2] Two Noble Kinsmen [GE's note]. 5.3.51–3. Romantic drama attributed to John Fletcher and Shakespeare, thought to have been written about 1613 and published in 1634. GE has altered the quotation.

[3] A Vorticella is a bell-shaped, one-celled animal living in stagnant pools or as a parasite on other animals. Lewes's *Sea-side Studies* describes vorticellæ and other microscopic organisms in anthropomorphised terms.

[4] John Milton. This pamphlet (1644) argues against restrictions on the freedom of the press.

[5] A Volvox is a genus of fresh-water algae.

[6] A Vibrio is a genus of bacteria.

[7] Residence of hack writers in late seventeenth- and early eighteenth-century London.

[8] A Monas is a class of one-celled organism.

[9] Or Chippewa, members of a tribe of Algonquian Native Americans.

[10] 1820–30.

Chapter XVI

[1] Perhaps an allusion to the prophetess Melissa in Ariosto's *Orlando Furioso* (1532).

[2] Literally, a gavial is a crocodile and a man-trap is a spring trap for catching human trespassers.

[3] 'The three percent consolidated annuities' were government securities in England which included a large part of the public debt.

[4] Name of the criminal whom the people chose to be released by Pilate instead of Jesus. He is mentioned in all four gospels (see for example, Matthew 27:17–23).

[5] Aristotle's *Nicomachean Ethics*.

[6] English statesman and author Thomas Babbington Macaulay (1800–59). See his 'Lord Clive' (*Edinburgh Review*, January 1840). Macaulay writes that after the death of Arungzebe: 'A succession of nominal sovereigns, sunk in indolence and debauchery, sauntered away life in secluded places, chewing bang, fondling concubines, and listening to buffoons.' Bang is the dried leaves of the hemp plant (hashish).

[7] Robert Walpole (1676–1745) was a dominant figure in English politics from 1721–42 (the Age of Walpole) who maintained his power by means of bribery and corruption. He was effectively the first Prime Minister.

[8] See Appendix 1 for a passage deleted at this point by George Eliot from the proofs of *Impressions*.

[9] In other words, for babies.

[10] *Macbeth* (1. 1. 11–12).

[11] 'The daisies of hell' and 'The delights of the devil' are mock variations on lines from the poems in *Les Fleurs du mal* (1857) by Charles Baudelaire, whom Theophrastus seems to be describing.

Chapter XVII

[1] The title derives from Edward Bulwer Lytton's science-fiction fantasy *The Coming Race* (1871).

[2] Trost means 'consolation' in German.

[3] Voltaire's *Candide* (1759, Ch. I).

[4] An impartial judge, from the Greek god, one of the three judges of Hades.

[5] Of the same kind.

[6] The 'unmoved mover' is an allusion to Aristotle, but the concept of 'moving its mover' may be a reference to Ludwig Feurbach's *Essence of Christianity*, a work George Eliot translated in 1854 (see especially Ch. XII, 'The Omnipotence of Feeling, or the Mystery of Prayer').

[7] Place in an organism where a germ may settle and develop.

Chapter XVIII

[1] The phrase 'Hep! Hep! Hep!' is an anti-Semitic cry which may have originated during the Crusades as an abbreviation of '*Hierosolyma est perdita*'

(Jerusalem is lost), or perhaps as a cry used for driving herds of animals. It is the name given to a series of anti-Jewish riots which broke out in Germany in 1819.

[2] Byron died in 1824 in Missolonghi, where he had gone to help train Greek nationalists fighting against Turkish rule. Greek independence was achieved in 1830.

[3] Italian patriot and republican Giuseppe Mazzini (1805–72) who was instrumental in the unification of Italy, which was achieved in 1870.

[4] In the 1820's, Austria was an 'alien government' present in some Italian states.

[5] Italian political philosopher Niccolo Machiavelli (1469–1527), Giulio Rubini (c. 1845–1917), patriot who fought with Garibaldi in the campaign to unite Italy, and Neapolitan insurrectionist Tomasso Aniello Mansaniello (1620–47).

[6] Probably J. R. Green, author of *The History of the English People* (1878).

[7] Scandinavian name of Anglo-Saxon god Woden (one-eyed).

[8] Probably a reference to the Indian Mutiny of 1857.

[9] King Nebuchadnezzar of Babylonia captured Judah in 586 BC, destroyed the Temple, and exiled most of the Jews to Babylon. After the defeat of the Babylonians by Cyrus the Great of Persia, the Jews were allowed to return to Judah and Jerusalem. The return to Jerusalem was spread out over decades. Ezra describes the return of the Jews (c. 397 BC) to a country in which the Temple had been rebuilt, but which was still dominated by pagan tribes. In addition to the Zealots (see note 12 below), there were a number of factions described by Josephus Flavius (c. AD 37–95) as fighting with the Romans between 63 BC–AD 70. His *The Jewish War* was a primary source of George Eliot's knowledge of Jewish history.

[10] The Seleucids were a Hellenistic dynasty established in Syria in 312 BC by Seleuces I. The Seleucids were an important power in the region and played a primary role in the Hellenisation of the Middle East. In 168 BC, Antiochus IV invaded Jerusalem and, in the following year, rededicated the Temple to Zeus and outlawed the Jewish religion. In 166 BC, Mattathias, a high priest, fled to the countryside with his five sons and began guerrilla war with the Seleucid conquerors. Mattathias died in 166 BC and Judas Maccabaeus took over leadership, reconquering Jerusalem in 164 BC, and rededicating the Temple. This is still marked by Chanukah. The family maintained control over the country until 63 BC when Pompey conquered it for Rome.

[11] The Zealots were a sect of Jews, driven by religious ardor and hatred of foreign occupation and paganism. Organised as a political party during the reign of Herod the Great (37–4 BC), they conducted a campaign of violence against Roman occupation, ultimately leading to the revolt in AD 66 and the destruction of Jerusalem and the Diaspora in AD 70.

[12] The reference is to the Roman desecration of the Temple in Jerusalem by the placement of a statue of the deified emperor, Caligula, in the most sacred part of the building.

[13] The reference is to the English Civil War (1642–8) when both Puritans

and Anglicans invoked biblical texts to justify opposing doctrines. James I, Stuart King of England (1603–25), was a proponent of the doctrine that kings drew their authority from God.

[14] Leaders of a rebellion against Moses and Aaron (Numbers 16:13).

[15] Extracting large sums of money on fraudulent, questionable, or arbitrary grounds. The reference is to the medieval, princely practice of forcing Jewish communities to pay large amounts of money to the local prince or King when money got tight in the royal household. These levies were not assessed against Christians.

[16] For nearly a millennium, beginning in the eighth century AD, Jews were considered unwelcome resident aliens in most European countries. Generally, they were not allowed to own land, or exercise most property rights granted to Christians. Moreover, Jews were not protected from attacks by their Christian neighbours. Some European kings and princes invited wealthy Jews, known for their commercial sagacity, to establish communities in their countries for the purpose of stimulating the economy. These Jews were given diplomas by the king, granting protection from attack, certain property rights, and often, the right to hire Christian workmen.

[17] Noah curses his son Ham (for seeing his father's nakedness) to be 'a slave of slaves' (Genesis 9:25).

[18] Matthew 27:25. The words of Jewish observers at the crucifixion of Jesus, taken as a sanction to persecute Jews for the death of Jesus.

[19] Words spoken by Jesus on the cross (Luke 23:34).

[20] Catholic Emancipation was achieved in 1829. Jews were admitted to the House of Commons in 1858.

[21] In 1866, the government of the newly united Rumania, under Alexander Cuza, enacted a constitution specifically excluding suffrage to non-Christians. This was followed by other legal restrictions on Jews and by years of anti-Semitic riots, in which many Jews were killed annually.

[22] Literally 'common body'. From the phrase: *Fiat experimentum in corpore vili* (Let the experiment be made on some common body). The phrase derives from a quotation in Antoine du Verdier's *Prosopographie. . . des hommes illustre* (Lyon, 1603) 3:2542–43.

[23] Throughout the nineteenth century, Jews living in the Turkish seaport of Smyrna were accused of the ritual murder of Christian children. The most well known of these accusations were brought in 1872, 1874, and 1876, and the cases received worldwide attention in the press.

[24] The leader of the Liberal party in Germany in 1878 was Eduard Lasker (1829–84). The leader of the Republican party in France may refer to Léon Gambetta (1804–81), who was reported to be Jewish. The head of the conservative ministry in England was Benjamin Disraeli (1804–81).

[25] The Scottish Stuarts ruled between 1603 and 1649 and were restored to the throne after the Civil War and English Commonwealth, ruling again between 1660 and 1714.

[26] Germany, which achieved total unification in 1871.

[27] See Cowper's ballad 'John Gilpin' (1782) and 'Edwin and Angelina, or the Hermit' (1764) by Goldsmith (included in *The Vicar of Wakefield*).

[28] 'The Eastern Question' was the term used in Western Europe to refer to a host of political-territorial problems related to the slow dissolution of the Ottoman Empire. The European provinces of the Empire, including Bulgaria, Bosnia, Serbia and Hercegovina were in constant turmoil beginning in the 1850s. British and French politicians were particularly concerned that the Russians would overrun these provinces and upset the carefully worked out balance of power that had been established in Europe during the first part of the century.

[29] The worship of Moloch, a Canaanite God, was distinguished by sacrifices of the first-born. The Mosaic law specifically prohibits such sacrifice: 'And thou shalt not give any of thy seed to set them apart to Moloch.' Leviticus 18:21.

[30] Cf. Ch. II, n. 23. Some anthropological theories of the late nineteenth century saw Aryan civilisation as superior to those 'less civilised' cultures, which were organised matrilineally, inheritances being established through the male relatives of the mother, rather than through the father.

[31] Benjamin Disraeli was a Jewish convert to Christianity. Robert Walpole (see Ch. XVI, n. 7) and William Pitt, First Earl of Chatham (see Ch. II, n. 2).

[32] Jesus to his disciples (Matthew 10:6).

[33] Letter of Paul to the Romans (9:3–5).

[34] 27 BC–14 AD.

[35] John Stuart Mill's *On Liberty* (1859).

Appendix I

[1] From the essay 'Imagination', which served as a rough draft of 'How We Come to Give Ourselves False Testimonials, and Believe in Them' (XVI). This particular passage does not appear in the MS of *Impressions* and has not been published previously. Huntington Library MS [HM12993] p. 52.

[2] A plain in Attica where the Greeks won a victory over the Persians (490 BC).

Appendix II

[1] This passage appears in the MS but was deleted by George Eliot from the proofs for the first edition of *Impressions*. Upon sending a revised set of proofs to George Eliot on 21 March 1879, John Blackwood wrote: 'I incline to put in a petition in favour of George the III about whom there was a great deal of good and he fought well with his troubled brain' (*GEL*, 6:118). George Eliot replied 'Of course I do not refer to George III where I speak of 'treacherous and rapacious' monarchs. The examples of misapplied praise to which I refer in the first instance are spread over history in general' (*GEL*, 7:119). In a footnote to this letter Gordon Haight quotes the passage describing a king 'treacherous, rapacious, and ready to sanction gross breaches in the administration of justice' (XVI:131) and states: 'No change

was made in the proofs.' However, while George Eliot did not refer to George III 'in the first instance', she does seem to refer to him here in terms of 'arrogance, obstinacy, and dulness'. After Blackwood's comment, she attempted to revise this passage and finally deleted it.

[2] John Dryden, 'Absalom and Achitophel' (1681) (l. 10).

[3] Stuart King of England (1660-85).

[4] Shakespeare's *The Merchant of Venice* (c.1595).